THE SECRET OF SUNRISES

THE SECRET OF SUNRISES

A Novel

ELLIE BLOCK

This is a work of fiction. Names, characters, organizations, places, events, and incidents are either products of the author's imagination or are used fictitiously. Otherwise, any resemblance to actual persons, living or dead, is purely coincidental.

Published by Lake Union Publishing, Seattle

www.apub.com

EU product safety contact:
Amazon Media EU S. à r.l.
38, avenue John F. Kennedy, L-1855 Luxembourg
amazonpublishing-gpsr@amazon.com

ISBN-13: 9781662539367 (paperback)
ISBN-13: 9781662539350 (digital)

Cover design by Kimberly Glyder
Cover image: © Birgit Tyrrell / ArcAngel Images

Printed in the United States of America

For my mother, Clementine, whose humor, heart, and resilience inspired me beyond words.

1

Lying was a skill Catherine Moran never fully mastered.

As she stood outside her boss's office working up the nerve to knock, she wished she were better at it because she knew his latest pet project was bound to be a bust. Like a lefty attempting to scribble with their right hand, Catherine had no dexterity with deceit. Whenever she attempted to lie, her cheeks would balloon, the facts balling up behind her teeth, ready to burst free. At fifty-seven, Catherine should have had some finesse at stretching the truth, but honesty wasn't just a good policy as far as she was concerned—it was the only policy.

You can do this. Just be diplomatic, she told herself, stalling and anxiously smoothing out her sweater as coworkers passed by in the hallway.

Catherine was a senior researcher at the credit card company, and her boss's idea of offering high-net cardholders extra time to pay in exchange for staggeringly steep interest was a risky gamble. The likelihood that larger loans would skid into collections, even for the ultrarich, was as high as the rates he proposed to offer.

If you get fired, your own credit card bills will go through the roof.

Since moving her mother into a memory-care facility for patients suffering from dementia, she had been racking up debt at breakneck speed. Catherine knew all too well what would happen if she couldn't pay it off. With her hand poised by the knob, she took a deep breath and steeled herself to explain the hard truth to her boss as tactfully as possible.

Catherine softly rapped on his door.

"Come in," her boss called.

Poking her head inside, she asked, "You wanted to see me, sir?"

Willford presided over his spacious office from a stately desk. Bookshelves bracketed the room. Behind him, windows framed the Manhattan skyline, rooftops draped in a thick mantle of February snow. Willford had on his blazer, which was a rarity.

Uh-oh. I must really be in trouble.

"I'm not the one who needs to speak to you," he explained somberly. "This is Mr. Latham."

Imposing even when seated, Latham was stationed across from Willford, hands folded in his lap, a leather briefcase resting by his leg. Catherine didn't recognize his name. Apprehension flooded her body, cinching into a knot in her stomach.

Is this some C-suite higher-up here to drop the hammer? This must be bad.

Latham stood to greet her, offering his card. He had the stolid, heavy-lidded expression of someone who routinely told people things they didn't want to hear.

Willford got to his feet next, straightened his jacket, then abruptly excused himself. "I'll give you some privacy."

Oh, God. Is this a downsizing meeting? Am I about to be fired?

Anxiety hurtling straight to her head, Catherine glanced at Latham's business card. Under his name, it read **Estate Attorney.**

Hold on. Estate attorneys handle wills.

For a second, her heart faltered, thoughts darting to her mother. "Is she okay?" Catherine blurted.

Latham looked perplexed. "Who?"

"My mom."

"Ms. Moran, I'm here on behalf of your brother, Robert."

Catherine's mind reeled at the mere mention of his name. "Robert," she repeated to be certain she could still breathe.

After nearly five decades with no contact, she had given up on ever hearing from her brother again, even if she'd never stopped wondering where he was. Her knees threatened to buckle. It was as though every ounce of air had been sucked from Catherine's lungs.

"I regret to inform you that he has passed away."

"How? When? Where?" Catherine stammered.

Latham walked her over to the chair he had been in and gestured for her to sit.

"Robert lost his battle with pancreatic cancer. He didn't realize he had it. Sadly, due to a late diagnosis, he succumbed to the disease quite suddenly."

Stunned mute, Catherine slumped in her seat as dozens of questions ran through her brain rapid fire. Her emotions ricocheted from sorrow to anger to sheer bafflement. Words bottlenecked at her mouth, her lips refusing to form sentences.

"I understand that you and your brother were . . . not close."

Catherine looked up at him as if that were the understatement of the century. "Not exactly."

As children, they had been. They were ten years apart, and Robert had doted on Catherine more like a daughter than a sister. He would hold her hand when they crossed the street, fix the barrettes in her hair if they were crooked, tie her shoes until she learned how. That changed after their father stormed out of the house one night following a drunken argument with their mother and never came back.

Catherine was only seven when her dad ran out. Robert was seventeen. The age gap hadn't felt vast until their father was gone.

His absence elbowed in between them. Robert became more withdrawn. He spoke less, ignored her more. He behaved like a sullen lodger who shared the house with Catherine and their mom. The day after he graduated from high school, he left, too, almost six months to the day after their father.

Robert had waited until Catherine and her mother were asleep. A note on the table said he loved them. There was no mention of where he was going or when he would return.

She had mourned Robert's departure far more than their father's, crying under the covers every night for weeks. Catherine had barely known her dad. Drinking made him distant, surly, and inscrutable to a young girl who only understood how to wish things were better. Her brother, her protecter, she had adored.

Robert's departure was akin to a death. Between her father's exit and then her brother's, it was as if Catherine had been in a constant state of mourning ever since she was a little kid. Grief was woven into who she was.

"Your brother was very sick," Latham continued. "When he contacted me to legalize his will, he didn't have much time."

"Long enough to phone a lawyer. Not his mother. Or his sister."

A bitter taste burned the back of Catherine's throat, like she was choking on everything she wished she could tell her brother but would not have the chance to say.

For a few years following Robert's departure, the occasional postcard from distant lands would arrive. One from Greece had a photograph of a colossal stone temple. One from Japan featured a grove of cherry trees in bloom. From Italy, a picture of Mount Vesuvius hulking over a cityscape. Each card bore a few words about how beautiful the country was—nothing personal. They vouched that Robert was alive more than anything else.

Eventually, the postcards had stopped.

That was when Catherine adopted the morbid hobby of envisioning the different ways he may have died—drowning in the Aegean, tumbling off a snowy Swiss mountaintop, getting in a car crash on some foggy German autobahn—fantastical ends befitting a hero rather than the brother who had deserted her. To Catherine, being away in a foreign country was a somewhat acceptable excuse for him never coming home.

So was being dead.

"Sorry. That must have sounded callous." Catherine hung her head.

"It's understandable. This is a . . . difficult situation," Latham answered with a practiced tenor of support.

Feelings that had been boxed up in the imaginary casket she'd buried Robert in were rattling the hinges. Despite Catherine's passion for research, once she had closed the lid on her brother, she'd never wanted to dig up any details on him or unearth more about his past. Curiosity never got the better of her because resentment already had. It sank to the bone, an ache she had acclimated to. If her brother hadn't cared to reconnect, she vowed not to either.

Catherine hadn't cried over Robert at the countless funerals she'd had for him in her mind. She wasn't going to cry for him today.

"You're telling me my brother died a painful death, alone, and here I am complaining about who he called."

"I only spoke to your brother once. He had all the papers in order. You're his sole beneficiary."

"Me?" Catherine replied, dumbfounded.

"He has one thing in his will."

"Unless it's an apology, I'm not interested."

"I'm afraid it isn't. It's a boat."

"A . . . what?"

"A boat. In Key West. I have the documents for transfer of ownership and a note that your brother asked me to write verbatim."

Latham removed a folded scrap of paper from the breast pocket of his jacket and read it aloud. "Catherine will get it when she gets it."

He passed the paper to her, and she reread it, searching in vain for more meaning in the words or some hidden explanation. The paper felt lighter than air between her fingers, while the letters seemed to be made of lead.

Intentionally vague, confoundingly cryptic. That was Robert. Catherine could instantly tell it was a direct quote. However, she did *not* get it. "Wait . . . did you say Key West?"

Latham nodded, popped the latch on his briefcase, and handed her a file full of papers tucked into an envelope.

That was the first thing that made sense.

Their father had been obsessed with Ernest Hemingway's novels. The regal machismo and alluring far-flung locales were the opposite of the hardscrabble working-class town in New Jersey where they had lived, which was close to her mother's job on the bottling line at the Anheuser-Busch brewery, while their father took work welding wherever he could find it. He had selected Robert's name from the lead in *For Whom the Bell Tolls*. Hers came from *A Farewell to Arms*.

"Your brother paid the dock fees until the end of the month." Latham was trying to encourage her to see the upside.

Missing Robert had indentured Catherine to a permanent heartache that seemed as woefully one sided as her love for him. Hating her brother year in and year out hadn't stanched the hurt. Pretending he was deceased didn't make the anguish more tolerable.

"Dock fees," Catherine echoed as the reality of the situation descended on her like the snow flurries falling outside in a cold, darkening blur.

"Robert stuck me with another bill I won't be able to afford and another mess to clean up." She sighed. "Well, that's what he was good at: leaving things behind."

2

A cumbersome silence hung between them as they stood by the elevator, waiting for Latham to take his leave. Catherine didn't mind waiting. She'd been holding her breath in anticipation of things that didn't happen for as long as she could remember—her father's return, her brother's reappearance, an improvement in her long-suffering mother's mental health. A few more minutes wouldn't faze her.

"Did my brother purchase a cemetery plot?"

"He was cremated, according to the wishes set forth in his will," Latham explained while putting on a heavy jacket to brave the elements.

A lump of sadness formed in Catherine's chest. Her hands felt numb, as if the blood refused to reach them anymore because it needed to stay close to her heart. "What about his possessions?"

"Donated to charity," he informed her as he bundled a scarf around his neck.

"Are there other family members listed in the documents? A wife, maybe? Children?" Catherine impatiently started opening the envelope he had given her.

Latham's response halted her. "Your brother made no mention of any other family members, and there is no forwarding address."

The answers pained and irked her equally.

Robert left little trace of the life he had lived without her, no clues to his past, as if on purpose to prevent her from discovering what he had been doing for all those decades. Catherine felt shortchanged for the umpteenth time.

The elevator bell dinged, and the doors opened.

"If you have any other questions, don't hesitate to call." Latham shook her hand sincerely before entering the car. "You have my sympathies."

Other riders made space while she stared at Robert's file; then the doors slid shut before Catherine could thank him.

Dazed, she stood there in a state of shock.

Her arms were leaden. Her legs wouldn't move. The buzz of the fluorescent lights overhead became a cacophony in Catherine's cloudy mind. She fixed her eyes on the paperwork until the stupor could wear off.

An address was listed at the top of the page, the location of her brother's boat at the Garrison Bight Marina in Key West.

You could sell it and put the cash toward all the bills.

Catherine was so embarrassed by the thought that she looked around as if someone could have heard her think it.

A tug-of-war started in her conscience. On one side was her anger at Robert, heaving hard. On the opposing end was her grief, a weight that wouldn't budge.

Her brother had taken a lot from her—holidays that always felt hollow, tarnished by his absence, happy memories that never materialized, the person she might have been if he had stayed. He may as well have packed up her childhood in his bags when he departed.

Can you get rid of the lone item he has left on this earth?

Robert owed her an incalculable debt. The boat, no matter its worth, could not put a dent in paying it off. Any fleeting regrets she had about selling the boat dissipated once Catherine remembered that the monthly payment for her mother's room and board was looming.

Call the dock. See if they can broker a deal from out of state. They may still be open now.

She was scanning the file for a contact number when Willford rounded the corner toward the elevator and nearly bumped right into her.

"My condolences to you and your family, Cath," he retorted, almost sternly.

"Catherine," she reminded him.

Willford flashed a forced smile after the slipup.

She didn't like nicknames—not Cath, Cat, Kathy, or Kit—and resented her own name almost as much as she resented her father for saddling her with it and running out on the family.

Brave yet modest, the fictional Catherine was a nurse who'd shown fortitude when the protagonist faltered, and she remained stoic even in the face of giving birth to his stillborn baby boy. However, she was renowned for not changing during the novel. She turned over no new leaves, blazed no untrodden trails, made no miraculous revelations. That Catherine was simply a foil to the disillusioned soldier at the heart of the story, a prop playing second fiddle to a flawed man.

Catherine resentfully saw herself in her namesake, and the similarities she perceived were salt in a long-gaping wound. It felt as if her father had carved out her personality as well as her future before she could.

Robert, on the other hand, had relished the connection to his famous moniker, a self-sacrificing teacher, dutiful yet disenchanted—a rare breed in Hemingway's pantheon of dashing heroes. Where her brother aspired to be like the character he was named after, Catherine tried to shake off the association as though it were gum on her shoe.

"Time heals all wounds, as they say," Willford added.

Catherine should have appreciated clichés. Condensing something expansive and complex into a palatable sound bite was part of her job. However, from her experience, that platitude wasn't even true.

Time healed some wounds quickly. Others left indelible scars.

When Catherine was five, she'd fallen off the front stoop of their house. Robert had waved her over, saying she could ride his bike with him; then she'd missed the bottom step in haste, splitting her knee wide open.

She should have gotten stitches, but their mother was at work, and Robert begged Catherine not to call the brewery because he was supposed to have been babysitting her. To stop the bleeding, he wrapped an entire roll of medical tape around her knee. When their mother came home, Catherine covered for Robert by claiming they were playing a game where she was a mummy. A horrible liar even back then, she was the one who had gotten in trouble for wasting the bandages.

To make it up to her, Robert had allowed Catherine to ride on his handlebars for a week. The long, craggy mark on her knee that remained to that day was worth what Catherine got in exchange. Biking along the streets with Robert, wind in her hair, him holding her close, was one of her most cherished memories.

"Take tomorrow off," Willford recommended, checking his cell phone.

At first, she appreciated the gesture. Then a sense of its cheapness set in.

Catherine could tell that Willford's custom suit cost more than the rent on her one-bedroom apartment. His watch probably retailed for the price of a compact car. She didn't even own a vehicle. Everywhere she looked, Catherine calculated costs, both literal and proverbial—it was an occupational hazard.

Willford pressed the button to summon the elevator. "The report on the new payment plan isn't due until Monday."

She'd been about to acquiesce to her first day off in ages until he added the deadline, which chafed. It was adding insult to injury.

Though they had worked together on numerous projects, Willford treated her with the arm's-length professionalism of a boss who wouldn't deign to get friendly with his employees. Catherine figured he felt guilty about passing her over for the director title twice. In light of Latham's visit, he seemed doubly uncomfortable around her.

Catherine loved her job because data didn't lie. Facts provided a comforting stability. But she'd sacrificed so much with minimal respect or reward. Now her nerves were too raw to hold back.

"I'm going to need a week."

Willford's face fell.

Catherine was the best researcher in the department. With the deadline fast approaching, her being gone would greatly hamper any progress on the project that he was pinning his hopes on, regardless of how harebrained his proposal was.

"It's imperative that I go to Florida to settle my brother's estate. I'm sure you understand."

This wasn't an outright lie. It also wasn't the truth. Catherine's cheeks started to puff, so she pursed her lips hard.

You'd better hope the lawyer didn't mention the boat to him.

She braced herself for Willford's answer.

"You are, of course, entitled to whatever vacation time you've accrued." He slipped on his gloves preemptively to signal that his part of the conversation was about to come to an end.

"I have a month."

Willford chewed the inside of his cheek. "The company has the utmost respect for circumstances such as these," he replied in a measured tone. "Since we're in the middle of a pivotal project and staff evaluations are coming up next quarter, I'd hate not to have you here to provide your valuable input."

This was less a threat than a proposition, a carrot he was dangling.

Catherine had been passed over for director of research two years running. After over a decade with the company, logging countless hours and forgoing time off, the twin rejections were consecutive slaps in the face. She desperately wanted the title as well as the raise that went with it. Willford was the one who would decide whether she received it.

You scratch his back—take off Thursday and Friday and get back by Monday—then he'll scratch yours.

"Well . . ." Catherine acted as if she were mulling over his offer, tapping Robert's will for emphasis. "It'll be tough to accomplish everything in a few days. But I think I can manage."

Relief washed over Willford's face as the elevator arrived with a ding. "You're a real team player. My sympathies to your family and have a safe trip," he told her, like it was an order.

For Catherine, who planned every aspect of her life down to the tiniest detail—like investigating which laundry detergent provided the most washes per container and analyzing what label maker had the widest selection of fonts—there wasn't anything safe about a spur-of-the-moment decision such as this. The thought of it made her a little queasy.

"Thank you, sir," she stuttered.

She exhaled as soon as Willford disappeared behind the closing elevator doors.

Catherine was about to get the time off that she'd been pining for and maybe the director title too. Then she remembered why she was going to Florida in the first place, and her spirits deflated. She gazed mournfully at the legal documents in her hands.

Besides the boat, they were all that remained of her brother.

3

Catherine shut the door to her office firmly, as if it could keep out the sorrow that was threatening to make her crumble into tears. She tossed the file with Robert's information onto her desk, bumping the keyboard and switching on the screen saver. It was a photograph of a lone palm tree arching over a languid stretch of empty coastline, sun cresting on the horizon. The picture was as close to a vacation as Catherine had come in years.

Sitting below the image of a golden beach and crystal-blue sea was a teetering pile of documents, hard copies of the work she would have to churn through during her trip to Florida. Frost cast a haze across the bottom of the window beside her desk. Sitting on the sill was a potted plant, which looked sickly. Fluorescent lights were no substitute for sunshine.

Gloria, the executive assistant for the research department, knocked, then popped her head in while scooting her rolling desk chair up to Catherine's doorway, squeaky casters heralding her arrival. "You still here?"

Her thick Bronx accent turned every syllable into a battering ram. While Catherine was used to it, strangers who got Gloria on the phone frequently asked her to repeat herself.

"Unfortunately," Catherine replied.

"What's wrong? You look like you seen a ghost."

If you only knew.

Gloria was a curvy beauty who had brains but hid them and proudly did the bare minimum. She would not make or get coffee, declined to lift or carry objects heavier than an envelope, and refused to get within ten feet of the copier on the days she had her nails done, claiming the lid chipped her polish. Gloria didn't get away with things because she was pretty. She got away with them because she had the confidence not to care.

"I, uh, had a talk with Willford."

"About his dumb idea?"

"I lied." The words popped out like a cork. "I told him the high-interest-rate plan could work. Maybe."

Now you're lying about a lie! You are terrible at winging this.

If she told the truth, then Gloria would insist that Catherine tell her mother immediately. She would lock Catherine in her office until she did. But the dementia made her mom edgy and unpredictable. How would she absorb the blow that her son, who had left a lifetime ago, had passed away?

Catherine had gone to great lengths to protect her mother, and she needed time to figure out the best way to break this shattering news.

"You *lied*?" Gloria raised a penciled-in eyebrow. "What happened to the office Girl Scout who always does the right thing? You're the Goody Two-shoes who went back into the restaurant after the Christmas-party lunch to add fifty cents to the tip because you miscalculated after a second chardonnay."

"I only lied to buy time until I can be honest."

It was exactly what she was doing with Gloria, too, which Catherine felt ashamed of.

Gloria groaned and gave her an arm-waving double thumbs-down while making a theatrical 360-degree spin in her chair.

"Look, finding new ways to do less is the most productive thing I accomplish at this job."

"You do have a knack for that."

"But Willford makes me look like a model employee. He rewards you for all your hard work by giving you his. He's a lazy blowhard who banks on people not challenging him. He should have been fired a long time ago. Coming from me, that's saying something."

"All I can do is zip my lips and keep my head down until this is over."

"That's all you ever do."

Sadly, Gloria was spot on. That was all Catherine had been doing since childhood.

"Maybe if you did speak up for a change, you'd finally get that promotion."

"Maybe I still can," Catherine countered sheepishly, thinking of what Willford had said. "Hold on. Why are you still here? You're usually standing by the door, counting the seconds until it's five o'clock."

"I got a date. We're meeting for drinks a block away. I keep telling you, you gotta put up a profile on a dating app. How else are you ever gonna meet a nice guy?"

"I have enough problems as it is. And I doubt a profile that says 'Never married, no kids, numbers nerd with occasional hot flashes seeking a man who's okay with me spending half my time at a nursing home' would get any matches."

"Just say 'Sexy spinster.' Guys will think you're a DJ."

Catherine frowned at her.

"You've got the dark hair, the blue eyes, no saddlebags, no stretch marks, and no crow's-feet. Okay, maybe you got a crow toe."

Catherine frowned again.

"See. There it is!"

"Men can be confirmed bachelors. Why can't I be a confirmed bachelorette?"

"Because that sounds like the name of a Lifetime movie. Or a porno."

"Dating just isn't on my to-do list right now."

"That's the problem." Gloria batted her false eyelashes vehemently. "Your back goes out more than you do."

Catherine's daily life had shrunk to a predictable loop from work to home to her mother's memory-care facility. Even her girlfriends had quit including her in activities because she usually canceled, insisting she had to visit her mom or catch up on reports. Though boyfriends had come and gone over the years, they had always been like stops on a train that seemed bound for a station much farther away. At her age, she wondered if she had missed her destination a long time ago, so it was easier not to think about dating at all. What Catherine's humdrum routine lacked in excitement, it made up for in a sense of control, something that was hard to come by.

Her cell phone rang from her purse, playing a muffled bar of "You're Nobody 'Til Somebody Loves You."

"Dean Martin has been crooning for the last hour," Gloria informed her.

"Giving my mom her own ringtone may have been an error in judgment."

"Teaching her to text was the mistake."

Catherine put her hands up in surrender. "She's lonely."

"No, she's bored. Believe me, I know the difference."

The diagnosis of dementia had been agonizing yet not surprising. Breaking her hip the prior year was the final straw. At eighty-four, her mother could no longer live safely on her own.

Finding an affordable memory-care facility had been a battle. Gloria had pitched in to help compare prices while Catherine had compiled a spreadsheet categorizing everything from staff-hiring policies to complaints lodged with the Better Business Bureau. Shady Ridge was an unpretentious yet properly maintained facility an hour outside the city. A nurse was available twenty-four hours a day, and her mother had a private room that overlooked scenic woodlands. Regardless of the cost, which was forcing Catherine to put off the thought of retirement for the foreseeable future, she couldn't bring herself to move her mom again to a place that was less likely to bankrupt her.

The dulcet tones of Dean Martin sounded again. Gloria rolled her eyes. "I'm out. Wish me luck! I'll let you know how my date went tomorrow!"

"Okay," Catherine called as Gloria rolled away, well aware she wouldn't be there the next day to hear the details.

Catherine's phone bleated with a new message. She instinctively grabbed it to call her mom. Fear stopped her cold.

Her mother overreacted to even the tiniest things. A misplaced remote control, a tissue box that was too far away, a cup of coffee that was too hot—they could each turn into epic catastrophes.

What havoc would the genuine tragedy of Robert's death wreak on her failing mind?

Staring longingly at the palm tree on her screen saver, Catherine procrastinated by dialing the number for Garrison Bight, the dock where Robert's boat was moored.

The line rang and rang. If someone picked up, that might stop her trip in its tracks. Catherine closed her eyes and let the ringing continue, as though waiting for a slot machine to stop spinning to see whether she had won or lost.

No one answered. Catherine eventually hung up, unsure whether she should be annoyed or relieved. She had only a few days to get to Florida, sort out selling the boat, then get home if she wanted a shot at the director position that would let her mom stay at Shady Ridge. Catherine weighed her options. Telling her mom, then hopping on a plane seemed cruel.

Not telling her was too.

Decision cemented, Catherine dove into making travel arrangements. Booking a ticket for that night was a snap. Finding someplace to stay was not.

February was high tourist season in Key West. Most of the hotels didn't have any rooms available, and short-term rentals were sold out. She had multiple windows open on her computer, trolling for reasonable rates while the beeps of incoming messages chimed from her purse like a ticking bomb.

She didn't have to listen to the voicemails to know what they said. Typically, her mother called to prattle about the gossip at Shady Ridge. Sick spouses, visits from relatives, or someone hogging the popcorn on movie night set the rumor mill churning.

Her mom's texts were usually minute-by-minute updates. An hour later, what she'd written would slip her mind; then she would resend the same message. That was especially wrenching, each text a testament to her mother's deteriorating mental state.

"If you have nowhere to stay, you can't go to Florida, and there's no point in telling her anything tonight anyway."

Though logical, the excuse was a cop-out. Catherine's phone chimed with another plaintive ping. Time ticking away, she gulped down the guilt and switched off her phone.

Snow was collecting in the corners of her windowsill. Her potted plant seemed to shrink away from the glass. Catherine moved it onto the desk, close to the images of glistening coastlines, coral reef diving excursions, and people sailing or swinging in hammocks, as if that would take off the chill.

Lodging options in Key West were slim. On a budget as tight as hers, they were scant.

After scouring every hotel on the island, Catherine could see that exorbitant penthouse suites were the only rooms left, most touting hot tubs overlooking the ocean, in-room spa treatments, and private butler service. There were luxurious photos of breezes blowing through gauzy curtains and trays of chocolate-covered strawberries resting atop plump king-size beds. Catherine could practically smell the ocean through the screen. She had a pang of envy.

The room rate was listed under the tempting images and tantalizing descriptions.

"Four grand per night?! I'd have to sell a kidney."

Her credit cards were nearly maxed out. This trip would strain her already strapped finances.

If Key West was such an expensive place to stay, it must have been an expensive place to live. *How had Robert afforded it?* she wondered.

A movie-reel mash-up of images flickered in her imagination, framing a version of what she envisioned Robert to look like, walking on a beach, then fishing, then striding along the island's colorful thoroughfares, like pastoral stock footage of a person she had never met yet whose life seemed enviable. What had Robert done for a living? Where had he lived? Did he have a family? And most pressingly, what kind of boat had he owned?

First, a yacht sprang to mind, yet that didn't strike her as his style. Maybe a deluxe fishing cruiser or some sleek sailing vessel. She didn't know much about boats, less about the island, and next to nothing about her brother, except for his love of Ernest Hemingway and Hemingway's love of Key West. From the pictures online, Catherine was starting to see why.

The place was a paradise, and paradise didn't come cheap.

There wasn't a single hotel room to be had. Bed-and-breakfasts were her last resort.

When she did a new keyword search, quaint converted houses with gingerbread moldings materialized. Some had wraparound colonnade porches, while others had sundecks with conch shells and salamanders stenciled on them. Beguiling snapshots of whitewashed porticos and antique four-poster beds gave Catherine hope, which was instantly dashed by the daily fees, all decidedly beyond her budget.

Discouraged, she was about to give up when she stumbled on the Abbott House.

Much less grand than the others, it was the runt of the Victorian litter. No spiral turrets or fanciful fretwork there, just a plainly shingled, two-story facade with hanging ferns in front. However, they offered accommodations for a rate that meant Catherine wouldn't have to starve during her stay.

Normally, she would have cross-referenced reviews and mapped the inn's location in relation to sightseeing hot spots, but she felt like she didn't have a minute to spare. An available room and complimentary breakfast sealed the deal. Catherine clicked through a payment screen to make her reservation, then experienced a cramp of dread.

She still had to call her mother. But she still couldn't face it.

4

It was still dark out when Catherine's flight landed in Key West. As she headed for a cabstand, her hastily packed tote slung over her shoulder, a gust of balmy air wafted across her face like a welcome greeting. The wind was tinged with the scent of sea salt. A sprawling mural on the side of the airport read **Conch Republic**. It looked like a waving flag, as if to proclaim this wasn't merely an island, it was a nation.

"Need a ride?" a cab driver called through his open passenger-side window from where he was idling along the curb. He had a goatee that was as gray as his hair, a potbelly that strained his T-shirt, and a Buddha-like smile to match. A bobblehead doll of Jimmy Buffett stood proudly on his dashboard.

Catherine checked the time on her phone. It was barely seven o'clock in the morning.

"I'm staying at a B and B. Except they're not open yet. I don't have anywhere else to go." Catherine felt as pathetic as the statement sounded.

"You do now! I can take you to the Southernmost Point to watch the sunrise. Should be any minute. Great way to start the day!"

That perked her up. "I like that idea."

Catherine hopped in. Soft jazz hummed from the radio, and the car smelled of coconuts from an air freshener adhered to the plastic partition between the front seat and the back. As the taxi wove over dewy roads, she squinted to make out the ornately painted bungalows and stately Victorian homes in the misty predawn haze. Flowers were in bloom everywhere, and mature trees spread their branches over the sidewalks, as if protecting them. She rolled down her window to get a better view.

"You ain't cold?" he asked. "I can put on the heater."

"Where I came from, it was below zero. To me, this is hot."

"Must be true what they say about your blood getting thin in warm climates. I shiver when the temperature drops below seventy."

Perhaps Catherine's blood had grown thick from living in a city with a climate that could be as unforgiving as its pace. Her skin had thickened too. She wasn't unemotional or insensitive, just desensitized from years of feeling things she didn't want to feel. Despite her exhaustion, being away from everything felt like waking up.

"You in town for vacation or for work?"

Catherine was conflicted. "Both."

"Been here before?"

"Never."

"Then you came to the right cab! I've lived here over thirty years. Learned a thing or two about the place. We have the third-largest coral reef in the world, but if you see it, you'll think it's the biggest. We have free-roaming chickens called gypsies, but they can't tell your fortune. We seceded from the United States in 1982, but that didn't quite stick. And we've been home to illustrious American characters like President Harry S. Truman, Tennessee Williams, and Jimmy Buffett." He bowed deferentially at the bobblehead doll on his dash. "Oh, and Ernest Hemingway, of course. You a fan?"

"Of President Truman, Tennessee Williams, Jimmy Buffett, or Ernest Hemingway?"

"Any of them!"

"Jimmy Buffett doesn't seem too bad," she said with a respectful nod to the bobblehead, who appeared to nod back.

He continued touting the island's history jovially. "We host the Fantasy Fest Parade, our version of Mardi Gras. Our beaches are mostly made of sand imported from the Caribbean. We have the nation's largest historical-wooden-structure district. We also have the most bars and churches per capita in the nation. Oh, and Key West was originally called Cayo Hueso by the Spanish. Means 'Bone Cay.' The land was littered with human remains. Natives used it as a graveyard."

"That's . . . a little-known fact," Catherine replied, unnerved, given why she had come.

"Yeah, Key West was an island nobody wanted. In the 1800s, the governor of Cuba deeded it to an officer of the navy, who sold it for a one-masted sailboat."

"Guess I'm not the only one who came here to sell a boat," Catherine muttered. "Would you mind turning down the music a little? I need to make a call."

While he obliged, Catherine dialed. Her mom picked up on the first ring.

"Where have you been? You were giving me a heart attack."

Catherine girded herself to tell her mother about Robert. She felt like she was pulling air up from her toes to her lungs in preparation. She gripped her cell phone so tightly that her fingertips began to burn. "I'm sorry. It was . . . an eventful day. Listen, Mom, I need to tell you some—"

Except it was too late. By not answering her mother's calls or texts, Catherine had spring-loaded her to explode with information. In a breathless tizzy, she cut Catherine off before she could finish.

"Hon, you are not gonna believe this. Mrs. Higgins, you know, the one with palsy and the catheters?"

Realizing she wouldn't get anywhere until she appeased her mom, Catherine gave in. "The woman you won't play cards with because you think she doesn't wash her hands after she goes to the bathroom?" She had memorized all the characters in her mother's senior soap opera.

"She touches those tubes, then the cards, then her hands shake. How is that sanitary?"

Afraid her mom could completely lose her train of thought, Catherine urged her back on track. "You were saying about Mrs. Higgins?"

"She fell down the stairs. Bing, bang, boom. There were ambulances, a fire truck, the whole enchilada. And wait until I tell you what I learned on that morning talk show I watch. There was this lovely Indian man, some fancy-pants author who they called a 'wellness guru.' Whatever that means. His name was Dr. Tupac Shakur, and he was explaining how—"

"You mean Deepak Chopra."

"No, no, Dr. Tupac said—"

"Deepak Chopra is into spirituality. Tupac Shakur was a rapper. But he's . . ."

Catherine stopped herself before she could utter the word "dead."

"You think I don't pay attention?" Her mom flew into a defensive fit. Doctors had warned that she could easily become agitated. The anger wasn't a conscious response. Lashing out was now a reflex. "You think you can send me away like a horse you're shipping off to the glue farm."

"Horses would go to the glue *factory*. Like a hundred years ago. And, no, I moved you to Shady Ridge to be sure you had the best care."

"I wouldn't call it the best. They overcook the fish. It's as rubbery as a spare tire."

"Fine," Catherine sighed, placating her. "What did Dr. Tupac Shakur say?"

The cabbie eyed her in the rearview as she shrugged in defeat.

"He was talking about how to be Zen in the workplace. That's why I watched the entire segment. Because I know you hate that Gloria woman who's your secretary."

To avoid another outburst, Catherine didn't bother correcting her.

"He said that when a coworker is hard to get along with, you have to treat them like they're your neighbor. You pretend there's a fence around you. Good fences make good neighbors."

Her mom had a valid—albeit roundabout—point regarding boundaries. They had been blurry for Catherine since childhood.

Once she entered high school and was allowed to be home alone, her mother switched to the night shift for higher pay. She would return from the brewery as Catherine was getting ready to leave for class in the morning. Catherine would prepare breakfast for them, then run a pot of hot water for her mom to soak her feet in while they ate.

Standing on a bottling line had nearly hobbled her mother. Hard work and hard knocks had taken a toll on her body. Her mind grew less sharp. It could have been the exhaustion of her job or the debility of being abandoned by her husband and son in quick succession. She left pans on the stove until they burned. Only the smell would alert her—or Catherine—that she had been cooking. She would wear the same clothes two days in a row and not realize it until Catherine reminded her. There were a million times when Catherine found herself wishing she could shout for Robert to open a jar for her, pitch in with raking leaves, change some filter in the water heater, or move something heavy. She would catch herself, then indignantly bite her tongue.

Although her mom was the provider, she wasn't the caretaker. Catherine became the adult early on. She had only gotten to be a daughter and a sister until she was seven. Catherine was so accustomed to being indispensable yet invisible that she saw herself like one of those silhouette optical illusions where it's hard to tell if the real image is the dark one or the light one.

"Wasn't that smart, what Dr. Tupac said?"

Catherine could feel the words piling up like a logjam in her mouth, yet nothing came out.

"Wish I had a fence between me and Mrs. Higgins. A soundproof one. She snores like a chainsaw. I don't want to hear that."

What her mother wanted to hear wasn't the same as what she was willing to hear. Catherine couldn't predict how her mom would react to Robert's death. Would her temper flare? Would she refuse to believe it? Would the heartbreaking finality of his passing evaporate from her mind without sinking in?

It felt wrong to say anything if Catherine wouldn't be there in person to console her mother when she learned that the son she'd never forgotten—when she had forgotten so many other things—was gone forever.

"You there?"

"Yes, it's uh, a . . . fuzzy connection," she murmured. "Can I call you back later?"

"Sure. Love you, Catherine," her mother said.

"I love you too."

They hung up as the taxi pulled to a stop. Catherine was lost in thought at how things had completely spiraled out of control since she found out her long-lost brother was deceased. Silence ballooned in the cab.

The cabbie cleared his throat. "Monument's right there. Home of the Southernmost sunset, as the saying goes. In my humble opinion, the sunrises are far better."

"Right. Sorry."

"Wanna know a secret? That isn't really the southernmost point. The real one is on Ballast Key. Except that's owned by some rich, old fart who won't let anybody on his property."

"Then the monument is . . . a fraud?"

To Catherine, that was tantamount to saying close enough was good enough. Fudging the details would have gotten her fired. Bouncing a check would have put her mom out on the street. She abided by rules. When people got away with breaking them, Catherine felt she was being penalized for playing fair.

"The difference between a truth and a lie ain't facts."

"It's not?" she asked with an incredulous huff.

"It's how one makes you feel compared to the other."

That stopped Catherine's rising irritation for a second. That notion had never occurred to her.

"Forget the clichés—a fresh start, a new beginning, nature's daily do-over, God's mulligan. None of that does our sunrise justice. This is the best one you'll ever see, even if it's not where you thought you'd see it. The truth only helps if it makes you feel better." He gave her a knowing wink in the mirror.

Catherine held that sentiment as if she were holding her breath, unable to take it in or let it go, until she finally exhaled for real.

"Well, we're already here so . . . can I leave my stuff with you?"

"Of course. Meter's runnin'!"

In the wan light stood an immense stone statue in the form of a bullet, painted in bands of red, yellow, and black. At the bottom, it read "Home of the sunset." Yet here Catherine was at sunrise, feeling like she was at the wrong place at the wrong time yet again in life.

Dozens of tourists were sitting on a cement wall that faced the water, cell phones out, ready to record. Eventually, the sun began to crest, casting brilliant rays over the horizon. An uproarious round of clapping started as it broke free of the waterline. The sky was steadily blossoming into a warm orange. Dawn painted the undersides of the clouds pink.

It took Catherine a moment to realize she had never watched the sun rise before, not on purpose. For a second, she felt humiliated, as if she had willfully been deprived or skipped it intentionally, yet seeing this sunrise seemed to make up for every sunrise she had missed.

Captivated by the sheer spectacle, Catherine went to take a photo, and the low-battery warning on her cell sputtered. She desperately tried to get her phone to restart. Then the screen went dark and stayed dark.

"Great."

She pawed through her purse for her charger. It wasn't there. Forgetting her phone charger meant her mom wouldn't be able to contact her. That spelled trouble.

Distraught, Catherine jogged back to the cab, jumped in, and began rifling through her bag. The cabbie stared via the rearview mirror, bewildered, as she tossed clothes everywhere. To her dismay, the charger was nowhere to be found.

"Uh . . . you okay?" he inquired, as one of her bras dangled from a headrest.

"Not really. Come to think of it, I'm not sure I ever have been."

Her brother had ruined an enormous chunk of her life. She wasn't going to let him, or a missing charger, wreck her trip too. Catherine was going to make the best of this. She would find Robert's boat. She would find someone to buy it. And then she was determined to enjoy the vacation that she so richly deserved, even if it was only a couple of days.

Now it simply had to start.

5

Worrying only made the situation worse. Catherine couldn't help it.

"Could you have left the charger on the plane?" the cabbie asked in a coaxing tone.

"No. Maybe." She thrust a plastic baggie full of toiletries at him to hold as she turned her purse inside out, raining down lint and a dime into her lap. He shifted in the driver's seat to take in the chaos she was creating as she searched her luggage.

"Do you want the paper bag from my take-out food so you can breathe into it?"

"I'm not hyperventilating."

"Yet."

Catherine passed him a pair of shoes. Then a skirt. Then a top. "It's got to be in here somewhere."

"We can swing by a convenience store to get you a new one."

"No, forget it. Let's go. I'll buy one after I've checked into the Abbott House."

"The Abbott House?" The cabbie suddenly sounded as antsy as she was.

"Yeah, it's on—"

"Oh, I know where it is."

"Now you're making me nervous."

"Did you already pay for the room?"

"Am I going to need the paper bag?"

"Based on what I know of you from the last hour, probably."

Catherine flopped back in the seat as they drove to Amelia Street, where the homes were packed as tightly as books on a shelf, each with a narrow collar of scrubby vegetation out front instead of grass. There stood the same house Catherine had seen online.

The difference between the pictures and the real thing was that a section of the roof was completely caved in. A few errant boards protruded from the shingles. It was as if a meteor had plummeted right into the house. The potted ferns from the photos online had been replaced by bright-fuchsia azaleas, meant to distract the eye from the giant blue tarp nailed to the roof that fluttered and bloated with the whims of the wind. They didn't.

"Place got hit hard by the last hurricane we had."

"They couldn't have fixed it before people were paying to stay under it?"

"Unfortunately, there's no place else to go. People been camping on the beaches until the cops roust 'em because they can't find a room. The island's totally sold out."

"Can I give you my number in case you hear about any vacancies?"

"Your phone is dead. Remember?" He passed her a business card with the cab company's name and number on the front and his information on the back. "Try me later. I'm game to give you whatever scoop I got."

"Thank you, Kenny," she said, reading the name he had written. "I'm Catherine."

"Pleased to make your acquaintance. Better take this, too, or my wife will think I'm switching teams." He passed her the toiletry bag full of face cream and mascara as Catherine started dolefully repacking her clothes.

"I know you're bummed about the accommodations. But you'll barely be there except to sleep. Listen, tourism is all we got down here. It's our lifeblood. Heck, it's the soul of Key West. If people don't make enough during the high seasons, it's almost impossible to survive."

Part of Catherine's job was understanding how precarious debt made people's lives, how it shaped their spending. She had been scraping away at her own savings since moving her mom into Shady Ridge. If she missed one paycheck, she would be on the ropes. Catherine couldn't imagine how it would feel to live like that all year long. She was afraid she would soon learn if selling Robert's boat didn't work out in her favor.

Had her brother been in the same position, doing seasonal work that left him in limbo for months at a time? Catherine felt a splinter of pity, empathizing about something she couldn't even be sure was true. Then that sentiment sharpened into a sting because she doubted that he had ever empathized with her.

"Money can't buy happiness, but it makes the misery easier to live with."

"You can say that again."

"Maybe the folks who run the Abbott House just got behind. Happens to the best of us."

Her credit card bill proved Catherine was behind too.

"If it's any consolation, I've heard they make a mean French toast."

"The last thing I ate was airplane pretzels, so that's one in the plus column for the Abbott House."

"It's all gonna work out." Kenny pretended he had pom-poms to limply cheer her on.

"It will," she told him as she paid the fare, hoping to convince herself more than him.

Catherine got out and watched him drive away. Once Kenny was gone, a harmony of crickets and birds swelled, like an orchestra tuning up. The sun was poking over the treetops.

The front door to the Abbott House was locked when she tried it. She knocked lightly. There was no response.

This is not an auspicious start to your trip.

Since it was ten to eight, Catherine assumed somebody had to be preparing breakfast. She tromped around the side of the house along a narrow brick path that let out onto a tiny yet exquisitely cultivated backyard with a dipping pool, a wrought iron patio set, and trellises festooned with flowers. A fountain burbled tranquilly. Relieved by the beauty concealed behind the disastrous facade, Catherine dropped her bags where she stood to take it all in.

"I'm going to hazard a guess that you aren't the new gardener," a male voice politely intoned.

She turned to see a short, plump man wearing a vibrant Hawaiian shirt and an impish grin.

"This place is amazing."

"Why, thank you!" He did a curtsy. "I'm Fred. Compliments will get you everywhere, including an invitation to breakfast."

"That's what I'm here for. I booked a room, only I—"

"Tried the front door and it was locked? Arnie!" he called, then quickly lowered his voice to a mock shout. "How are guests going to check in if they can't *get* in?"

A tall, flinty man with a mustache and a similarly loud Hawaiian shirt appeared in the doorway, wiping flour from his hands onto an apron emblazoned with the saying **It's Called a Diet Because the Other Four-Letter Words Were Taken.**

"Good morning," Arnie said with a jolly finger-waggling wave. "You must be Catherine. Come in! The French toast is almost ready, and the strawberry butter is fresher than the mouth on this man of mine." He elbowed Fred while ushering her in the door.

"Ooh, she looks a little like Vivien Leigh, doesn't she? High cheekbones and that hint of damsel in distress."

"Who?" Catherine asked blankly.

Fred seemed stricken. "*Gone with the Wind*?"

"*A Streetcar Named Desire*?" Arnie tried, aghast.

"Sorry. I don't know the name. But the 'distress' I've got covered."

"We are going to pretend we didn't hear either part of that sentence." Arnie shut the back door behind her.

Catherine entered a sliver of a kitchen that was decked out in 1950s style, complete with seafoam green cabinets, a vintage refrigerator, and a matching stove. A vast collection of kitschy salt and pepper shakers dotted the countertops, the open-faced cabinets, and every shelf on the wall. The smell of strawberries and hot food was as distracting as the decor.

"You'll have to forgive us for the whole roof situation," Fred whispered. "We didn't want a crew of men banging away up there. They would wake the guests."

"Correction. We wanted the first part. Not the second."

"Honey, *ixnay* on the flamboyant gay," he mumbled.

"I don't care what you say as long as you feed me," Catherine said.

"Of course, darling. I'll show you to the dining room. I redid the wallpaper last Christmas. It's divine. The kitchen is Arnie's domain. The rest of the house is mine."

Fred led her through a hall into the main part of the house. "The girl is wilting, Arnie. ¡Ándale, muchacho!" Aside, he whispered, "He goes loco when I speak Spanish."

The interior of the Abbott House was a jewel box, compact yet decadently decorated. The dining room table was a long mahogany antique, the chair seats covered in chintz to coordinate with the deeply hued floral paper on the walls. Even though Arnie and Fred were wearing nearly identical shirts, their interior design tastes appeared to differ drastically.

"Your Spanish is *horrible* for a gringo who lives this close to Cuba."

"You love it," Fred insisted.

Catherine was about to take a seat when a corgi dog toddled out from under the table, belly almost brushing the ground. He snorted as though she had ousted him from his favorite spot.

"Forgive Truman." Fred petted the dog on the head as he wobbled toward the kitchen.

"Oh, is he named after Harry Truman?"

"Nope. Capote. He's short and moody, and he bites."

Arnie flounced into the room in purple oven mitts, carrying a piping-hot dish of French toast. "Plates, Fred. And utensils. Por favor."

Fred scuttled into the kitchen, then returned to set the table. "You'll burn your tongue if you're not careful. Try a parfait while the rest cools."

Arnie arrived with a cut-crystal glass layered with fruit and heaping dollops of fresh cream. "I whip the cream myself," he relayed with pride.

"He excels at whipping things," Fred added wryly.

Catherine dove in. The parfait was delicious. Between shoveling bites into her mouth, she asked, "Are you a professional chef? Because this is beyond fantastic."

"Her I like, Fred. Tell me I don't look a day over thirty-five, and you can have seconds."

Both men were in their late sixties, yet they genuinely did seem younger.

"I bet they card you when you buy alcohol," Catherine said to humor Arnie.

"It's official. We're keeping her," he pronounced.

The men slipped into the kitchen, then reappeared with trays of scrambled eggs, crisp bacon, and a smattering of muffins, along with a platter of maple syrups in a variety of flavors.

"This is regular. This is vanilla passion fruit. And this has a hint of rum."

"You may want the one with the liquor. Arnie will start asking you if he favors Rudy Valentino in a certain light. Better to be tipsy for that."

"Who?"

"No. Nope. Pretending I didn't hear that either." Fred plugged his ears.

Stairs creaked, announcing the arrival of a pair of sisters in their sixties who looked similar enough to be twins, with their stick-straight white-blond hair, beefy limbs, and broad shoulders.

"Ladies, this is our new guest, Catherine," Arnie announced.

Fred pointed out each of the sisters. "This is Ina and Lita from Saint Paul."

Ina had a fanny pack around her thick waist, and Lita was wearing an oversize T-shirt with a tabby curled up under the phrase **Nobody's Purrfect.**

"Pleased to meet you. Doesn't this look fantastic?" Ina sang, her Minnesota accent giving the phrase a bouncy cadence. She was more interested in the food than the introduction.

"Doesn't it, though?" Lita agreed, their voices almost identical.

"We're here on a yearly trip," Ina said.

"We pick a new place every year." Lita pushed past Catherine with barely a glance.

"This year it's Key West," Ina stated.

"This year it's Key West," Lita echoed.

Catherine wasn't sure if she was delirious or if Lita was intentionally repeating her sister.

"Lita works at a drugstore," Arnie explained. "And Ina is an avid crafter."

"Scrapbooks," she corrected. "Sounds easy. But it's an art form."

While Ina plunged into a lengthy description of her scrapbooking, Fred and Arnie listened attentively, nodding at all the right places. Sleep-deprived, Catherine got lost in the details about stickers, pinking shears, and highlighter pens. She dug into the French toast, which was delectably airy, devouring three thick slices in record time. The mix of whipped cream and syrup she was wolfing down sent her brain spinning from sweetness. Her eyes started dipping shut.

"Say, does anybody have a phone charger I can borrow?" Catherine asked, drowsily interrupting Ina midsentence. "My mom has dementia, and my brother died, and I have to sell the boat he willed me, but my mom doesn't know, and I need to call her," she blathered.

Taken aback, Ina's fork clinked loudly against her plate, while Arnie's eyes bulged.

Catherine was only distantly aware that she was slurring her speech. "I've been awake for over twenty-four hours, and I'm—"

Fred abruptly started hurrying her upstairs. "Pooped! We understand. Don't we, gals?"

As they mounted the steps, Catherine felt as though she could pass out. "My bags?"

"I'll bring them up."

"My room?"

"Right here, darling."

He guided her into a powder blue bedroom with a carved oak headboard, a fluffy white duvet, and lace eyelet drapes. A dressing table topped by an oval mirror, and a wicker nightstand with a lamp rounded out the furnishings. Catherine shuffled, too lethargic to pick up her feet.

"I'm glad I'm here," she cooed as she fell onto the bed while slipping off her shoes.

"We're, uh, glad you are too," Fred sputtered.

Before he could close the door, Catherine was fast asleep.

6

The southern sunlight had a brightness that refused to be ignored. It was so intense that it bore through the blinds, waking Catherine from a deep slumber. She rolled over to catch a few more winks, thinking she had only been dozing for an hour. Then she squinted at the bedside clock.

"Two forty-five?"

Catherine hurled off the covers and bounded out of bed to discover her bag by the dresser. Her phone was resting on top, attached to a charger. The battery was back to life. She hadn't even heard Fred or Arnie come in.

As she powered up the phone, Catherine tried to ballpark how many messages and texts awaited from her mom. Five would be a low estimate. Ten was the norm. Fifteen was what she was prepared for.

"Twenty-three. That's a new record."

One text was from Gloria. It read "Where are you? My date was amazing! He even paid for the food. The last guy I went out with stuck me with the check after trying to convince me to buy into a multilevel marketing scam for joint pain relief. If I marry this new guy, will you come to the wedding? Also, would you be interested in any joint pain relief cream?"

Catherine cracked up and shook her head. Oddly, that was the precise second when it hit her that she wasn't at work. She truly was on vacation. For a moment, a weight was lifted, and she felt lighter, almost buoyant and untethered.

Then the phone beeped, signaling her inbox was almost full. That brought her slamming back to reality.

It was hard to resist the temptation to check the other messages from her mother. Once Catherine started, she would be sucked in and feel duty bound to reply. The texts tugged at her heart even when they were incoherent or downright crazy. They were like the tap-tap of Morse code signaling that her mom was isolated and alone. Catherine knew exactly how that felt and didn't wish it on her mom. However, she needed to get a handle on the boat situation first. Once that was done, Catherine could tell her the truth.

She swallowed hard, then switched off the ringer until she was ready to return the calls.

From outside, bicycle bells trilled. Catherine peered past the window's lacy curtains and saw a family riding single file down the street on beach cruisers, each in a different sherbet hue. That was when she remembered her first view of the house from outside and realized that her room was beneath a portion of the roof that had been ripped off by the hurricane. The ceiling overhead, however, was unmarred.

"Of course I got this room."

She had been sleeping under a wrecked roof. It was hardly the worst of her problems.

Her hair was a mess, and she was sweaty from the plane ride, but Catherine decided a shower could wait if she was heading into the ocean anyway. Brushing her teeth, however, was nonnegotiable. The mounds of sugar she'd consumed before passing out had pickled the inside of her mouth. Her head was hazy from the rich food and the grueling trip.

The inn's one communal guest bath was right outside her room. Still in her clothes from yesterday, Catherine gently bumped open the door, expecting to see a slew of damp used towels and other people's shampoo bottles strewn about.

To her surprise, the bathroom was immaculate.

It was appointed with ornate tiles surrounding the claw-foot tub and a sink inset into a marble-topped bureau that was converted into a vanity. Embroidered hand towels lay beside the basin, along with Parisian-milled soaps in lavender and honey. As Catherine brushed her teeth, her marketing mind wondered why there weren't pictures of these amenities on the website. They made her feel like a welcome guest rather than some average traveler.

Careful not to disrupt the scrupulously clean bathroom, Catherine splashed a little water on her cheeks but couldn't bring herself to use the delicate hand towels. She wiped her face on her shirt instead. The image that met her in the mirror when she glanced up was pale, fatigued. The lines on her face seemed more pronounced. With her hair twisted into a sloppy bun, Catherine was beginning to resemble her mom.

If she looked like her mother, would she suffer the same memory problems that she did?

Who would take care of her if she were to succumb to the same fate? Robert's absence cut deepest when she considered the future compared to what it could have been if he'd stayed. Every insecurity, feeling of worthlessness, and inability to trust was born on the day he left, reverberating into each day that followed, echoing how alone she was and would be. The thought depressed Catherine as much as the visage that met her in the mirror.

"Nothing a couple of hours on the beach can't fix."

In the hallway, she noticed the door to the room beside hers was ajar. She peeked inside. Ribs of lath hung from the ceiling, providing a gaping view into the rafters with glimpses of the sky beyond. The furniture was draped in plastic to protect it from further damage. Catherine felt bad for Fred and Arnie. The repairs appeared as if they would cost a fortune.

After throwing on her bathing suit, a clean T-shirt, and a pair of shorts, Catherine yanked the folder with Robert's documents from her laptop case and slotted it into her purse. Getting the difficult stuff out of the way was her first order of business.

She planned to visit the dock and inspect the vessel, then run the numbers on comparative sales figures for similar boats later that evening once the sun had gone down. She also had to keep up on the research for Willford's new payment plan, which was dry and technical, the written form of anesthetic. That could wait. Soaking up every possible ray of sunshine was her priority.

Catherine gathered her purse, tugged on a baseball cap bearing her company's logo that she'd gotten at a holiday party, then set off for the day with Kenny the cab driver's business card in hand.

"Just get it over with," she urged herself, pushing aside any trepidation as she descended the staircase. "Then you'll be done with the boat—and Robert—forever. Get it out of the way and get on with your vacation."

"Get what out of the way?" Fred yodeled from downstairs.

He and Arnie were sitting in the front room, reading sections of the newspaper with Truman asleep at their feet. Carved wood furniture with tufted upholstery and swagged floral drapes gave the space the spirit of a turn-of-the-century parlor with the warm charm of a bygone era. Bouquets of flowers in elegant vases dotted antique end tables.

"Nothing," Catherine told them, self-conscious after being overheard.

"There she is!" Arnie cheered her arrival.

Fred folded his paper shut. "We were giving you until sundown before we called the paramedics."

"What did I do? Sleepwalk into the kitchen for more food?"

"He's being melodramatic," Arnie insisted.

"Well, after your outburst . . ."

"Announcement." Arnie amended Fred's choice of words.

"Ina told us how she'd seen an episode of *Dateline* about meth addicts, and she pegged you for a closet tweaker because you were twitchy and skinny."

"Me? I'm the most straitlaced, buttoned-up, dependable person you could meet. I don't even jaywalk. I file my taxes early. I proofread my emails twice. I alphabetize my spices."

"Well, you've officially won my respect," Arnie stated. "Mainly for the spices thing."

"Admit it. Is this your long-lost love child?" Fred prodded his partner.

The entire breakfast incident flooded back to Catherine with embarrassing lucidity, especially being hustled away from the dining table like a ranting lunatic. She was mortified.

"I apologize for ruining breakfast."

"Ruin it? You rescued us!" Arnie declared. "We didn't have to listen to Ina jabber away about that god-awful scrapbook anymore."

"Puffy paint. Glitter glue. Those sound like party drugs from the eighties."

Arnie cut him a look. "Is there something you haven't told me?"

"Countless somethings, darling."

"*Anyhooo*, Ina's crafting story put the *oy* in 'annoying.' You liberated us from boring-convo bondage."

"Remember, we don't speak disparagingly about our guests," Fred scolded, whacking him lightly with the paper. "About your . . . announcement?"

Catherine took a perch on a brocade settee. The men deserved an explanation since they had been so kind.

"It's true. My brother passed away."

In unison, both Arnie and Fred stood, ready to swoop to her side and console her. She put a hand up to stop them. Both backed up a pace.

"He abandoned me and my mom when I was a kid. Same as my father. He was an asshole."

She took no pleasure in bad-mouthing Robert. It felt wrong, despite how he had treated her and their mother. It seemed almost blasphemous to talk badly about him because of his recent passing.

"An asshole who left you a boat?" Arnie swapped a puzzled look with Fred.

"Tactful," Fred said between his teeth.

"It's a long, sad story. I'll spare you the details."

He took a spot next to her on the settee. Arnie followed, then rubbed her back and said, "Catherine, doll, it's okay to be sad."

"No, it's not. I did it for decades, like some crappy part-time job that had no benefits, no vacation days, and zero pay. Being upset never did me any good."

The finality in her voice silenced the men, warding off further attempts at sympathy. Admitting that aloud, Catherine couldn't help but pity herself. She'd made a career out of missing her brother. She was ready to quit.

After a minute, Arnie nudged Fred, who said, "Listen, I owe you an apology as well."

"For what?"

"For expediting your exit this morning, stage left." Arnie motioned toward the dining room. "We've had prior guests write negative things about the inn—and us—online. The comments hurt our bookings. We had vacant rooms for weeks. Somebody posted that we're too 'over the top.'"

"You guys?" She feigned astonishment.

"Over the top? For Key West? Here we could pass for heterosexual."

"It's more that we don't make everybody feel comfortable," Fred clarified. "We figured that was why business was down. Without paying clients, we can't get the roof repaired, so we couldn't afford to have you make a bad impression on the current guests. That's why I was hiding you away in the bedroom like Blanche from *Whatever Happened to Baby Jane?*"

"Never saw it. I'm guessing that's not good."

"You never . . . ?" Arnie seemed traumatized by her admission.

Fred shushed him. "Catherine has more important things to worry about than diva movie trivia, darling."

"Speaking of which, thanks for charging my phone. I'm going to call a cab and head over to the dock to inspect the boat before I put it up for sale—then I'm hitting the beach. Any places you can recommend?"

"But . . . ?" Arnie was holding back. He appeared keen to encourage her to keep Robert's boat. Catherine could tell he didn't want to say it in front of Fred.

Fred shot him an admonishing glance. "We have towels if you need them."

"How about sunscreen and a beach chair?" she asked, chancing it.

"Done and done," Arnie told her. "It's the least we can do. We're giving you the SPF 70, or you'll broil. Zinc for her nose?" He deferred to Fred.

"That goes without saying. We can't have her coming home beet red and blistered. Ina will think she was involved in some drug-lab explosion."

"Then you could tell new guests that the roof is my fault," Catherine suggested.

Arnie burst out laughing.

"For someone who's been put through the wringer"—Fred chuckled—"you certainly haven't lost your sense of humor. Come on. Let's get you fixed up!"

Catherine had, indeed, lost a lot, more than she cared to tally. Maybe today she would find something that would balance the scales in her favor.

7

Being doted on was a new experience for Catherine. She let Fred and Arnie load her up with big beach towels in wacky floral patterns and a travel-size cooler stocked with bottled water and chilled grapes, as well as a folding beach chair in a zany palm tree print, which she could easily carry on her shoulder along with her laptop case.

It was a relief to have somebody take care of her for a change.

After a call to summon Kenny, the couple walked Catherine to the door, barraging her with advice the way overprotective parents would.

"Fred, does she look too much like a homeless one-man band minus the bass drum and slide trombone?"

Catherine glanced down at everything they had saddled her with, concerned.

"It is . . . a lot. Are you going to topple over, dear?"

"I don't think so."

"There! She's fine. So much to do and see," Fred extolled. "There's Fort Zachary Taylor, the butterfly conservatory, the Conch Tour Train, or a stroll down Duval Street."

"There's Mallory Square, the Key West Lighthouse, seeing the rescued sea turtles at the aquarium, and of course, the Ernest Hemingway Home to see the famous six-toed cats!"

They all sounded appealing until the last option.

Catherine's expression must have betrayed her. "I'll pass on that one."

"Not a fan? I get it," Arnie whispered. "A brawler, a bragger, and a drunk. Much ado about an egomaniac, in my opinion."

Catherine could have kissed him for confirming her opinion; then Fred said, "Last week, you declared that Ernest Hemingway was a 'retro zaddy.'"

"Don't quote me after four rosés. Maybe I like toxic masculinity." He blew a kiss to Fred pertly. "Anyway, there are plenty of other places to go!"

"Oh, but don't give money to the panhandlers," Fred warned. "Most of them are pickpockets."

"So are the jugglers."

"And the sword-swallowers."

"You just wanted to say 'sword-swallower.'"

"Perhaps."

"Remember to reapply the sunscreen every two hours," Arnie reminded her. "Or else you'll go from fair to flambéed fast. The sun here in Key West is set to air fryer mode."

"Don't forget your ears. People always do the face. But they forget the ears."

"You just wanted to say 'do the face,' didn't you?"

"I was on a roll. Couldn't stop myself."

"If you see any handsome men, don't forget to flirt. Key West has a bountiful selection."

"Blonds, brunettes, tall, short, muscular, slender," Fred declared, dreamily envisioning a roster as he listed it.

"It's like IKEA for guys." Arnie gave her a wink.

"It's Guy-KEA!" Fred proclaimed.

"The men are cheap, foreign, and fall apart easily?" Catherine wrinkled her nose.

Arnie shook his head and stifled a chuckle.

"I haven't had the best luck in the romance department," she explained. "Some guys want kids when they already have an AARP card. Or they're afraid of commitment. Or they're looking for an open relationship when they need blue pills to keep up with one woman, let alone more. Or they're still hung up on their ex. Or still married and cheating. It's always some lame excuse for being delusional enough to believe they have a shot at dating younger women way out of their league."

"Then date younger men. They never grow up anyway."

It was Fred's turn to shake his head.

"Looking for love really isn't on my radar right now, given the circumstances."

"Neither Mr. Right nor Mr. Right Now is wrong," Fred reminded her.

"We want you to have a fantastic time," Arnie cooed. "Forget your troubles. Come on. Get happy!"

"Enjoy the seafood," Fred insisted. "Have a daiquiri. Or three!"

"Get out of your comfort zone. Get wild. Go on an adventure. That's what a vacation is about."

This was news to Catherine. She thought she was supposed to lie on a beach towel and vegetate. That was her version.

Meeting men was the furthest thing from her mind until Arnie and Fred had practically made it her duty.

Every time friends attempted to set her up or cajole her into joining a dating app like Gloria had, it made her feel ancient, undesirable, and more out of touch. A part of her had always expected to remain single because the important men in her life had left. So why would any man stay?

Arnie opened the inn's front door for her ceremoniously, like he was presenting every amazing thing the island had to offer just beyond the threshold.

"You'll be okay," Fred said.

She wasn't sure if he meant she would be fine getting around the island on her own or that she'd have no problem weathering whatever the sale of Robert's boat would bring up emotionally, which was bound to be deeper and choppier than whatever water it was docked in. She hoped he was correct on both counts.

"I'd say 'Don't talk to strangers,'" Arnie began, "but it's Key West, baby. You absolutely *should* talk to strangers!"

They shut the door behind her as if pushing her off the proverbial plank.

Cars cruised along Amelia Street as the ocean breeze rustled palm fronds overhead, casting jagged shadows of leaves that raked across the sidewalk. The sun beat down on her like a reprimand. Catherine clomped down the front steps in her flip-flops. She couldn't see how she would have the courage to talk to anybody now that she was feeling shy and decidedly pale.

"Maybe a tan will help."

Kenny soon rode up and tooted at her, wearing a friendly grin and a Miami Marlins baseball cap, brim cocked low.

"You must be one hell of a packer because I don't remember seeing that chair in your bag this morning."

She slid the gear into the back seat with her. "The owners were really generous, and they lent it to me along with these magazines, the mini fan, the towels, everything."

"Does that mean you don't want to hear about a room with a balcony and a view at the Sheraton?"

"There's a vacancy?"

"And a tiki lounge. And a pool with a swim-up bar."

Catherine had a twinge of jealousy.

"I took some guy to the airport twenty minutes ago. He told me he walked in on his girlfriend with his best buddy doing the nasty in the bathtub. The room was on his credit card. The girlfriend got the boot. The buddy got a knuckle sandwich. *Voilà!* Vacant! The Sheraton has flat-screen TVs and a spa. Probably a smidge pricier than this place but not an arm and a leg."

She debated the decision for a heartbeat.

The amenities did sound cushy. However, Catherine felt loyal to Fred and Arnie for taking such good care of her. They weren't worth trading in exchange for a pool and premium channels.

"Thanks. But I think I'll stay at the Abbott House. You were right about the French toast."

"Can you say that 'you're right' part again?" He held up his cell phone. "I want to record it to prove to my wife that it can occasionally happen."

Catherine wondered if she was right too. About not telling her mom as soon as she had found out about Robert. About selling the boat. About how she felt so profoundly conflicted about his death.

A gnawing sense of regret had taken up residence in the back of her brain, making her question her intentions.

"So?" Kenny asked. "Where are we off to? Plenty of primo beaches on Key West to pick from."

The dock or the beach?

She had to choose.

Catherine was certainly curious about what type of vessel Robert had owned, but she was keener to learn what, if anything, of his might still be onboard. The lawyer had said his possessions had been sold off, but perhaps something remained, something that would give her more insight into the life he had lived in secret. She was also eager to put that part of the trip behind her, dreading what the experience would stir up.

"Garrison Bight Marina, please."

"There's no beach there," Kenny replied, confused. "Do you mean—?"

She cut him off. "I have some business to attend to. Ten minutes. Tops. You can keep the meter running again."

Kenny stayed conspicuously mum on the matter and slid the cab into drive.

"'Keep the meter running' is my favorite phrase. Say no more."

Outside the taxi's windshield, people were happily crisscrossing the streets while sightseeing and zipping along on bicycles. A vibrant energy bubbled in the air. Between the movement everywhere and storefronts clad in a dizzying array of colors from canary yellow to Caribbean blue, the streets seem to effervesce with activity. She wanted to be a part of the action, to do what the tourists were doing, not what she had to do.

Watching them, Catherine realized that Fred and Arnie hadn't exaggerated about the number of attractive men on the island. There were tons everywhere, many in swim trunks, bare chested with sun-kissed skin, and many seemed to be around her age. Arnie's buffet of brawny options was living up to the hype.

She spotted Kenny scrutinizing her in the mirror.

"What? Was I drooling?"

"If you're looking for dates, most of those hunks play for the home team, if you take my meaning."

"Ah, good point."

"The handsome ones usually do around here."

"I thought you said you weren't switching sides," she teased.

Kenny patted his belly. "I know when I'm outta my league! So . . . you ever been to Garrison Bight before?" he asked, turning from joking to slightly suspicious.

"No."

"You runnin' drugs?"

"Of course not!" Catherine was flabbergasted. "Why does everybody keep insinuating that I'm some kind of dope fiend?"

"You are wound a little tight."

"I like to think of it as being attentive."

"And you are kinda finicky."

"I prefer prudent," she countered.

"And you seem like you need a—" Kenny stopped himself short. "Vacation."

Catherine knew what he was going to say. She glowered at him.

"I'm supposed to be on one, thank you very much."

"Funny way to start it."

"What's the big deal? Is this dock in some shady neighborhood?"

"It's over on the causeway. Neighborhood isn't sketchy. A few of the folks who dock there, that's a different story."

What sort of boat did Robert leave me?

Catherine had been banking on an outboard she could sell to a family who enjoyed waterskiing. Now she had visions of some slick cigarette boat complete with hidden compartments and a motor with enough horsepower to outrun the Coast Guard.

"I have to go," she confided. "It's a . . . family matter."

Her tone was evidently enough to sway Kenny into softening, though he still appeared wary.

Calling her brother "family" stuck in Catherine's throat. It may have been true. It didn't feel like a fact.

"You're the boss."

"I'm going to record the 'You're the boss' part, then play *that* for your wife."

Kenny smiled at her in the rearview mirror and gave her a salute.

"Then aye-aye, Captain. Full steam ahead."

8

The northern edge of Key West was a different island altogether. The coastline was fringed with marshy swathes of tall grass and mangrove islands, where leggy trees held their foliage aloft of the water. Framed in the windshield of the cab, a low-slung plane of glassy sea was flattened under an unfettered sky.

"This here's the backcountry," Kenny explained.

"Why is it called that?"

He scratched his head. "I don't have an answer other than that's what it's always been called. Locals also refer to it as 'the flats.' Water's gin clear, and people come from far and wide to fish for the 'Key West Grand Slam.' That's tarpon, permit, and bonefish. No place else in the world can you catch all three in one day more months outta the year than here."

Catherine stared out her open window, lost in thought, the breeze caressing her face. She removed her hat to feel the wind run through her hair. Miles of ocean met miles of sky in a pale line of blue on blue. The panorama was epic in its proportions. When she was at home in Manhattan, her life was completely compartmentalized, right down to the cubicle she slaved away in ten hours a day. Here, boxing in the beauty would be impossible.

"Am I wasting my breath, or did you stow a reel and bait in that bag of yours too?"

"No, no, I'm interested. However, it's unlikely I'll be doing any fishing on this trip."

"Then you gonna tell me why we're going to a dock?"

A spasm of shame crept up her shoulders. The truth had turned grating. Facts that were so often her friends and allies now felt like an assault on her nerves.

"I have to sell my brother's boat."

"With his permission?"

"He willed it to me."

Kenny dipped his head compassionately, then doffed his cap to her. "My condolences."

"Any chance somebody there might be interested in buying it? I'd prefer to get this whole thing over with as quickly as possible."

"You know much about the engine, the hull, the transoms, the electronics, the masts, the length, or the age?"

The litany of criteria made her head swim and her spirits sag.

"Not a thing."

"Then it depends on the boat. Garrison Bight's got dry- and wet-slip storage and a full-service mechanical department, and they sell everything from Carolina Skiffs to Sea Chasers."

"I'm not fluent in boat speak. You're saying it's possible?"

"Bingo!"

He pulled off the main road into a parking lot with a dock house and tackle shop, and an enormous boat-repair building made of corrugated steel striped in teal and white. Individual docks fanned out like spokes on a wheel. Rows of ships of every shape and size filled the water, masts slicing into the horizon.

"Try the dock house. They should be able to put you on the right track."

"Wish me luck," Catherine said, pulling out the folder full of Robert's documents.

"Hold up. I'll do you one better." He shifted on his hip to look at her squarely, then squinted.

"What's wrong?"

"Put your hat back on and wipe that zinc off your nose. Do not, under any circumstances, remove your sunglasses. And take this." Kenny handed her a pen as if it were a weapon.

"You think they'll offer me a deal to sign on the spot?"

"If they did, it wouldn't be one worth taking. Listen, no matter who you talk to, write a bunch of notes on those papers. Look important. Don't let anybody see what you're writing. Scribble gibberish if you got to. You're a woman walking into a marina, trying to sell a boat you've never seen. That's chumming the waters."

"I know what that is! From Shark Week!" Catherine said, impressed with herself until she realized what Kenny was driving at. "Oh. You mean they're going to eat me alive."

"Not if they think you work for a collection agency. Or an insurance company. Tell them you have verification of ownership. You'd have the right to board. Acting professional might spook 'em into negotiating a decent price if they're open to buying."

"Only I won't know what a reasonable price is until I research what other comparative watercraft would sell for, as well as any associated taxes or fees for transfer of title."

"Keep that business lingo up. It'll sell the whole act."

"First, you make me think I could get shanked here because the people are shifty, and now I'm supposed to smooth-talk them into believing I'm some boat aficionado?" Catherine rubbed the zinc from her nose, then checked her face in the rearview mirror. Between the shades and the cap, she seemed to be in disguise. "I look like I'm going to play golf."

"Perfect. They'll think you're rich."

"I should warn you I'm a really bad liar."

"Sink-or-swim time."

"I should've packed a life jacket. Will you wait for me?"

"Of course. Gotta see how this turns out."

"Want to tag along? For moral support?"

"Hell no. I won't pass as your chauffeur."

Uneasy, she made a beeline for the marina's tackle shop, which doubled as a convenience store. Shelves full of snacks stood opposite displays for lures and spools of fishing line. Through a side window, Catherine could see a forklift hoisting a motorboat onto a tall dry dock where other boats were being stowed. The noise of power tools drummed in the distance.

"Can I help you?" A guy behind the counter with a buzz cut eyed her hard.

She clearly wasn't their average customer.

Catherine raised the folder, pen pressed to the paper at the ready. "Yes, I'm here to inspect a boat that belonged to"—she pretended to read the name off the file—"Mr. Robert Moran."

He paused for a second, deliberating. Catherine understood why Kenny had advised her to leave the sunglasses on. If the clerk could have seen her eyes, he would have seen the fear.

"You'd talk to Vic about that." He dialed a number on the phone. "Send Vic to the store, will you? Got a lady to see him."

The way he enunciated the term sounded like code for a person not to tangle with.

Score one, Catherine told herself, clutching the folder to her chest and trying to keep her breathing even.

Moments later, in walked Vic, a towering, barrel-chested man in oil-stained shorts and dusty work boots. He had a dark tan and a deeply furrowed brow. This man didn't strike her as the type who was easy to scare. Or easy to fool.

Panicking, Catherine shoved her hand at him to shake. "Good afternoon, sir."

Vic pumped her arm, his grip calloused. "What can I do for you?"

"Would you be kind enough to show me to the boat owned by Robert Moran?"

Guarded, Vic asked, "Are you a friend of Bobby's?"

Hearing her brother called by a nickname she had never used with him threw her. Catherine and her mom called him Robert or Robbie. Her sudden annoyance at the man's familiarity with her brother made the lying come more naturally.

"I currently hold the title to Mr. Moran's boat." She tapped the folder with the pen imperiously. "If you would be so kind as to take me to it, I would appreciate that."

He noted the logo on her cap, exactly the way Kenny had said he would, then traded glances with the clerk at the register, who stared back with a shrug.

"Sure," Vic replied dully, as if he had more important things to do. "Follow me."

Catherine tailed him out the door, sunglasses sliding down her nose because she was sweating profusely from the stress. Her cheeks kept ballooning because of the lies, so she was purposefully sucking them in and clenching her jaw.

Keep it up. Don't get flustered. This is almost over.

Seagulls wheeled in the sky. Their guttural calls filled the silence between them as they walked. They passed a series of pleasure ships and yachts as they proceeded away from the main marina toward the last dock, the briny odor of the ocean thick to the point of being acrid. Fuel slicks created rainbows on the surface of the water.

Vic's footfalls were weighty on the wooden dock. He maintained the lead but would glance back at her intermittently. "Bobby's property up for auction?"

His interest was evident, yet his voice remained gruff.

"There may be an opportunity for select buyers to place early bids," she replied coyly.

"We consign boats here. Always looking to replenish our stock."

"I'll bear that in mind."

She played it cool. However, they had been walking for a while, and the tension was fraying her nerves.

Where is this boat already?

"Last one on the left," Vic told her, gesturing in that direction with a furtive glimpse at her folder. "You're free to go aboard. Assuming the paperwork's in order."

"It most certainly is."

Since that wasn't a lie, her response came out confidently. Then Catherine pivoted to look where Vic had pointed.

Sitting in the water beyond a string of motorboats and two-tier fiberglass cruisers was a dilapidated fishing trawler with rusty metal rims and a jumble of tatty nets hanging off splintered masts, which appeared as though they might snap like toothpicks. Stenciled on the weather-beaten stern over a ghostly outline of the vessel's old name was a new one: **SAME SHIP, DIFFERENT DAY.**

"*That's* Rob—Mr. Moran's property?"

Catherine was furious and freaking out, simultaneously.

"You gave Bobby proper notice, right? He knew this was coming?"

"He knew," Catherine said, incensed.

I wish I had.

She'd often fantasized that Robert followed her upbringing from a distance, maybe watched her from outside the house or peeked in on her from a window during class. He'd often had to walk her home from school when she was young because their parents were working. He never seemed to mind and would pepper her with questions about what she had done that day. Robert would attentively listen to her explain what she had learned, then would quiz her on math equations or spelling. She didn't feel like a burden to him or a pest. His patience and interest were how he showed he cared. While her dad treated her like she existed only when his eyes happen to fall upon her, Robert always saw her.

Her dad she had long given up on, but her brother's postcards had given Catherine hope that a part of him did still care. She reread them over and over again, seeking some furtive clue meant solely for her, some hint that only she could figure out. By leaving her the boat,

Catherine believed Robert had finally sent her a message. Except it was completely incomprehensible, if it was there at all.

"You see the shape it's in." Vic ambled up to the side, picked off a sliver of peeling paint, and flicked it into the water. "I can give you five thousand even. Take it off your hands. Let you get on to more pressing matters."

The first bid is always a low bid.

Though she was no expert negotiator, Vic's price sounded high, given what horrendous shape the trawler was in. Nevertheless, her gut told her not to accept the offer.

"I'll be in touch," she replied, voice steady, even though she wanted to burst into tears. She'd been banking on a far bigger profit.

As kids, she and Robert often watched *The Price Is Right*. Back then, the prize catamarans went for tens of thousands of dollars. She remembered bickering with him about which contestant was closest to the price and who would come up short. Catherine had been too young to know what anything cost and would always overestimate the value of a television or a barbecue, winding up way off the mark.

Now here she was, years later, misjudging value yet again.

Her dreams of paying for her mom's room at Shady Ridge through the end of the year were snuffed out. Five grand would not go far. Then there were the bills from this trip. Catherine's heart sank.

Half of her wished Robert's boat would too.

9

Laughter was the last thing on Catherine's mind, yet that was all she heard.

It was the seagulls in the sky above. It might as well have been Robert cracking up from the beyond.

A giant pelican was perched on a piling on a neighboring dock. Between the long bill and sturdy build, the bird seemed like it was in charge, that this was its territory. It blinked at her, then looked up at the seagulls overhead as if to agree that they were annoying.

"Joke's on me," Catherine muttered to herself once Vic had trudged back to the dock house.

She kicked the side of the trawler, cursing it.

"*Same Ship, Different Day* . . . sounds about right."

The pelican flew away, as if it didn't want to stick around for this disappointment either.

"You think this is funny, Robert? You disappear for decades—then out of the blue, you leave me a floating heap of junk? Hilarious."

Infuriated, she put the folder in her purse and climbed aboard, steadying herself on the small section of the stern that wasn't covered in bird droppings. The rear deck was a patchwork of worn plywood sheets with buckets of mechanical supplies holding down the corners. Rivets in the side panels were corroded, ready to pop from their sockets. Red fishing buoys were piled in an empty crab trap.

"What a charming seafaring vessel. Why yes, I'd love the grand tour."

There wasn't much to see.

The filthy deck and shabby wheelhouse took up most of the thirty-foot vessel. Narrow planks ran along the sides, where a person could walk to the prow. That certainly wasn't something Catherine was going to attempt. She went toward the door to the wheelhouse and was about to turn the knob when it turned first.

Catherine let out a gasp and backpedaled.

In the doorway stood a handsome sandy-haired man in cutoffs and a threadbare Chicago Cubs T-shirt. Fred and Arnie were right. There were good-looking guys wherever she turned. Only she wasn't expecting one on her brother's boat.

Their gaze met, and Catherine could feel herself blushing.

"You lost, Miss?"

Her pulse pounding, it took a minute for Catherine to catch her breath. The man was tall, broad shouldered, and around her brother's age. He had the face of a sailor, with a hard-set jaw and skin that had been weathered to a permanent tan. He stared at her with light-blue eyes, unblinking, sizing Catherine up.

"This boat belongs to Robert," she stammered, edging toward the dock. "Who are you?"

"Might ask you the same?" He glanced around furtively after noting her cap. "Is this a repo?"

After playing the part with Vic, Catherine wasn't sure if she should keep the pretense going for this guy, so she didn't answer.

"Bobby was always on time with the payments. If it is, I'm going to need to see the papers."

"Was he really?"

Catherine folded her arms, aggravated that her brother had been responsible when it came to bills but not his family.

Confused, the man cocked his brow. "This is private property. Please don't make me call the cops. That's the last thing I want to do."

"Be my guest. Because you're right. This is private property. *My* property."

"I get it. You're on vacation. Had a long night of drinking. Hangover must have you a little turned around. Well, let me set you straight."

He put his strong hands on her shoulders to spin her toward the dock. Catherine wanted to melt for a second, then dodged out of his reach.

"I'm not drunk. Robert's dead."

The stoic man appeared as if he had been punched in the stomach. "What? No, that can't be true."

"I'm his sister. He left me this piece of crap in his will."

A flicker of emotion rippled across the man's face. His jaw muscles flexed. He and Catherine locked stares, an unspoken battle of wills. "You're lying."

"I'm not good enough at it to bother."

"I talked to him—"

"About a week ago?"

Wary, the man peered at her. It seemed to disturb him that she was a step ahead. Catherine got the sense that he usually had the upper hand. "Robert was probably already in the hospital."

"With what?"

"Pancreatic cancer."

The words seemed to slam into the man's chest. In despair, he whispered, "Oh, no. Did he . . . ?"

"Robert wasn't aware he had it."

Catherine could hear how cold she sounded—mean, indignant, horrid. However, she was powerless to be anything except blunt. She was afraid she might well up.

"There must be a mistake. I've known Bobby for years."

"Years?" That was an affront to her. "How long?"

"Long enough," he countered, cagey. "He's been letting me stay here and paying me to restore this ship since last fall . . ."

"Restore it? And this is what you've accomplished?" She panned around, arms out, presenting him with the run-down state of the boat.

"Excuse me?" he growled.

"Are you going to tell me I should have seen it before you got started?"

That was, indeed, what he'd planned to say. Catherine could tell.

Outmaneuvering him for a second time was making the man mad and making her feel more in control. "Robert was sick, and you were what? Taking advantage of him?"

Clearly offended, he took a menacing step toward her. "I would never do that to Bobby. You have my word."

"I don't know you, so your word doesn't count for much."

"The feeling is mutual."

His comeback silenced Catherine for a moment.

"This has got to be some sort of mix-up or mistake. Bobby was always on top of everything."

"Not everything." The edge in her voice seemed to make the man bristle.

He was a stranger, a strong one at that, and Catherine realized she ought to be careful, especially after Kenny's warnings.

Nevertheless, the kinship this man apparently felt toward her brother enraged her. What made him so special that Robert would befriend him and allow him to live on the boat? Catherine couldn't fend off her jealousy. It turned her spiteful. "Then let me show you your good pal Bobby's last will and testament, as well as the documents proving that this boat is now mine."

Catherine went to remove the folder holding the papers Latham had given her when a gust of wind caught the file and sent it sailing overboard.

"No, no, no!" she shouted, watching helplessly as the papers fluttered into the ocean.

Instantly soaked, they bobbed atop the water along with dead leaves and briny foam. Catherine scrambled after them. She was about to plunge her hand into the bay, except the papers were rapidly being carried away on the tide.

She bent far over the side, ready to dive in when the man yanked her back.

"Don't," he cautioned.

Wrestling away from him, Catherine leaned precariously toward the water. "Afraid I'll prove you wrong? I need those documents."

In a single effortless swoop, he picked her up, feet dangling in the air; then before she could exhale, Catherine was on the other side of the boat.

"You fall in and you'll be sick for a week. Water around the dock is full of diesel fuel. And sewage."

Panting, enraged, Catherine pushed him off her and adjusted her clothes. As much as she wanted to think he was bluffing, her gut said he was telling the truth. She had never hated someone so much for *not* lying to her. And for saving her.

Over his shoulder, Catherine saw that the papers were drifting farther into the bay. She darted around the man and started digging through scrap piles, looking for something long to harpoon them with. She found a net on a pole and tried slapping the water with it to get the papers to come her way. However, they were already gliding in different directions, out of reach.

"Don't you have anything with a hook on it? This is a fishing boat for Pete's sake."

The man had gone out of his way to prevent her from going overboard. That was where his helpfulness ended. "No documents. No boat. I'm staying." He folded his arms smugly.

The papers were a few boat lengths away, blithely rippling in rhythm with the waves. They were gone. Though not for good.

"Until the estate attorney emails me new ones," she sneered.

"Then I guess I'll see you tomorrow, Catherine."

Stunned, she spun to face him. "I never told you my name."

"Bobby did. I know you're his sister. You have his eyes."

Her anger subsided for a split second, softening into hope. The thought that Robert had spoken of her, perhaps fondly, turned on a light in a forgotten corner of the dark part of her heart.

"Only I don't believe for a second that he left you this boat. He loved it—" The man cut himself off.

His impassive expression cracked slightly, and Catherine saw a glimmer of regret in his eyes. "More than me," she said, finishing his sentence.

"I didn't mean—"

Catherine turned her back to him as her chin started to quiver.

Could this have been a colossal joke Robert was playing on her? Why give her the boat when he was aware there was somebody bunking onboard? Was his goal to humiliate her?

Robert rarely teased her when they were kids. He would sneak food off her plate or try to get the best seat on the sofa first or beat her to the bathroom, but putting her in a position to be embarrassed didn't seem like the person she remembered. Then again, she had no idea who her brother had become over the intervening years.

Catherine's thoughts were whirling uncontrollably. She snatched up her purse and catapulted herself over the stern onto the dock, unwilling to let this obnoxious stranger see her cry.

"Pack your bags," she shouted into the wind. "Because I *will* be back with those papers. Count on it."

10

Catherine slammed the door to Kenny's cab so hard that the entire car shook. She wiped her eyes and sniffled. She didn't bother trying to conceal that she had been crying.

Kenny hemmed his lips, unsure how to comfort her. "What happened? The boat sank?"

"If only I were that lucky."

"Did they give you a piss-poor offer?"

"Worse. The thing is older than Noah's ark, there's some guy living on it, and all the papers I had that verify I own it blew into the ocean."

Along with the documents was the estate attorney's business card. Catherine had to track him down immediately. While dialing her cell phone, she told Kenny, "Drop me off at whatever beach is close enough to the Abbott House for me to walk home, please."

No doubt worried, he shifted the taxi into gear. "I take it you don't know the guy staying onboard?"

"Nope. But I do know I do *not* like him."

Kenny pulled onto the causeway as Catherine apprehensively listened to the line ring on her phone. The seconds drew out and distended. Tension burned in her shoulder blades. The cloudless sky was so vacant that it seemed like a wall pressing down on the water.

Gloria didn't waste her breath with a 'hello' or pleasantries. "Where the hell are you?" she demanded.

"The whole department has got their thongs up their butt cracks because of this idiotic project, and they're going bananas because you decided to dip out right in the middle of the insanity and leave them in the lurch. Oh, and your mother has been calling here every hour on the hour, claiming you need a new fence for your neighbor. I wasn't sure if she was off her meds, so I played along. I told her I'd google chain-link suppliers. What in the name of Beyoncé and all that is holy is going on?"

There was no stopping Gloria as she plowed onward. "Meanwhile, I got a situation of my own. I think I'm in love with that new hottie I went on the date with. His name is Tito. He's a Taurus, only has one baby mama, and he lives in Queens. Says he's a facilities manager and a limo driver on the side and that he wants to take me for a ride. Think that's sexual or is he just being a gentleman?"

Desperate as Catherine was to interrupt, Gloria continued, undeterred, the way her mom would. Horning in wasn't an option. "Here I am, busy trying to get people on this floor to believe there's been a gas leak. That way I can go home early to get ready for our second date. I'm walking around sniffing the air and pretending to cough." She choked a bit and asked aloud, "Doesn't anybody smell that? Smells like gas."

"Wait, Gloria. Let me—"

She returned to the line, whispering, "Nobody's biting. If I wasn't fielding calls from your mom and lying about where your scrawny butt was, I might be more convincing. I feel a fake fainting spell coming on any minute. Only I gotta wait until somebody is walking by my desk."

"Gloria!" Catherine hollered. "I need your help, and I need it fast."

The line went silent for a half second. "What's the matter? Are you in jail?"

Catherine explained what had transpired over the last twenty-four hours—the news of her long-lost brother's death, the boat, the deal with Willford, and the sudden trip to Key West. She saw Kenny keeping tabs on her in the rearview mirror, listening attentively along with Gloria.

"Wow. Guess I won't have to fake that fainting spell," she said once Catherine was through. "But come on, you didn't tell your mom that your brother is dead? That's cold."

"I couldn't. Not yet."

Clearly, Kenny was thinking the same thing. He glanced at her in the mirror, though he kept his lips sealed. Gloria, on the other hand, did not.

"Baloney! This is family. You can take some time off from sunbathing and be straight with her. She's bonkers, but she's your mother. She's all the family you got."

The word 'family' felt like a sharp jab to her ribs.

Family was a vague concept to Catherine. Because her father and brother had both been gone for such a long time, they seemed to be related to her by default rather than a real bond. Her mom was the only one left. But she wasn't entirely there either. Catherine had parents, yet somehow, she felt more like an orphan.

"Just get Latham to email me the documents."

"Are your fingers broken?"

"No. Just my heart. Please?"

That hard truth dilated in the silence.

"Fine," Gloria snapped after a second.

The judgment in her voice was unmistakable; then came the sound of computer keys clacking as Gloria searched for the lawyer's contact information online.

"I'll get you what you need. That doesn't mean I'm onboard with this."

"I'm not onboard either. But I have got to deal with this boat. You're the best, Gloria."

"Tell me something I don't know."

When Catherine hung up, Kenny whistled to fill the void in conversation. The Jimmy Buffett bobblehead appeared to rock to Kenny's tune gleefully.

Outside the taxicab's windows, the verdant marshland had given way to commercial buildings and tracts of houses that blocked the vista of the seaside. It was as if Catherine had been dumped back into the everyday world, her vacation put on pause after the papers had flown from her grasp.

"Do you think I'm a terrible person?" she asked Kenny.

"I once took a gold-digging cutie-pie to the mansion of an old guy who I was pretty sure she planned to rob. I've picked up alcoholics from a night's stay at the city drunk tank, then dropped them off at bars in time for happy hour. I've even driven men to their mistresses' houses after I watched them kiss their wives goodbye at the front door."

"Is that a yes or a no?"

"You don't strike me as a bad egg. Just remember that the road to hell is paved with good intentions."

Another canned cliché, Catherine lamented in frustration.

Though she might not have wanted to hear it, perhaps she needed to.

"It's only for one more day."

"You do what you got to," Kenny replied as compassionately as he could. "But if I agreed with you, we'd both be wrong."

Catherine always did what she had to. She rarely did what she wanted. She was the reliable one, the trustworthy one, the accountable one. Everything and everyone else came first. Her needs hadn't been a priority for years. She wasn't even sure what they were anymore.

Neither Kenny nor Gloria understood that telling her mother about Robert would be difficult for a number of reasons. She was frail, unpredictable. What if she forgot and Catherine wound up having to deliver the same awful news over and over again? Or worse, she could become hysterical and hurt herself while Catherine was half a continent away.

The risk outweighed her regret. Catherine was damned if she did and damned if she didn't; she would feel guilty either way.

As the cab cruised away into the heart of Key West, tourists were meandering around, taking in the sights. The slow pace, such the opposite of New York City, telegraphed that they were on vacation. One girl was helping another tighten the strings on her bikini top. On a corner, a fruit vendor was cutting a pineapple open for a delighted little boy and his dad.

Catherine watched them with a yearning envy.

She had only ever been on one family trip in her life. The summer before her father left, they went to Long Beach Island on the Jersey Shore. Catherine had been six years old and could now vaguely recall filling a plastic pail with sand, the gummy sweetness of saltwater taffy, sea salt sticking to her legs after Robert walked her hip deep into the ocean and stood behind her so the waves wouldn't knock her over—snippets of memories sewn into a story like a patchwork quilt of moments.

Was that what her mother would do once she learned Robert was dead? Piece together the facts and whatever fiction her faulty memory summoned up? It was an ordeal Catherine was not excited to endure.

"I changed my mind."

"About calling your mom?" Kenny asked, optimistic.

"About my next stop. Can you take me someplace where there's a fax machine? And a beach? And something to eat?"

She wanted another hard copy of the documents, but she was also ravenous and didn't want to miss out on the last of the afternoon sunshine.

"Anything else? Holy Grail? Body of Jimmy Hoffa?"

"How about a football helmet?"

"What for? Might mess up your tan lines."

"I'm going to need it when the big man on the boat finds out he has to leave."

"You didn't say he was big."

"Rude too."

"Quite the combo."

"I'm from New Jersey. Rude, I can handle. Big and about to be evicted? That's why I might need protection."

As she spoke, the taxi pulled up to a magnificent, sprawling hotel with a cream stucco facade, arched windows, and majestic palms lining the walkway to the main entry.

"Where are we?"

"Your laundry list. This place has everything on it."

The sign on the lawn read **WALDORF ASTORIA CASA MARINA RESORT AND BEACH CLUB**. Catherine recognized the name. This was the hotel that had the dream room with the regal decor and the butler on call that she had salivated over back at the office.

Of all places.

A white-gloved valet was attending to a gorgeous couple exiting a Mercedes coupe ahead of the cab. The woman was in stiletto sandals and a chic sundress. The man had on freshly pressed khakis and aviator shades. Catherine glanced down at her rumpled T-shirt and saggy shorts.

"Are they going to let me in the door?"

"About that . . ."

Catherine sank in her seat. "How much humiliation can I take in a single day?"

"Hear me out. Walk in and head straight back to the left. There's a bar and lounge there. You can ask the concierge to accept your fax, grab a bite, then head to Higgs Beach right over there." He motioned a short distance away. "You're not a guest, but they can't kick you out if you're a paying customer."

"Can I even afford a glass of water here? It's the Waldorf!"

"You can now." He switched off the meter, cutting himself out of a forty-dollar tab.

"Kenny, no. You've been schlepping me around for the last hour. I couldn't."

The valet waved them up, and Kenny rolled forward.

"I'm not usually one for giving advice, and if I do, I suggest you take it with a grain of salt. And a slice of lemon. And a shot of tequila. So here goes: The right thing and the easy thing are never the same."

Aware he was right in more ways than he could know, Catherine pulled a twenty from her wallet and gave it to Kenny as a tip.

"They never have been."

11

Extravagance wasn't in Catherine's vocabulary. For her, buying an extra latte per week or splurging on a mani-pedi with a coupon qualified as self-indulgent. The Casa Marina Resort was a monument to luxury. Lush greenery ringed the rounded drive, and the air was redolent of tropical flowers.

"Welcome," the valet in a monogrammed polo said as he opened the cab door. Catherine clambered out carrying her laptop case, a beach bag, the folding chair, and the flower towel flung over her shoulder. "Do you have a reservation?"

"For a late lunch," she replied, winging it.

Despite how disheveled she was, the valet pointed her toward the door. Catherine padded into the lobby, her flip-flops thwacking against the glossy floors. When she tried to walk more softly, the folding chair slid off her shoulder, almost clattering to the ground.

Don't make a scene.

Compared to the vivid colors splashed around elsewhere in Key West, the hotel was an oasis of soft taupe hues, caramels, and burnished browns. The dark coffered ceilings contrasted against the clean white walls and minimal furnishing, transforming the space into an art gallery where the idyllic views of the water were on display. Catherine was too. She stuck out like a sore thumb. Head down, she did as Kenny directed, heading for the bar area in the back.

The dimly lit room had the ritzy ambience of a private club. All the tables were empty. A female bartender in a crisp polo bearing the hotel's crest on it was arranging glasses.

Catherine sidled up, then asked, "Is the kitchen still open?"

"Always." The cheery bartender handed her a menu.

She took a spot at the bar and got out her laptop. "I need to receive a fax . . . ?"

"This is the number you can have it sent to." The bartender graciously passed her a glossy card. "The concierge will bring the papers to you once they arrive."

She dialed the number for Latham that Gloria had texted her. While the line rang, she did a search for fishing-boat prices. Up came photographs of the latest-model cruisers, which started at over $20,000. Catherine meant to type "trawlers" instead of "boats," but before she could change the keyword search, the lawyer's assistant transferred her through to him.

"What can I do for you, Ms. Moran?" Latham sounded surprised to hear from her.

"You probably aren't going to believe this," she began.

Catherine described what had occurred since yesterday. She tried to keep her voice low, yet she sensed the female bartender was tuning in to the bizarre saga—and seemed less stunned than the lawyer did.

"My, my," he retorted. "I was just contacted by someone from your office, and I'll have my assistant get those documents to you immediately."

Relieved, Catherine read out the hotel's fax number, then thanked him, adding, "Please put a note at the top asking to have them brought to the bar."

"I could see how you might need a drink. You may have to get the authorities involved to remove this man from the boat," Latham went on. "Technically, he's a squatter. You can have him arrested if you see fit."

Catherine had been kidding about the football helmet. Having an attorney underscore the serious nature of this matter made it more distressing.

"Let's hope it doesn't come to that."

"Let's hope," he echoed.

By the time she had hung up with him, her stomach was churning from stress. Although everything on the bar's menu sounded scrumptious—chilled melon soup, duck confit tartlets, lobster on a bed of greens—Catherine's appetite had evaporated. She couldn't really afford the food she wanted anyway, so she asked for a BLT on wheat. Even that was exorbitant.

"That's quite the commotion," a male voice pronounced.

Catherine turned to discover a distinguished-looking man standing behind her. He had silver hair and wore a stylish linen suit. His proud posture gave him an air of refinement, yet his placid expression said he wasn't trying to be impolite. She was certain Arnie would have swooned for him. She wasn't far from that herself.

"That's putting it mildly," Catherine conceded, subtly trying to brush back stray hairs and pull herself together.

The bartender ducked into the kitchen to place her order, leaving Catherine alone with the man, who seemed to have materialized out of nowhere. He folded his hands in front of him as if patiently waiting for her to say more. Only Catherine just grinned at him awkwardly, unsure what to do next. She didn't have enough steam left for more lies.

"A valet can take your things to the beach when you're done with your meal."

Uh-oh. He thinks you're a guest.

"Oh, it's no trouble." She didn't want to admit that she wasn't staying at the hotel. Not for fear of being booted out but because she was enjoying how well they treated her.

"I have one of your cards," the man stated.

"My . . . ?" It took a second for Catherine to realize he was talking about the credit card logo on her cap. "Oh, yes. I hope we're giving you satisfactory service."

"Exemplary."

"Are you in town on business or pleasure, if you don't mind my asking?" He gestured at the images of boats for sale on her open laptop.

"Both, it seems," she said, motioning to her phone and the call he had overheard.

"Of course," he replied courteously.

A woman dressed the same as the bartender entered. "Your fax from New York."

"Thank you," Catherine said; then the woman was gone as quickly as she had arrived after a brief blink at the man.

He must be a manager. And he seems to believe you're somebody important.

Maintaining the charade that she was a paying guest made her antsy. She was inadvertently doing the same haughty shtick from the docks. Worried her luck might run out, Catherine folded the faxes and anxiously began rambling.

"It's almost criminal to accept a fax these days. Given the environmental impact, of course. While a single tree can produce over twelve thousand pieces of paper, that pales in comparison to the two hundred billion pieces that are used to send faxes within the continental US each year."

The man raised both brows. "You know quite a bit about paper."

Embarrassed, Catherine explained, "I'm a researcher. For . . ." She pointed to her hat.

"I see. The company is fortunate to have you."

Catherine wished her boss, Willford, were of the same opinion.

"I'd like to think so. Any brand driven by consumer needs would be remiss not to invest in research. It might appear to be a tiny piece of the pie, but between evolving customer preferences, fluctuating marketing allocations, and innovation by competitors, it's crucial to survival, let alone success."

You're babbling. This guy already assumes you're footing the steep cost to spend the night here. No need to oversell it.

"True," the man agreed. "However, upper management tends to focus on the big picture."

"Thinking globally and acting locally is as beneficial for our forests as it is for any firm."

"Why is that?" he inquired, his interest piqued.

"A one-size-fits-all approach rubs modern consumers the wrong way. Studies have shown that they want to feel special, catered to, unique. It's like dating. Would you go out with somebody who was more interested in your money than your personality?"

Are you the right person to be making relationship analogies?

"Savvy advice. What would you say most companies are doing wrong?"

"Ignoring the customer closest at hand. Hard data has proven that word of mouth is exponentially more powerful than most TV ads or social media. Why not look out your front door before shelling out a fortune to advertise? Take that woman, for example." Catherine motioned at a well-coifed older lady in a silky swimsuit cover-up who was breezing past the door toward the pool. "If she tells her friends what a fabulous time she had here, terrific. They'll probably book a room. However, if the man who runs the bike shop down the road recommends this hotel to tourists, they'll trust him because he lives here. They'll pay top dollar for firsthand advice. Given that travelers over fifty have more disposable income and spend almost double what younger people do on international travel, they're the demo that will drive tourism dollars, and that's who the smart marketers are targeting."

"I admire the way you think." The man smiled at her sincerely.

It was gratifying that somebody appreciated what Catherine had to say for a change.

The food arrived, saving her from droning on any longer. The bartender presented Catherine's order, which was garnished with speckles of parsley as well as scrolls of shaved carrots that lay on the plate like confetti. This was the fanciest BLT she had ever had.

At the Waldorf, a humble sandwich was its own party.

"I'll let you enjoy your meal. Should you require anything else, don't hesitate to ask."

The bartender nodded deferentially at him; then the man glided out of the lounge.

"I didn't even hear him come in," Catherine remarked.

"That's how he is." It was all the bartender was willing to say on the subject. "Would you like something to drink? Sparkling water or a spritzer perhaps? We have a signature grenadine martini or a blackberry-truffle martini with Godiva white chocolate liquor if you favor something on the sweet side."

Could this place get any better?

Catherine was torn between feeling deprived that she couldn't indulge in everything on the menu and being thankful that she hadn't been kicked out.

"I'm fine with water," she replied between bites.

When she was done scarfing down her sandwich, the bill didn't leave much left over for a tip. Catherine scraped together a respectable amount, then bundled her bags onto each shoulder.

"Is it nice? Working someplace as gorgeous as this? Or is it still work?"

"It's a job, all right," the female bartender admitted. "But hey, I'd take eight hours on my feet with that view over anything else."

Beyond the windows, the sand sparkled. The sea beckoned. Hammocks were strung between palms, inviting guests to laze in the sun and let the breeze rock their cares away. The bartender had confirmed Catherine's fears: that any occupation was, indeed, more bearable when it was done in a place that beautiful.

She tried not to think about returning to her cubicle and the grind that her life had crumbled into. It was like stubbing her toe on reality.

"Ms. Moran?" A guy in a white polo with the hotel's emblem on it was standing at the entry to the lounge. "I'm here to take you to a cabana. One has been reserved for you."

"For me?"

"Like I said, that's how he is." The female bartender repeated her earlier statement about the man in the suit with a wink.

"Ready?" the guy in the polo asked, taking the beach chair from her as well as her bags.

Catherine could put off dealing with the man on the boat and returning her mother's calls. But she couldn't postpone what she would be returning to. She decided to enjoy her vacation while it lasted.

"Lead the way."

12

Appearances could be deceiving. Catherine had assumed the hotel's dignified facade was the showpiece. She was wrong.

The front was nothing compared to the back. Reflecting ponds and towering palms flanked a main walkway that led visitors to two large pools and an expanse of pristine beach with a private pier. Catherine had never been anywhere this stately or exclusive.

Even though the guy in the polo was toting her brashly colored menagerie of bags, Catherine felt exposed, as if security might run up to cart her off for being a gawdy gate-crasher.

"Here we are," he announced.

The cabana was draped in creamy cotton fabric, and inside sat a sculptural chaise longue facing the ocean. Sunbathers were soaking in the rays around the pools, where a handful of children played quietly. The grandeur of the resort seemed to browbeat the kids into being on their best behavior. While Catherine would have preferred to sit by the water, she couldn't turn down this lavishly private little hut that she had to herself.

The guy in the polo delicately placed her bags on a side table, then watched as Catherine flung the wildly patterned beach towel Fred and Arnie had loaned her across the chaise.

"Um . . . we have towels. If you'd like some."

This was less a suggestion than a recommendation.

Catherine noticed that the other guests were lying on bright-white towels that bore the hotel's name. Suddenly, she felt tacky using the one she had brought.

"Sure. This is, um, my backup," she said, grimacing inside at the ham-handed comment.

Having not grown up with money, Catherine was insecure about how she conducted herself around people who had. Before the company sent her on her first business dinner, she had looked up silverware place settings online and memorized what utensils to use for the various courses. The restaurant turned out to be less formal than she had expected, yet Catherine never forgot the difference between the demitasse spoon and the dessert spoon.

Putting on airs felt forced to her, yet pretending to be something she wasn't came naturally. She had faked being a normal kid in school while taking care of a mother at home, pretended she was over her father's and brother's absences, acted like she was okay being single, and feigned that she was perfectly fine with her current title at work when it incensed her that she wasn't already a director.

Catherine may have been a bad liar, yet she excelled at living lies. Although she rarely knew how to act, she had become an accomplished performer, a paradox that wasn't lost on her.

The guy in the polo promptly presented fluffy white towels from a nearby stack. Catherine could smell the scented fabric softener on them. When she reached for them, he looked at her as if she was doing this wrong.

"Let me get that for you." He unfurled the towels across the chaise with practiced flair. "Any important colleague of the manager deserves the best."

"Important colleague?"

"He doesn't do this for everybody."

She tried not to let the confusion show on her face. What had she done to earn the VIP treatment other than being polite? she wondered.

"Will there be anything else?" he asked.

It took a second for it to dawn on her that he was waiting for a tip. Comfort had a price. She sorted through her wallet for a five-dollar bill, which she handed to him. "No, that'll be all."

The conceited reply was as cringeworthy as her last one.

Catherine flopped onto the chaise with the ocean framed between the panels of canvas fabric. She took off the cap and laced her hands behind her head. Relaxation couldn't come soon enough.

Regrettably, it didn't come at all.

Even though her phone was off, in her head, Catherine could hear the beeps of waiting voicemails like never-ending drips from a leaky tap. The faxes seemed to harp at her from her bag, along with the reports she was supposed to be reading for Willford. The idea of figuring out how to appeal to high-net cardholders in precisely the type of place they would be staying made her spirits flounder. She had to force herself not to think about anything except unwinding. That in itself was becoming work.

Catherine switched positions on the chaise, took off her shorts and tee, slathered on sunscreen, tried paging through the tabloids Fred and Arnie had given her. Nothing worked. She was too distracted to be distracted.

Maybe a walk on the beach would clear her mind.

She left her belongings in the cabana, reasoning that nobody who could afford to stay at the Casa Marina Resort would be remotely interested in her paltry stash. Then the New Yorker in her made Catherine reconsider. She tugged on her shorts, stuffed her valuables in the pockets, and hid her laptop under the hotel towels.

That was her problem—getting the what-ifs out of her mind for more than a minute.

Catherine was in a constant state of concern—about bills, her mother, her job—so she had acclimated to it. Fretting was her status quo. Shaking off the anxiety was easier said than done.

She felt her feet sink into the sand, the fine grains welling up between her toes. The sound of waves softly crashing and ebbing at the shoreline lured Catherine closer. Water lapped over her legs, brisk yet refreshing. A breeze gently buffeted Catherine's skin. Even though she was usually stuck in her own head, the sensation of the wind and the water pulled her into her body and into the present.

Yet Catherine's mind wandered to the past.

The man on the boat had referred to her brother as Bobby, as had Vic from the dock. The nickname perturbed her, as if Robert were a totally different person than how she remembered him. She wondered what his job had been, what hobbies he'd enjoyed, what kind of music he'd listened to or food he'd liked. Then she looked down at her feet and wondered if her brother had ever been on this very beach and stared at the same patch of ocean. So many blanks to fill in, and she had nowhere to start.

As a kid, Robert had loved the water. Most of the pictures in his baby book were of him in the tub, shampoo lathered in his hair, plastic toys floating in the bath amid the suds. Catherine used to sneak the family photo album off the high shelf where her mother hid it after her father had run out. She had poured over the snapshots, straining to remember the ones she was in or making up stories for the ones she wasn't.

There weren't many pictures of her dad. The handful of photos showed him talking or staring off, an ever-present cigarette between his fingers and beer in hand, shoulders slouched as if he had just finished with a long day of work. After numerous attempts to locate him through online research, she'd come to the sad yet likely conclusion that his alcoholism eventually rendered him homeless and that he had probably passed away, a nameless, unclaimed John Doe. Though there was an abstract grief to that realization, Catherine's father was almost a stranger to her, familiar simply because he looked like Robert, heavy brows, a sharp chin, and the same smallish dusky-blue eyes they all shared.

In her brother's pictures, he clung closely to their dad, jockeying to be near him in the frame, while their mother stood by their father's side, donning an obligatory smile. The only photographs of Robert alone featured him in a pool or in the ocean on that trip to the Jersey Shore. It was as if a force of nature, such as water, were the one thing that could keep him apart from his dad.

Robert had been a natural swimmer and tried to teach Catherine. The local pool was free to kids on certain days in the summer, and she had memories of wading in the shallow end as Robert waved for her to come deeper. He would scoop her up in his arms, trying to take her in over her head. Frightened, Catherine would start to cry and beg him to bring her back. Then she would watch him frolic from a distance, afraid to join him.

Getting close to her brother meant she would have to do something that terrified her. That was their relationship in a nutshell—Catherine on the sidelines and Robert in the thick of things. She regretted not letting him take her into the deep end.

Perhaps if he hadn't had to go it alone there, Robert wouldn't have left.

Catherine stood at the edge of the ocean for what had to be hours. Her feet should have hurt from standing. They didn't.

Or maybe they did, and she didn't feel them because her heart hurt more.

The sun was starting to set. The transition had been so gradual that Catherine hadn't noticed until some of the hotel guests came to join her by the waterline. It was as breathtaking as the sunrise she had seen earlier, this time in reverse, a natural spectacle whose grandeur defied description. Gold bands turned to pink, then to red, like the clouds were melting heat into twilight.

While the dusky haze turned purple, drifting down the coast, the other guests decamped and Catherine tromped back up the beach toward her cabana. Her bags and towels were undisturbed. The pool was empty, as were the chairs surrounding it. Lights shone in the rows of windows at the rear of the hotel.

She imagined people in their suites getting ready for a night on the town and wished she had someplace fun to go. Not that there weren't plenty of restaurants and bars on the island, but going alone didn't appeal to her. This was another part of the trip Catherine hadn't thought through.

Despite daydreaming about a vacation for years, she didn't have any inkling of what she wanted to do.

Catherine collected her belongings and walked along the path with the palms and the reflecting ponds. Lit from below, they took on an ethereal radiance. The resort was so enchanting she didn't want to leave. Except she had to.

She stopped at the sleek concierge desk on her way out.

"Can you tell me how to get to Amelia Street from here?"

A woman wearing the hotel's monogrammed attire smiled. "I can show you on your phone."

Catherine fished out her cell. The battery was sapped again, as if the island were keeping her disconnected on purpose. She shrugged bashfully. "Directions will have to do."

"We have complimentary maps."

The concierge plotted the course on the glossy grid of Key West, then gave it to Catherine to keep. "Or I could have the valet order you a car."

Despite Kenny's generous gesture, she had already burned through that day's budget. She would have to hoof it.

Covering, Catherine said, "It's a nice night. Perfect for a walk."

Within minutes of leaving the hotel, every step in her flip-flops was uncomfortable. Her feet hadn't ached before, but they did now. She shifted the bags and the beach chair from shoulder to shoulder. They kept slipping from the sunscreen she had slathered on, making it hard to maintain a steady pace. The heat of the day had simmered down to a warm embrace. If Catherine wasn't so sore, she would have enjoyed ambling back to the inn at a leisurely pace.

"Some New Yorker you are. A couple blocks and you're down for the count."

Catherine felt a level of exhaustion she had never experienced before. She couldn't tell whether it was from the news about Robert or the years of stress finally catching up to her in a wave as dense as cement and just as heavy.

The walk home was a metaphor for the entire trip—she would have to put aside the hurt and put one foot in front of another if she wanted to get where she needed to go.

13

Catherine followed the map and found herself among a crowd of beachgoers heading home for the night. It was like a concert had let out. Surging masses of excited people filled the streets. She gazed at the families and couples wistfully. They were sunburned, content, heading to dinner together or off to the bars to party.

Catherine hadn't really felt alone until that moment.

Limping slightly because a blister was forming between her toes, she wove from road to road, passing fanciful homes and brazenly painted bungalows until she finally made it to the Abbott House. The front door was open, so she let herself in. Though the light in the parlor was on, no one was around. Starving and tired, Catherine wished she had saved the carrot garnish from her BLT.

"Home so early?" Arnie poked his head out of the kitchen, wearing yellow rubber dish gloves as well as a new apron, which read **Don't Make Me Poison Your Food.** A skull and crossbones were stamped at the center.

"I was famished until I saw . . ."

"Oh, this?" he said, tugging the strings. "It's to keep Fred in line. Reminds him where his bread is buttered. Literally. How was your day?"

He waved her into the kitchen and patted a diner-style chrome barstool for her to sit on. The seafoam cabinets were iridescent in the evening light. His crowded collection of salt and pepper shakers seemed to have multiplied since she last saw them. Pairs of penguins, ducks, mice, aliens, and gnomes peered down at her in tandem. Arnie was completely at home in the eccentric space.

Pots were boiling on the stove, and warmth radiated from the oven, cutting through the cool air being pumped out by the air-conditioning system. The smell of roasting chicken and vegetables made Catherine's stomach rumble. She hoped Arnie didn't hear it. He was rigorously washing the dishes under running water and setting them in the washer, as if they couldn't be clean enough. Now Catherine knew who kept the bathroom spick and span.

"Meet any eligible bachelors?" Arnie inquired.

"Actually, I did meet two men today."

Clearly thrilled, he twirled on his heel. "Details!"

"One was a little older than me and runs a hotel. He even let me use a private cabana."

"Glamorous! Who doesn't like a little sugar with their daddy?" he joked.

"The second is illegally squatting on my brother's boat, and I may have to call the cops to kick him off."

"What?!" Taken aback, Arnie put his scrubbing on pause. "Yay on the cabana. Nay on the squatting. That puts the *ick* in 'tragic.' Wait, was the second guy cute?"

"Uh, empirically speaking, sort of."

Infuriating as the man had been, it was true. He was more handsome than Catherine cared to confess.

Arnie pursed his lips. "Describe."

"Did the part about the police slip your mind?"

"I need a mental picture. Are we talking dashing and mysterious à la Humphrey Bogart in *The African Queen*? Or strapping and buff, like Matthew McConaughey in, well, everything?"

"I haven't seen *The African—*"

"Criminal," Arnie gasped. "I mean your movie-trivia background. Not the dreamboat on the boat."

"It's more of a nightmare. The thing is about to fall to pieces. I thought I could sell it to pay for my mom's memory-care facility—only I doubt it'll fetch much. I really needed that money."

Catherine couldn't hide her disappointment. Arnie shut off the faucet and removed his rubber gloves to give her a hug.

She was afraid she would start crying again as he held her.

"Can I tell you something . . . personal? Fred doesn't want me meddling in your business, what with the problems we've had with guests, except I can't help myself. I'm a meddler. I meddle. There, I said it."

He pulled up a barstool next to hers.

"I'm also not exactly what you'd call manly. Never have been. I would dress my G.I. Joes in Barbie clothes and put on plays for my parents, making my sisters act out the male roles. It should not have come as a shock to my parents that I was gay. Somehow it did. My father didn't speak to me again. Ever."

The loss still clearly affected Arnie. It dimmed his spirit when he spoke of it. Catherine could commiserate.

"When my dad died, I asked my sisters if I could have his shaving kit. He had this English-leather dopp bag that I adored, with silver scissors and a badger-hair brush and a heavy razor. I knew he missed out on having a father-son relationship, watching sports, doing guy stuff. The only truly masculine thing we ever did together was when he taught me to shave. To this day, I can't part with that dopp bag. Which is why I want you to think long and hard about selling what your brother gave you. If it isn't going to make you much money, why not keep it? Yes, the way he treated you and your mother was wrong. It was almost unforgivable."

"Almost?" Catherine blotted her eyes. She was wrestling with the same question.

"I'm not saying you need to forgive him overnight. But once his boat is gone, what you have of him will be too."

Arnie's story touched her. Regardless of whether she agreed with him, she was stuck.

"Whatever I'd get for the boat is more than I have. I can't afford the dock fees on top of everything else. I'm having trouble keeping my nose above water as is."

"There's got to be some sort of compromise. Take this kitchen, for example. I let Fred decorate the entire house in exchange for having a madcap space to call my own. He detests this room. I hate the rest. It works because I have one place that's truly me."

"That sounds less like finding the middle ground and more like a landslide for Victorian decor."

"Precisely!" Arnie declared as he hopped up to check the chicken in the oven. She caught a glimpse inside. The skin was a golden brown, and the vegetables were bubbling in the drippings. Catherine started salivating.

"Fred *thinks* he won," Arnie went on. "He didn't. Even I couldn't take a whole house full of seafoam and tchotchkes. That would put the *God* in 'gaudy.'"

"You're saying compromise is essentially a cunning deception?"

"Men," he retorted with a flap of his hand. "Letting them believe they've won is half the battle."

"What battle?" The back door swung open, and Fred entered with multiple pints of ice cream from a local shop. "Oh, hey, Catherine!"

"To get our dear guest to join us for dinner." Arnie eyeballed Catherine to play along, which she was happy to do, given how enticing the food smelled.

Fred stowed the ice cream in the freezer portion of the vintage fridge, singing, "You must stay. We're going to watch *Roman Holiday*. Somebody's on an Audrey kick." He made an obvious show of pointing at Arnie.

"He means a Gregory Peck kick."

Catherine looked at them blankly, sorry to disappoint them about films yet again.

"Egad, Fred," Arnie sighed, clutching his Hawaiian shirt as if this were an emergency. "This calls for a cinematic intervention. The poor girl doesn't know who Gregory Peck is."

"Then dinner and a movie with us are a must," Fred asserted. "Unless, of course, you have other plans."

"It's the best offer I've had in a while."

"Take a lesson from Ms. Hepburn and maybe that will change." Arnie winked at her.

"Promise you're not going to Eliza Doolittle her," Fred implored.

"What does that mean?" Catherine asked.

"Don't you worry your pretty little head about it." Arnie traipsed across the kitchen, bumping Fred out of the way with his backside. "You, read this closely." He tapped the saying on his apron, as well as the skull and crossbones.

Although Catherine wasn't sure what they were up to, as she sat in the kitchen with them, she thought this was what it must feel like to prepare a family meal—dishes clinking, cupboard doors open, pots percolating on the stove.

That wasn't how it had worked in her house.

Of the scant recollections she had of her father, one was of him sitting at the kitchen table reading the newspaper, a six-pack ready to be polished off, while her mother reheated leftovers as Catherine colored on the floor. Both her parents seemed so large to her back then, looming overhead, neither speaking nor acknowledging the other.

At the time, she thought that was what adults did at dinner. Now Catherine understood they had been ignoring one another, tolerating each other's presence out of convenience or habit. While they didn't fight, they didn't connect, either, not deeply. They had lived in parallel, rails that were close but could not meet.

Too young at the time to fully comprehend how strained her parents' marriage was, Catherine now wondered what Robert had experienced growing up in that environment.

Was it the bad memories that had driven him away? Or was it an acute awareness of memories that could never be made?

Watching Arnie and Fred working together on the entrée, chatting, and getting out plates gave Catherine a twinge. She'd never had such a homey experience. A small bite of what she had missed out on was better than no taste at all.

14

Romance wasn't Catherine's thing. At least, when it came to movies.

"You're going to love this," Arnie insisted as he and Fred guided her out thc back through thc tiny gardcn, food in hand, folding TV trays tucked under their arms. A pair of matching blue bicycles were leaning up against the exterior. Monogrammed baskets read "His" and "His."

"Don't spoil it!" Fred pushed open the door to the garage.

"Are we eating in the car?" Catherine asked.

The garage had been converted into a media room, complete with comfy chairs, a giant flat-screen television, and framed posters of old Hollywood films lining the walls.

"Do you come out here to get away from your guests?"

Fred said, "No," right as Arnie said, "Yes."

Catherine cracked up. Though their shirts always matched, the couple's opinions didn't. The three of them sat in a row in front of the screen and set up their TV trays; then Fred plucked a DVD from a bookcase full of them. "It's a good thing Arnie's organized."

"He wants to say obsessive compulsive."

"The movies are alphabetized," Fred explained. "We have over five hundred classics."

"I do that with my books, and I color-code my files," Catherine volunteered. "Makes them easier to find. It's pragmatic."

"A woman after my own heart. See, Fred! I'm not fussy. I'm pragmatic!" Arnie declared, pulling a miniscule set of salt and pepper shakers from his pocket.

"You don't go anywhere without your own seasoning?" she asked.

"Please don't get him started," Fred begged. "Spices, condiments—they are his personal crusade. Peace in the Middle East, starving children, and global warming be damned. An unsalted potato or a flavorless side dish: To Arnie, those are travesties."

"I'm going to bite my tongue because we have company, but yes, I believe the difference between food and a meal is the opportunity to attune one's dish to their liking. Call me crazy."

"'Crazy' wouldn't cover the half of it." Fred clucked under his breath.

"Should we put in the movie?" she refereed.

"Let's," Arnie said.

Sulking, he had Fred do the honors and made a production of sprinkling salt and pepper on his food while the opening credits rolled. Between the bouncy orchestral music, the shots of Rome, and the costumes, everything was made more escapist because it was in black and white. Catherine had trouble tearing her eyes away from the screen to eat.

As a kid, she hadn't gone to the movies much, not unless she saved up her allowance and went with her school friends. The television, however, was eternally on. In the months after her father ran out, she would let Robert pick the programs to keep him around. Sitcoms, sports—she didn't care as long as he would sit with her on the couch.

That was how they spent time together once her dad was gone—not talking.

Sometimes Robert would comment on a baseball game or guess who the bad guy was in some murder mystery; then she would seize the opportunity to discuss something. Although the conversations had rarely lasted more than a few sentences, they were a step up from being ignored.

Catherine got a kick out of Fred and Arnie's banter. She envied it. Although they had obviously seen *Roman Holiday* countless times before—Arnie's lips moved as he soundlessly quoted the actors' lines—they were entranced. She was too. She barely blinked.

Audrey Hepburn, the bored, sheltered princess, believed she had fooled Gregory Peck, the savvy newsman, into thinking she was an average girl. Yet he knew precisely who she was. Each character assumed they had pulled the wool over the other's eyes.

That gave Catherine an idea about the boat and the handsome man onboard.

Suddenly, she bolted up from her seat, nearly toppling her TV tray.

"What's wrong?" Arnie asked, alarmed, as Fred paused the movie.

"Can I borrow one of your bicycles?"

Catherine couldn't afford to pay Kenny to drive her where she wanted to go.

"It's nearly nine o'clock, and you want to go for a ride in the dark in a place you've never been to before?" Fred asked.

"Blame Audrey."

Intrigued, Arnie was willing to indulge her. "Take mine."

"Yours? They're both blue, and they both say 'His.'"

"Arnie's has a bell," Fred informed her, still befuddled.

"I'll be back before the end of the movie," she called, dashing out the door.

Catherine jogged inside to grab her purse, which she had left on the kitchen counter, then walked Arnie's bicycle alongside the house to the street, where she hopped on only to find the seat was too high. Her feet barely skimmed the pedals. After a few adjustments, Catherine was on her way.

The evening air was cool against her skin. Landmarks were harder to distinguish unless the headlights of passing cars brought them into view. At a stop sign, she paused to get her bearings.

Night birds sang, and tourists were milling around the streets. Musicians staked out different corners, attempting to wow the crowds for spare change. The farther Catherine got from Old Town, the fewer people she saw.

Each house she rode by, she questioned whether Robert had lived there. With every restaurant, she wondered if he had eaten there. Catherine oddly expected to make out some lingering trace of him despite the fact she might not even have recognized Robert himself if he were alive.

Her brother seemed to be everywhere yet nowhere, a feeling she was thoroughly acquainted with.

As Catherine approached an intersection, she worried the sedan in front of her couldn't see her. She rang the bell. It warbled and the driver waved.

The heady smell of salt in the air signaled that she was getting close. As Catherine crested the causeway, her legs began to burn. The blisters between her toes were smarting. This was way more of a workout than she had planned. She pedaled onward.

At last, the marina came into view.

Coasting into the parking lot, she recalled what Kenny had said about the locals, that they weren't all on the up-and-up. Afraid of leaving Arnie's bike unattended, she rode it down the row of docks, bumping over the planks. Most of the boats stood dark, water sloshing against their hulls. A handful of them were lit from within. A radio played from somewhere. Catherine felt less alone.

She wasn't certain if that was a good thing or a bad thing.

Upon nearing her brother's boat, she got off the bike and walked it the rest of the way. There were lights on inside. She debated what to do next.

Should she shout out? Knock on the stern? Short on options, she rang the bell on the handlebars as loudly as she could, the tinny trilling incessant.

Eventually, the man who she had encountered that afternoon appeared in the doorway to the wheelhouse. He did *not* look thrilled to see her. His hair was mussed, a fresh grease smudge was streaked across his Chicago Cubs T-shirt, and he was rubbing his oil-stained hands on a rag.

"Nice ride," he said archly. "Yours?"

"No, it's . . . never mind. I'm here to talk to you."

"Okay. Talk."

Catherine gathered the courage to make this lie convincing. She had one shot. "I spoke to my attorney, and he won't be able to get me that paperwork for a couple of days."

A satisfied smirk curled on the man's lips, though he didn't respond.

You've got him on the hook. Reel him in.

"In light of the delay, I have a proposition for you."

"I'm listening."

"You knew my brother. I didn't. At least, not as much as I wanted to. I was hoping, maybe, you could tell me about him, what he was like."

A guarded glint flashed in his eyes. "In exchange for?"

"Time. I already have a buyer for the boat."

His expression shifted, slight yet perceptible.

Vic had, indeed, made her an offer, meaning this wasn't a total fabrication. What mattered was that the man believed her. The intensity with which he was listening to Catherine, his light eyes riveted to hers, telegraphed that he did.

"Go on," he said.

"You were my brother's friend, so I'm not going to kick you out with no place to go. But I need to sell it."

"Why?"

She was surprised by the temerity of the question and almost offended. "Why do you care?"

"Because I've poured more blood, sweat, and tears into this boat than anything else in my life." He held up his hands to show her the fresh and healed cuts as proof.

Catherine glanced around at the run-down boat, unconvinced and unsure if he was trying to pry.

"*This* is your greatest accomplishment?"

He glowered, then took a subtle swipe at her. "Just want to be sure it goes to someone who will appreciate it."

"Unfortunately, I don't have a choice in the matter. I need to sell for financial reasons."

"How soon?"

"By Sunday."

The short timeline seemed to hit him in the gut.

"My mother is in a special facility for dementia. It's . . . not inexpensive." Catherine calculated her words to keep from revealing too much. She felt humiliatingly exposed already.

He seemed to take in that admission with conciliation. "Not much of a swap."

"You got a better one? Or another place to sleep?"

He wiped his hand on the rag again, then extended it toward her to shake. Catherine leaned over the stern and slid her hand into his. He gripped her palm hard, holding it longer than necessary; the warm roughness was a comfort that took her by surprise, especially after how he had been acting toward her.

"Deal."

"Deal," she said, breaking the grasp first skittishly.

"Be here tomorrow morning at ten."

"Tomorrow morning?"

Beach, sunshine, tanning, fruity drinks—thoughts of her day circling the drain swirled in Catherine's head.

"I have work to do on the boat."

"But it's about to be sold?"

"A couple of things aren't finished. Bobby wouldn't want it that way."

Both went quiet for a moment. It pierced Catherine to hear this stranger talking about her brother's preferences when she hadn't the foggiest idea what they would be.

Catherine grudgingly agreed. "Then I'll see you at ten."

He nodded, seemingly waiting for her to leave. She stole a glance at him. He was still staring, his eyes like magnets.

Uneasy under his lingering gaze, Catherine climbed on the bicycle and pedaled away, wheels squeaking. Exhilaration welled in her chest. She would finally get to learn more about her brother, firsthand knowledge from an actual friend of his. But she didn't know if she could trust the guy to be there when she got back. She didn't know if he would go nuts and torch the boat before morning out of spite.

It dawned on her that she didn't even know his name.

"This movie stuff is a lot harder than it looks."

15

Catherine was ready for the finale—of the movie and the day.

Eager to tell Fred and Arnie how she had expertly taken a page from one of their favorite films and turned it to her advantage, she threw open the garage door only to find that they were gone. The TV was off, the trays put away, and the den was dark.

Disappointed that she had missed the ending, Catherine went through the back door into the kitchen. Nobody was there either. The sink was empty, the counters were clean, and the pairs of salt and pepper shakers were all aligned perfectly, like an army of watchful eyes to make sure the kitchen remained spotless.

Catherine cut through the dining room to discover that the lights were on in the parlor. She burst in, declaring, "I did it! I tricked him! Just like Audrey Hepburn did with Gregory Peck!"

There sat Ina and Lita on the settee, their faces waxy pink from the sun, their expressions disapproving.

Catherine realized that she sounded like the unstable addict the sisters assumed she was. Fred and Arnie were across from them in their favorite chairs with Truman by their feet, captives to the conversation, which Catherine had clearly interrupted.

"Isn't she a hoot, ladies?" Arnie forced a laugh. "We were telling her about . . ."

The sisters stared at him, stone faced. Fred quieted him with a glance.

"A tale for another time," he trailed off, giving up.

"Ina and Lita were regaling us with the details of their day." Fred attempted to conceal his exasperation. "You were saying? About the sharks?"

"A viewing tour on a catamaran in the backcountry," Ina began, delighted to regain the stage after Catherine's disruption. "Hard to get tickets. We were lucky."

"Hard to get. Very lucky," Lita restated. "We saw turtles, dolphins, and three different sharks: a nurse shark, a lemon shark, and a blacktip. We don't have those in Minnesota."

Catherine had been to the backcountry. And she had been on a boat. However, her version was not like a vacation. Theirs was.

With precious little time left on Key West, she was jealous.

"Did you know that the nurse shark is able to breathe while remaining still by pumping water through its mouth and gills?" she offered, trying to ingratiate herself to the sisters. "Most sharks will die if they don't keep moving."

Ina harrumphed to voice her displeasure at Catherine horning in on her moment.

"I saw that on Shark Week. Wholesome, quality programming," she added. "I promise I'm not on drugs. I've just been sleep deprived. And I'd barely had anything to eat."

In a mock whisper meant to be heard, Ina said, "On *Dateline*, they said that meth makes people stay awake for days on end. Takes away their appetite, too, don't cha know."

Her accent sounded sweet, yet Catherine couldn't miss the condemnation.

"We are on Social Security and saved up all year to take this trip," Ina explained indignantly. "If we wanted to bunk with weirdos, we'd stay at the motor lodge with the bikers and the hookers."

Fred appeared to sink into himself with dismay.

"Wait! Please! I'm sorry! I don't want you to sleep with bikers and hookers. I'd love to hear more about the blacktips," Catherine exclaimed. "They're responsible for the majority of human attacks off the coast of Florida."

"Not helping," Arnie cautioned out of the corner of his mouth.

The sisters stood up from the settee simultaneously, as though conjoined at the hip.

"*Uff da.* You can't trust the skinny ones as far as you can throw 'em."

Lita nodded, as if that closed the case; then they went for the stairs. "We will be turning in for the night."

Dejected by the mess she had made, Catherine flopped onto the spot where they had been sitting; then Truman trotted over and licked her leg like a condolence.

"I apologize. I thought I could get on their good side. Even the dog feels bad for me."

"No," Fred exhaled. "You haven't showered, and he smells the salt on your skin. You're like a corn chip in flip-flops to him."

She was humiliated. "How can I make it up to you?"

"It's okay." Fred excused himself wearily.

Only Catherine could tell it wasn't.

Truman followed him for a few steps. Arnie didn't.

"I really screwed up, didn't I?" she asked softly once Fred was gone.

Arnie pinched his fingers to indicate a smidge.

"It's our job to be friendly and accommodating. It's part of running a B and B. Acting wowed by boring stories or astonished to hear about places we've been a million times. It puts the *host* in 'hostage.' We only have four rooms for rent, so reviews mean everything to our reputation online. One bad post can spoil the bunch. It's a lot of pressure to pretend like you care when, for the most part, you don't."

Catherine felt guilty for putting their reputation at risk. Of all people, she knew from her work how critical public perception was for the success of their business. She wanted to help them, not get them in hot water.

"Be a doll and try to act normal around the Sisters Grimm from here on in?"

"I'll do my best."

Compared to her mom, who was always saying something inappropriate, or Gloria, who didn't care who she offended, Catherine considered herself to be polite, professional, and courteous. Since landing in Key West, she was coming off as the complete opposite and making things worse—for Fred and Arnie as well as herself.

"Is there anything I can do to make it up to Fred?"

"His love language is sweets. He already polished off the ice cream he brought home."

"What about you?" she asked, contrite.

"I'd say 'Surprise me'—however, we've had enough surprises."

"Too many," she admitted in earnest. Catherine didn't recognize the person she had turned into since she was told Robert died.

"I know you're going through a lot. Grief doesn't bring out the best in anybody."

"I wish things could have been different with my brother. Now they can't be."

Arnie leaned in, almost confidentially. "Let me tell you a little secret. Fred gave me a Hawaiian shirt for our first Christmas together, and it was so hideous I almost dumped him. I refused ever to wear one. I adore that tiny donut hole of a man, but he doesn't always show his love the way I need him to. He does, however, love me the best way he knows how."

He popped the collar on his current Hawaiian shirt to prove he had become a convert.

"Love is like Christmas presents. You give people what you think they want and hope they're happy with what you picked for them. Only sometimes it's like Secret Santa. You get stuck with some gag gift you can't wait to toss into the trash. We can't expect people to treat us how they should, but they may be trying as hard as they can. It truly is the thought that counts."

Catherine felt how right he was deep in her bones. She desperately wanted to believe that Robert had loved her in his way, even though he'd abandoned her. Maybe there was a gift yet to be found.

"I'm going to hit the hay. Don't stay up too late." Arnie rose and gave her a peck on the top of her head.

"Should I turn off the lights?"

"Aren't you the most responsible guest we've ever had? Not to worry. The lights are on motion sensors in case any guests stumble down to the kitchen in the middle of the night for a snack. We can't afford anyone tripping, falling, and suing us, or else the roof will never get fixed, and I'll have to turn the hole into the biggest planter in the state of Florida. Wait, that could—"

"Make Fred have an aneurism?"

"Yeah, probably not my most brilliant idea. Come on, Chubs," he said to Truman. "Let's go night-night."

The dog followed Arnie and fumbled up the first few stairs, not nimble enough to reach them; then Arnie had to carry him the rest of the way, stumpy legs dangling uselessly as he licked Arnie's face.

Catherine sat in the parlor alone, feeling far from responsible. She barely recognized herself. It wasn't just the unattractive T-shirt tan, the greasy skin from layers of sunscreen, or the rumpled attire. She wasn't acting like her normal self at all. Who was this stranger she had become?

She'd been thoughtless, reckless, and selfish. She had withheld information or suppressed the truth since she had learned of Robert's death. She also hadn't returned any of her mother's calls.

Her cell was in her pocket. Preparing for an onslaught, Catherine dialed her voicemail.

The text count had climbed. Ditto for the messages. Her mom had been dialing her relentlessly. The early voicemails she'd left were short and casual. The later ones grew more and more fraught.

"I know they must have given you a lunch break," her mother moaned in message number nine. "You couldn't call your poor old mother? Who's in a nursing home?"

"For the millionth time, it's not a nursing home. It's—"

Catherine had to take a few breaths to calm herself down.

One voicemail was a rehash of what was served for dinner at Shady Ridge and who her mother sat with in the dining hall. The one after that reiterated who she was seated beside as well as a graphic description of how the woman chewed with her mouth open.

"Delete, delete, delete!"

She couldn't get rid of the messages fast enough.

Without warning, the lights shut off, plunging Catherine into darkness. It mirrored how she felt—like the lights had been snuffed out on the hopes she had of one day reuniting with her brother. She sat there moping for a minute, then flapped her arms in frustration to reactivate the motion sensors.

With a pensive sigh, Catherine called her mom.

After a few rings, she picked up, her voice groggy. "Hi, honey. I fell asleep. How are you?"

"Oh, I'm, um . . ."

"Listen, I can't really talk. I gotta get up early. Mrs. Higgins is coming home from the hospital in the morning. Everyone's taking bets on her condition. Cast, sling, bandages, walking boot, neck brace, or any combination. I'm thinking neck brace for sure. The pot is already up to forty bucks."

"That's . . ." Catherine wanted to say *macabre*. Instead, she went with "a lot of money." Given what she had to tell her mother, she was in no place to judge.

"Okay, I'll let you get some rest."

"You all right?"

Here was another golden opportunity for Catherine to come clean.

Her confidence deflated. Or perhaps it was her conscience. She vacillated between fessing up and stringing along the sham that everything was normal.

Catherine defaulted to a lie.

"I'm fine, Mom. I'll call you tomorrow."

"Not if I call you first."

She said goodbye then into the phone, the sweetness making it even more difficult to withhold Robert's death from her.

The lights went off again without warning after Catherine hung up. She was back in the dark.

When her mother eventually did find out about Robert, she would want to know when Catherine had found out and why she hadn't told her sooner. Catherine hoped her mom's memory would give out the way it often did.

Then maybe she would forget to hate her for what she had done.

16

Nobody was talking. The sounds of utensils and chewing were all that could be heard at the breakfast table. Ina and Lita sat opposite Catherine. Her hair was wet from a morning shower, and rivulets of water were dripping down the back of her neck, but she didn't dare wipe them for fear of acting like some fidgety junkie.

Arnie entered from the kitchen, carrying a tray full of fresh yogurt topped with raspberries and mint. He grimaced, likely at the dreary atmosphere that had settled upon the room.

"How's the food?" he asked, upbeat, plainly attempting to boost the mood.

"Tasty," Ina stated.

"Tasty," Lita echoed.

Catherine enthusiastically nodded in agreement but kept her mouth shut. She was being vigilant about her behavior around the sisters and was at a loss for what to say that wouldn't cause a problem.

Fred came in with a tray stacked with delicate miniature waffles. He caught the somber vibe like a drink thrown in his face. "Did you oversalt the quiche?" he whispered at Arnie accusatorily.

"I most certainly did not."

"Then why isn't anybody speaking?"

Feeling as though she was to blame for the uneasiness, Catherine piped up. "What do you ladies have planned for the day? Anything exciting?"

"Snorkeling," Ina replied curtly between bites of a scone.

"We've never been snorkeling." Lita took a scone and followed suit with her sister.

"I understand that's a great place to see barracuda and the goliath grouper that Key West is famous for."

"Yes, we're looking forward to it," Ina answered, a little less sharply.

"We like to try new things," Lita added.

Catherine glanced at Fred to see if he approved of her comments. Arnie held his breath. To her relief, Fred seemed grateful that the tenor of the table conversation had turned slightly more cheerful.

"Let me clear these empty platters," Fred said.

"The mini cinnamon buns will be coming out of the oven any minute," Arnie announced.

He nudged Catherine's shoulder appreciatively while collecting the dirty dishes.

"Do you two like swimming?" Catherine ventured.

"I do," Lita intoned happily.

"But we are extra careful," Ina explained quickly, evidently ready to steer Lita onto another topic. "With sunscreen, I mean. Because we're fair skinned. Burn easily."

"That's smart."

Even though both sisters were already beet red, Ina warmed at Catherine's passing compliment.

Arnie returned with the tray of buns, icing dripping, cinnamon swirled to perfection. Catherine let Ina and Lita dig in first.

"May I take some to go, please?" she asked, careful to remain well mannered.

"Where are you gallivanting off to?" Arnie inquired, sounding overly friendly, which put her in a tough position. He apologized with his eyes.

Catherine had to think fast. Admitting that she was on her way to scam some stranger into telling her about her dead brother would *not* go over well. She fell back on a half truth.

"Ina and Lita had such a good time in the backcountry, I thought I'd rent a bicycle and ride over there myself."

The sisters nodded approvingly.

"Breathtaking views," Ina pronounced.

"Yes, fabulous," Lita echoed.

"Of course you can!" No doubt grateful to have dodged another breakfast fiasco, Fred popped a couple of buns into one of the inn's seafoam green monogrammed paper napkins for Catherine.

"Let's get you some tin foil for those," Arnie hinted.

She trailed him into the kitchen, where he immediately embraced her. "Thank you! You made Fred happy. I can tell."

"Just glad not to seem crazy for a change. But I need to get going. Where do you suggest I rent a bike? Cheaply, that is."

Catherine couldn't afford to continue paying Kenny to chauffeur her around, and she had been checking her cell under the tablecloth during the meal. Texts from her mom were stacking up. Apparently, Mrs. Higgins had returned from the hospital in a leg brace with a cast on her arm, so the forty-dollar pot went to some man that her mother was sure had cheated: high drama for Shady Ridge. The bombardment of phone calls was bound to begin shortly.

"I knew it! You're going back to see the hot guy on the boat."

"The hottest thing about him is his temper. Let's hope I don't wind up calling 911."

"Should I come along? You know, as your bodyguard?"

Catherine gave him a dubious smirk. "Exactly whose body will you be guarding?"

"Okay, okay, take my bicycle. Just don't let the old gals see you leave with it. Wouldn't want them to think I'm playing favorites. Even though you are my favorite."

Hearing that warmed Catherine's heart. At least somebody on the island liked her, because the man from the boat clearly wasn't her biggest fan.

Arnie escorted her through the dining room toward the front door. "Let's say goodbye to Cath. She'll be gone for the day. Renting a bicycle. Riding around. Doing . . . things," he heralded, theatrically.

Fred gave him a funny look as Ina and Lita waved, oblivious.

"You're going to blow my cover," she murmured as Arnie shoved the cinnamon buns into her arms and slammed the door on her.

"Subtle," Catherine said, standing on the front porch alone.

She crept around the side of the house, crouching as she went by the dining room windows, then wheeled the bike out the same way, buns resting in the basket along with her purse. The sun was already beating down stridently. Although she had her cap and sunglasses on, she'd forgotten to borrow sunscreen. She would have to buy some at the marina's shop.

"You're about to get that tan you've been after."

As she pedaled the same route from last night, Catherine mulled over what questions she should ask about her brother. From broad strokes to the mundane, she had an endless list. Excitement started to percolate at the prospect of finally learning more about Robert.

She passed a trio of street performers playing steel drums and had to weave through a throng of tourists clapping along to the tune. They had disembarked from a cruise ship and were all sporting the same free tote bag with the ocean liner's name on it. She rang the bike's bell; then the crowd parted, making a path for her.

If this were New York City, nobody would have moved for some dinky bell.

That reminded Catherine of Willford's project and the work she hadn't touched. She wondered how Gloria was faring and made a mental note to buy her a gift. But what? Having hardly seen the sights herself, she had no idea what a quintessential Key West present would be.

Crossing the causeway, Catherine realized that she ran the risk of running into Vic at the dock's convenience store. She wasn't sure she could pull off another performance, and she wasn't ready to sell him the boat. Her pit stop would need to be speedy.

When Catherine rode into the parking lot, a large fishing vessel had a group of men gathered around it. She recognized Vic in the mix. Something must have been wrong with the boat because they were haggling. Seizing her chance, she propped Arnie's bike against the wall and hurried into the shop.

She whipped off her cap as well as her shades, then took her hair out of the ponytail to look different than the day before. The same clerk with the buzz cut was at the counter. Catherine scooped up the closest bottle of sunscreen as he watched the melee through the window, barely acknowledging her presence.

"Here's your change," he said, his attention diverted.

Catherine was out the door before he had even shut the register drawer.

Halfway to Robert's boat, she paused to slather the lotion on her face and body, anyplace her skin was exposed, then kept rubbing in the greasy cream as she walked. Many of the ships that had been at the docks the previous night were gone, leaving Robert's trawler a lone eyesore.

Perched on a piling by the stern of Robert's boat was another pelican. It turned to look at Catherine as she approached, the noise of the bike's squeaky wheels drawing its interest. This one was particularly large, and its bill bore a distinctive red tip. It stared at her unnervingly, like it knew what she was up to. She felt as if it was barring her path, preventing her from going onboard.

Ringing the bicycle bell at the bird didn't work. Waving her arms didn't scare it away either. Neither did hopping up and down. The pelican was unfazed.

"What are you doing?" a voice asked.

It was the man she had met yesterday. He was standing at the cabin door, wearing swim trunks and a timeworn T-shirt that said **Napoli** in green, a mug of coffee in hand.

"Nothing."

"You were talking to that pelican."

"It was giving me a look."

He furrowed his brow. "Be kind to the pelican. They're a fortuitous sign."

"Really? Of what?" she asked sincerely, taking a closer look at the bird, who craned its neck, then resettled on its roost.

"Of sacrifice, atonement, and charity."

It felt like he was telling her something about himself without saying it outright; then he sipped his coffee in the silence. Catherine had done enough sacrificing, probably not as much atonement as she could have, and was in dire need of some charity.

"You okay?" he asked.

"Yeah, why?"

"You're . . . striped." He motioned to her arms and legs.

The sunscreen hadn't sunk in, leaving bright-white streaks across her body. Catherine tried rubbing the lines away as he watched, a bemused grin burgeoning as he took in the spectacle.

"You missed a spot."

"Where?"

He gestured at her entire face.

Embarrassed, Catherine massaged the sunscreen into her cheeks and wiped it from her forehead. "Is it gone?"

"Looks a little like sweaty clown makeup."

"Great. That's what I was going for."

Suddenly, the pelican flapped its massive wings, startling her.

Catherine recoiled, and the man on the boat chuckled. "Careful. You're even scaring away the birds."

"Maybe they're not the only ones I'm trying to scare off."

"It's going to take more than that with me."

17

Catherine hadn't traveled the globe, seen much of the country, or taken many trips in her life, but she did know that 'Napoli' was the Italian translation for Naples. That was where Robert had sent a postcard from after he left home, and here it was written on the man's shirt. She wasn't about to let that go.

However, she decided against badgering him about it right out of the gate.

"Permission to come aboard?" she asked from the dock.

"Sure," he said, taking a swig of his coffee.

"Quite the pun." She pointed at the boat's name as she stepped over the stern. Visible under the current name, *Same Ship, Different Day*, was the blurry outline of another in dark blue, which faintly read *Pauline's Escape*.

"Yeah, witty," he replied dryly.

"We haven't been formally introduced. I'm Catherine Moran. Which you already know."

"Travis Bradley."

"For you," she told him, holding out the foil-wrapped package. Her olive branch was Arnie's cinnamon buns. Only Catherine had forgotten that hers was packed with his. Travis popped them into his mouth before she could get any.

"You make these?" he asked between bites.

"A . . . friend did." Catherine wasn't willing to give away where she was staying until she knew Travis better.

"They're good."

"I'll tell him."

Travis tossed the last of his coffee into the bay. "So?"

"So . . . what?"

"What do you want to know about Bobby?"

"Oh, we're getting right into this. Well . . ."

Catherine searched for a place to sit down and settle in for their discussion. While she deliberated between using the seagull-poop-covered side rails or turning an empty crab trap into a makeshift stool, Travis started shuffling around the boat, taking out parts and sorting through junk-filled bins.

"I'm listening," he said.

Except he didn't seem like he was.

Laboring in the sun had turned his skin a golden hue. He looked over his shoulder and caught Catherine staring at the ropy muscles along his back flexing through the T-shirt as he bent to pick up tools that were strewn about.

Flustered, she sputtered, "Okay, Travis, what can you tell me about my brother?"

"Nope. That's not how this is going to work. You get three questions."

"Pardon me?"

He turned straight at her. "I thought about it, and to make this fair, I decided you can ask me three questions per day."

"How is that equitable?"

"Say you find out everything you want to know today. You could kick me off the boat by nightfall."

Catherine was about to protest that she would never do that. However, she had threatened him with that very fate less than a day ago. She kept her objections to herself.

"Explain the query guidelines and restrictions," she stated.

"The . . . ?"

"Strictures and constraints of what I'm allowed to ask. For example, does a two-part question count as a single question? If so, how am I to know what constitutes a multitier inquiry ahead of time? Additionally, are the limitations based on—"

"Stop. Three questions. Period. If I don't know the answer, it won't count against you."

"Can I sit down? Wait, that's not my first question. To be clear."

"Sure. Make yourself at home."

She took his dig in stride, then laid a tissue from her purse on a portion of the stern.

"How did you meet Robert?"

"Navy. Next."

"Hold on. If that's how you're going to reply, then you can forget our deal."

She briskly stood up, prepared to walk off. Travis stepped in front of her, his body alluringly close. She could smell soap on him mixed with motor oil. He met her eyes.

In them, she saw a silent plea to stay.

"Fine. I'll explain." Travis chucked a wrench into a tub of tools to punctuate the statement. "We met at Great Mistakes."

"That sounds like a rehab facility. Or a place where they hold bachelor parties."

"It's the nickname for the Great Lakes basic training facility outside Chicago. Wasn't close with Bobby back then. He was on track to be a sonar tech. I wanted to be a gunner's mate. That was the difference between us, to a T. He wanted to watch out for trouble, while I wanted to be in charge of the missiles and torpedoes. He was smart enough to know that a good defense is the best offense. I'm all offense."

"*You?*" she said sarcastically.

"Can't help the way we're raised, can we?" he hinted.

Catherine felt like she was dancing with him, but they were struggling with who would lead and constantly stepping on each other's toes.

"I wound up stationed in Italy with him a few years later."

Now Travis's shirt made sense. Robert's postcards did too.

They had been sent from naval bases. Wanting to join the military and see the world, that was what every Hemingway character did, so it was no surprise Robert had set off on a similar path. When Catherine's company had been doing a study on how to improve membership in the armed forces, she made a spreadsheet of bases around the globe. Catherine could have screamed at herself for not putting that together sooner.

"Bobby was the quiet type," Travis continued. "Did his job right. Kept to himself. Played a mean game of poker. Took my money more times than I care to admit."

A glimmer of happy memories twinkled Travis's eyes. Catherine didn't have any trouble picturing her brother as an expert poker player. He had always picked up games easily and aced his math tests in school without studying. Anything with numbers came naturally to him. Catherine too. She found herself starting to reminisce, then forced the conversation back on topic.

"Was he a jokester? Laid back? Upbeat? Did you meet any of his other friends around here? Or ever go to his house?"

Travis gave her an impatient look.

She rolled her eyes, then reconsidered. "All right, how would you describe him?"

"Honest, smart, and dependable." He ticked the adjectives off on his fingers.

The last one stung Catherine. Her brother had indeed been honest and smart. But he had not been dependable to her.

"Final question," Travis declared.

"How did you end up working for him on this boat?"

"That's more about me than Bobby."

"Are you declining to answer? We didn't discuss that contingency when we laid down the ground rules."

Travis finally stopped fiddling with various tools and took a seat as far from Catherine as he could manage, as if girding himself to explain.

"I ran into him here at the Green Parrot, a dive bar. We had some beers. Got to talking. Catching up. He told me he had a boat that needed fixing, and he remembered I was handy at repairing things. Said he didn't care how long it took or how much it cost and that I could stay there, too, if I wanted a place to crash. I was . . ." Travis appeared to mull over his choice of words for a minute. "In a tough spot, so I took him up on his offer."

"A tough spot as in . . ."

"As in that's my business." He inched away from her a little. "What? You never been in one?"

She was frustrated with his reply, yet she could relate. "Feels like I'm always in one."

"You Morans, you love making deals."

"Not sure I'm loving this one so far."

"This was your idea."

Catherine thought of how dumb Willford's plan was, and here she was, mismanaging her own half-baked scheme.

"Did Robert say where he got this boat or why he bought it or why he was in Key West?" She was dying to know more, even the smallest tidbit.

"You got your three. We're done for the day. And, no, I never met any of his friends or visited his place. Didn't get the sense those were things he wanted to share. Those last two were freebies."

He stood up, as though asking her to leave without saying it outright. He had won this round. Travis was clearly too savvy to let Catherine boot him off the boat if he could prolong his stay by whatever means necessary.

Though that bothered Catherine, she respected him for it.

Travis offered her his hand to help her up. She took it—calloused, manly. Catherine didn't want to let go. She also wanted to stay there for hours and wring every answer out of him she possibly could. That wasn't in the cards.

"What about you? What brought you to Key West?" she asked.

He dropped her hand. "Questions about me aren't part of the deal."

Self-conscious, Catherine quickly removed the tissue and searched for a trash can to throw it in. Travis was staring, so she balled it into her purse and clumsily hopped from the stern onto the dock.

Without warning, a loud horn blew, making Catherine jump and nearly sending her overboard into the bay. The sound came from the huge fishing trawler she had seen earlier. Using her hand to shield her eyes, she could see it moving in the distance. The vessel was being backed in toward the repair area.

"What's up with that big boat over there? Looked like a bunch of guys were fighting over it."

Travis seemed reluctant to answer.

"Give me a break. That question's *not* about Robert. Or you."

"It's a repossession," he replied tersely. "Vic, the guy who runs this marina, swindled some guy out of it. Paid a quarter of what it was worth. Cheats sellers by convincing them their boats are beyond repair. Bet he'll do some shoddy fixes, then sell it to some tourist for triple what he paid."

Travis didn't attempt to conceal his disdain.

Although Vic struck her as rough around the edges, hearing that he had undercut this other offer by that much and gotten away with it meant he played dirty when it came to business. Maybe she could get a lot more for Robert's boat than anybody was letting on. Including Travis.

"One thing Bobby warned me about when I first moved onboard was to watch out for Vic," he told her. "The mako sharks in these waters have got nothing on him. Bobby could tell a jackass from a gentleman in ten seconds flat. It's a skill most people would kill for. Myself included."

He stared at Catherine as if to say he remained on the fence about her character too. "That detail's on the house." The reverence in his voice was unmistakable.

"You talk about Robert like he's your hero."

"You talk about him like he wasn't yours," Travis shot back, stunning Catherine with the lengths he would go to to protect her brother's reputation.

She felt as if she had been hit between the eyes with his outrage. "For your information, your 'hero' abandoned his mother and his sister to fend for themselves when they needed him after our father ran out. Remember that the next time you try and defend Robert to me."

Travis's expression flattened with remorse as he took a tentative step toward her.

Before he could say another word, Catherine got on the bike, nerves jangling, and pedaled away.

18

If it weren't for the breeze, Catherine wouldn't have realized she was crying. As she rode Arnie's bicycle out of the marina parking lot, the wind off the water slid the tears sideways across her greasy cheeks. She stopped to put on her sunglasses so nobody would see.

"Who does he think he is?" Catherine snarled to herself. "He doesn't know the real Robert."

Maybe she didn't either. How could she? Her brother was like the million sunrises she only realized that she had missed after seeing one.

Unsure whether she could take another few days of Q and A with Travis's petulant attitude, Catherine decided it was time to line up another buyer for the boat, especially if Vic was notorious for underbidding.

But where? And how?

She pulled over to the side of the causeway and called the only person she could think of who might be able to help. Cars whizzed by as she dialed, whipping her hair against her shoulders. The line rang and rang.

"Hey, darlin'," Kenny sang. "Need a lift?"

"No. I need some advice. Got a minute?"

"For you, I got two."

After Catherine had given him the update, Kenny exhaled a long breath. "Now I get why everybody in town calls Vic 'the Ambassador.'"

"I'm guessing it's not due to his tact. Or his attire."

"I thought it was on account of him being in charge of the marina. But it's probably because he's a diplomat, the kind that always gets what he wants and can tell you to go to hell in the sorta way that you'll look forward to the trip."

"I'm already in purgatory with the headache this boat is giving me."

"Go see my buddy Ignacio at the A & B Marina, off Front Street. Tell him that you're best friends with my wife."

"Except I'm not. Why can't I just say I know you? At least that's true."

"One and the same. His wife gets her nails done at the same place mine does, and if Iggy believes you two are pals, he won't want to get his missus miffed for not lending a hand."

The thought of having to lie to yet another person stressed Catherine out. "How come everything has to be complicated down here?"

"It's not. It's just how it's done."

"That's oxymoronic."

"What did you call me?" Kenny kidded.

"I get it. I mean, I don't. And I do. It's the Key West way. Thank you," Catherine added sincerely. "For everything."

"Say, how was the resort?"

"Sensational. I got comped a poolside cabana."

"See, you're getting the hang of this place."

It didn't feel like that.

Back home, Catherine followed rules. She was a good daughter, a good employee, a good friend, all in the hopes that it would pay off in kind. For the most part, it hadn't. In Key West, she wasn't certain what the rules were. Or if there were any. All Catherine could be sure of was that she only had a couple of days to sell Robert's boat and to enjoy what was left of her vacation.

The ride to the other marina took her along the western edge of the island, a scenic trip traversing main thoroughfares and postcard-perfect side streets. She passed the stately homes on Eaton Street and caught some shade under old banyan trees that stood guard along the roads. Key West was under six miles square, a fraction of the size of the island she had come from, yet it reminded Catherine that a city as big as Manhattan could seem crushingly small because of the way she had been living in it, while a place this tiny could feel vast because of the freedom it afforded her. She wasn't crowded into a subway car or walking cheek by jowl with other commuters on Broadway. Instead, she was tooling around a sand-dusted stretch of asphalt on a bicycle. Catherine was on cloud nine—until she turned onto Front Street, where a giant red-and-blue sign loomed, emblazoned with the words **A & B Marina.**

That was the cue for her next performance.

This was far nicer than where her brother's boat was docked. Outside, signs for a lobster house, a steak house, a cocktail bar, an oyster bar, a sailing school, and a grocery store were stacked atop one another like an advertising totem pole. Where would this Ignacio be amid the many options?

Catherine hesitated about going inside to ask and leaving Arnie's bicycle unattended. The last thing she needed was for it to be stolen. She paced around until someone who wasn't dressed like a tourist came out.

"Excuse me," she said to a woman in a shirt with an A & B Charter Fishing Fleet logo on it. "Can you tell me where I might find Ignacio?"

"No problem! Follow me," the woman replied with a friendly wave, leading Catherine to a covered area for refueling. "Iggy, you got a visitor!"

A man with a cap on backward came to greet her, the hat's band framing his bushy brows and dark eyes. Flecks of gray in his short beard shone in the bright sunlight. He looked at Catherine quizzically, not recognizing her.

Showtime!

"Hi, there!" she said, chipper. "Kenny told me to talk to you. I know his wife. Do you have a minute?"

Ignacio warmed up as soon as Catherine mentioned Kenny's better half. "Sure, sure," he said, his accent making every word sound musical. He stepped out to join her on the dock. "What can I do for you?"

Struggling with how to condense the insanity that was her situation, Catherine decided to play it straight.

"I have a boat to sell. Honestly, it isn't in the greatest shape. I'm from New York City, and I can barely tell the difference between the bow and the stern, but I'm pretty sure the one bid I've gotten was too low. I want to see if anybody else might be interested." She dug the papers the attorney had faxed her out of her purse and showed Ignacio the information.

"What did you say is the name of this boat?"

"It's called *Same Ship, Different Day*. It also went by another name, I believe. *Pauline's Escape*."

Ignacio smacked the faxes. "Por supuesto. This I know. I hope you did not pay much money for this."

"Not a dime. Why?"

"This boat, it is kind of famous on the island."

"Famous?"

"Only not in a way that is good."

A flush of panic made her body feel burning hot. "Can we sit in the shade for a second?"

He escorted her to a nearby bench and leaned in to talk privately. "You have heard of this writer, Ernest Hemingway?"

"Yup," Catherine replied ruefully, now afraid she might faint.

"He had much success, many books, many travels, many wives. The story, it goes, his wife, Pauline, with her he was not always happy. To get away, he would go on long fishing trips with his friends on one boat, a favorite boat. They say it was called *Pauline's Escape*."

Catherine's queasiness suddenly morphed into unbridled excitement.

"You're telling me I own the boat Ernest Hemingway once fished on?"

Wagging his finger, Ignacio said, "No, no mija."

"But you just—?"

"This, it is a story. A, what do you call it . . . fish tale."

"A lie?" Her stomach turned.

"Tourists, they come to Key West to drink, to party, to hear about famous men, like Harry Truman, Ernest Hemingway. These tourists, they have money. Maybe many years ago, somebody finds an old boat. Paints this name on it. Tells people this story and says the boat belongs to this big writer. That Hemingway was on it. Then sells the boat for a high price."

"It's a scam?" Her hopes took a steep nosedive. "The boat never belonged to Hemingway, and it's worthless?"

"If there's no hole in the bottom, it's not worth nothing. It still floats." Ignacio's attempt to comfort her fell on deaf ears.

Had Robert randomly bought a boat with a sketchy connection to Hemingway?

Or had he been duped into the hoax because of his infatuation with their father's favorite author?

That didn't ring true. Her brother was a quick study. It was as though his math skills applied to adding up people's intentions and subtracting their motives. A neighbor once tried to get him to trade some of his better baseball cards for lesser ones by insisting the players would be Hall of Famers in the future. Robert didn't buy it. Had he lost that talent over time?

Clenching her teeth to stop herself from shrieking a string of expletives, Catherine had to remind herself, much as Travis had, that she didn't have a clue about the person Robert had become over the years.

"This boat, it has a new name, you say?" Ignacio asked.

"Yeah," Catherine sighed. She didn't see how it mattered.

"What is it again?"

"*Same Ship, Different Day*," she told him, enunciating.

He didn't understand.

"It's a joke. Based on the saying 'Same shit, different day.' You do the same thing repeatedly, day after day."

"Sí, sí, I get it." He finally understood. "Funny."

"Not really."

"But this name, it's not similar to Hemingway."

Admittedly, Catherine wasn't an admirer, yet she knew enough about the author to agree the new name had no obvious connection. "Not in any way I can think of."

Ignacio rubbed the stubble on his chin contemplatively. "Anybody who lives here, they have heard of this boat. Maybe the name is changed to mix people up."

That only made the whole sordid story more unsettling.

"You mean then it could be resold to some other fool who was dumb enough to believe the legend and pony up a ludicrous amount in order to own a piece of Hemingway memorabilia?"

Ignacio shrugged. "You know this now. Not everyone does. Maybe somebody like you, from far away, they want something from this Hemingway writer, and they pay."

Her choices were getting less desirable by the second. Off-load the boat to Vic for a rock-bottom price so he could turn around and make a profit at some sucker's expense or trick someone for the proceeds herself.

"I no say nothing. This, it is your business. *Your* business." Ignacio underscored the money aspect, implying that it was her prerogative what she did next.

Kenny had been right about sending her to see Ignacio, who had opened Catherine's eyes. But Kenny had been wrong about her. She wasn't getting the hang of this island.

Not by a long shot.

19

Bright sun, a cloudless blue sky, fresh air—nothing should have gone wrong on a day such as that. Except it had.

Catherine walked Arnie's bicycle along the dock, rehashing what Ignacio had told her about the checkered history of Robert's boat.

How can you wash your hands of this mess and just enjoy your vacation?

Travis had said the big trawler she had seen at the marina was a repo. If Catherine's job at the credit card company had taught her anything, it was that people didn't hesitate to contact a claims service if fees weren't paid promptly. Assuming she didn't keep up with the dock dues, Robert's boat would be put up for repossession as well. That might not happen for a month or two, but at least then it wouldn't be her problem anymore.

But was that an outcome she could live with?

She was too hungry to think straight. Since the dock's lobster house, steak house, and oyster bar were out of her budget, she got onto the bike and hoped to pass a reasonably priced sandwich shop. Deciding to head west on Greene Street, she happened upon a line of people surrounding a food cart in a parking lot. That was as auspicious a sign as any.

Nestled beside tall, slender palm trees, the stainless steel cart gleamed in the daylight, and the pink sign said **Garbo's Grill**. Customers who had gotten their orders were standing around, contentedly gorging themselves. With a menu featuring mahi-mahi burritos with mango and cilantro and strawberry lemonade at affordable prices, Catherine had hit pay dirt.

"The burrito, please," she told the woman in sunglasses working the cart.

What Catherine got was the most exotic, flavorful food she had ever tasted. After one bite, she realized why people didn't stray far once they'd gotten their order. It was difficult to walk away when all she wanted to do was savor her meal.

A few tourists were toasting each other with their burritos. Before Catherine knew it, hers was gone, devoured in a matter of minutes. She was slightly ashamed for having eaten that fast, but she wasn't alone. Between the breeze, the palm fronds swaying, the tang of the cilantro, and the cool sweetness of the mango, this was a vacation in food form. Catherine urged herself to relish the moment.

Easy as it was to worry about Robert's boat, she couldn't let her mind go there.

This meal wasn't lukewarm coffee and chips from a vending machine gobbled down in the break room at her office. This wasn't a frozen dinner she had nuked in the microwave after getting home at some ungodly hour after work. This was what Catherine had waited for.

She pulled a couple of singles from her wallet and stuffed them into the tip jar. The woman behind the counter flashed her a smile of gratitude. It was money Catherine shouldn't have been giving away, yet it was worth every penny.

Blissfully full, Catherine walked the bicycle along the sidewalk, passing souvenir shops that were tucked into old converted houses, wood siding slanted, windows crooked in their frames. Here, the ravages of nature and the march of time weren't forces to be fought against but rather facts of life to be admired and accepted. The town wasn't trying to be something it was not.

Catherine could relate to that.

Telephone wires drooped overhead, the tallest things in the sky for as far as she could see. The flatness made Catherine feel decidedly earthbound. In New York, the buildings towered above, and it was always as if she were at the bottom of a well. Here, she was finally on level ground.

The souvenir shops reminded her of Gloria. Catherine still wasn't sure what to get her. She decided to call and ask.

"Can you please pick up your phone," Gloria barked without greeting her. "I gave up leaving you messages after your mother called to inform me that she had already left you ten of 'em. I can't compete with that kind of crazy."

"She's in a tizzy about some woman—"

"Who came back from the hospital. Mrs. Higgins. I heard the whole saga. Tito has been calling me to plan our next date, but your mom keeps interrupting. I'm telling you this guy is a keeper. He pulled out my chair for me. Told me I looked pretty. Didn't give me dirty looks when I ordered an appetizer *and* a dessert."

Catherine could hear the excitement in her voice over the tourists whizzing by on rented scooters. Normally, Gloria only got jazzed when mass transit shut down due to weather or rolling power outages, which gave her a legitimate excuse not to come to work. This was different. She sounded sincerely elated.

"That's the best news I've heard all day. Has he asked you out again?"

"He was about to. Then your mother demanded that I find her the phone number for the FBI."

Either the sun was suddenly too hot, or Catherine was about to have a panic attack. Anxiety ratcheting up, she pulled over the bike and hid in the shade of a shop awning.

"Oh, God. What for?"

"She's convinced there's a conspiracy going on at Shady Ridge. That Mrs. Higgins's accident was no accident. She was getting really *Law & Order* and telling me she had evidence."

"Okay, I'll handle it."

"Why does your mom have my number in the first place?"

"Emergency contact. I'm at work more than I'm home."

"That's depressing."

"I know."

"Girl, you need a vacation."

"I'm trying to take one."

A couple passed by, licking ice cream cones, towels slung over their shoulders. Catherine wished she could relax and soak in the afternoon the way they were.

"Oh, before I forget, what do you want as a souvenir from Key West?"

"I'll take a T-shirt. Make it cute. Not trashy, like those ones with the picture of a skinny girl's torso in a bikini. Or a mug. Maybe a mug."

"One mug coming up. Send the rest of my mom's calls to voicemail and tell Tito I say hello!"

Ducking out from under the awning, back into the blare of the sunlight, Catherine was feeling the heat in more ways than she could count.

She dialed her mother's number as she reached the Maritime Museum. The stocky limestone structure hulked over a redbrick square where old cannons stood as sentinels around the perimeter. Propping Arnie's bike against a wall, Catherine took a seat on the brick steps that fanned outward from the museum. She wanted to go inside and see what was on display. The battle relics would have to wait. She had a feeling she was about to do hand-to-hand combat of her own.

"Hey, hon," her mother said, answering the phone merrily.

"Mom, are you all right?"

"Never better. Why?"

"Did you call Gloria and tell her you needed to speak to the FBI?" she whispered to prevent the group of tourists trampling up the steps from hearing her.

"Yes. But she overreacted."

"*She* overreacted?"

"Mr. Navarro is a cheater. He cheats at mah-jongg. He cheats at bridge. Now he randomly wins the big cash prize for Mrs. Higgins's injuries? Something is fishy. Mark my words, the fix was in."

"Then you don't really want to get the authorities involved, right?"

"Meh. I spread the word around here. The other residents won't let him get away with counting cards during casino night anymore."

Catherine should have been concerned, hearing her mother talk this way. However, it wasn't out of the norm. The maelstrom of extreme paranoia had passed, as it always did. Her mother wouldn't remember it come morning.

What was left in its wake was damage and devastation. Each day was a new hurricane of confusion. Or an unforeseen tornado of befuddlement. Or a typhoon of forgetfulness from out of the blue. Catherine lived in the wreckage, ever trying to rebuild amid the ruins and debris.

As she sat there in the sunshine, Catherine wasn't sure how many more storms she could weather. Between her mom's behavior, her boss's tacit pressure about his project, and the boat being practically valueless, she considered packing up and heading home early.

Maybe it was time to cut her losses.

"I'll tell you something, Cath," her mother continued.

Beleaguered, Catherine massaged her temples. "What, Mom?"

"I'm not going to let that Mr. Navarro get one over on me. I'll play it cool. I won't let on that I know he rigged the bet. I'll keep my eye on him. He'll slip up. The shifty ones always do."

In her mom's fanciful tale, Mr. Navarro was the villain; however, Catherine couldn't figure out who the bad guy was in her own story.

Was it Robert, who could have been conned or was in on the boat hoax? Travis, who was drawing out the days to keep a roof over his head? Vic, who'd given her a low bid for the trawler?

Or was it Catherine herself for lying to virtually everybody?

"When Mr. Navarro shows his true colors, I'll be there to catch him. Expose him for what he truly is. You can't let people get away with cheating. If you don't stand up to them, who will?"

For a change, Catherine thought her mother was absolutely right.

20

Patience wasn't Catherine's strong suit. She biked hard to the Abbott House, her legs burning from exertion, her arms prickling under the harsh sunshine. Incensed, Catherine made a plan.

Sweat and cheap sunscreen didn't mix well. Halfway home, her left eye started to burn. She could barely see out of it, which turned riding a bicycle across an unfamiliar town into a trial by fire.

Blinking and wiping her face, Catherine did her best to avoid oncoming traffic as well as pedestrians. Seeing clearly was getting harder by the second. She nearly rammed the handlebars into the side mirror of a parked car.

Catherine was grateful when she finally got to the inn safe and sound.

Both eyes watering profusely, she replaced Arnie's bicycle next to Fred's by the garage. Because shoving her face into the backyard fountain didn't seem the decorous thing to do, Catherine rushed into the kitchen, ripped off her cap, and ran for the sink, where she splashed water on her face, soaking herself and her clothes.

"Catherine, dear, are you having some sort of . . . meltdown?"

Squinting, she looked over and saw Fred in the doorway to the dining room. The counters were sluiced. There was a puddle on the floor. Water ran down her legs.

"I got sunscreen in my eyes. I feel like I've been maced."

He gave her a paper towel to blot her face, then unspooled more from the roll. "Wouldn't be the worst thing I've walked in on. I found a guest in here making a cup of tea at midnight in the buff. It was a woman. In her seventies. I wanted to wash my eyes out too. Let's get this cleaned up before Arnie has a conniption. I don't want him reading me—or you—the riot act because his sanctum sanctorum is in disarray."

Catherine bent down to dry the floors while Fred took care of the counters.

"Am I the worst guest you've ever had?" she asked, repentant.

"Not by a mile. We once had a guy come home drunk, singing 'Cheeseburger in Paradise' so loudly that the neighbors called the cops. Jimmy Buffett may be Jesus in Key West, but not everybody's a fan. Or there was the time when this family with a toddler let their little boy loose in the parlor and he started ramming a toy truck into the leg of my rare R. J. Horner rosewood slipper chair. Arnie had to hold me back. Oh, then there were the newlyweds who got into a hellacious fight and decided to have the marriage annulled."

"Who knew a bed-and-breakfast could be the stage for so much drama?"

"I certainly didn't," Fred lamented, tossing the towels in the trash. "I envisioned fabulous guests telling colorful stories, everyone gathered around the dining table, lapping up Arnie's cooking, laughing and enjoying themselves."

Fred's shoulders slumped, the disenchantment displayed by his posture. "Instead, we have to make endless small talk and look at pictures of people's grandkids while the guests complain about the food, damage the antiques, and steal the hand towels."

Catherine squeezed his shoulder supportively. "I can see why they steal them," she admitted, teasing. "They're gorgeous."

"Owning a B and B was our dream. Sank our savings into the house. Now with the Airbnbs undercutting our rates, we had no idea how tough it would be to make ends meet."

"I'm in the same boat. Pun intended."

She had moved her mother to Shady Ridge imagining she would love it there, maybe improve, start remembering more. Catherine was burning through what money she had in hopes of selling Robert's trawler in order to try and make both their lives better. However, the thing that was supposed to save her was only complicating the situation.

Fred wiped up the last of the water. "How are those peepers of yours? They're awfully red. Don't let Ina get a look at you. You know what conclusion she'll jump to."

"I can only really see out of one of them." Catherine tried closing her right eye, then the left to check her sight, making her dizzy. Wobbling a bit, she leaned on the counter for support.

"Steady there, matey. We have an eye patch if you want it. Came with Arnie's pirate costume from last Halloween."

"This really is a full-service bed-and-breakfast. I should put that in my online review."

"Don't you dare," he scolded.

"You ought to put more pictures on the website. The dipping pool, the fountain, the claw-foot bathtub, the French soap . . . those are selling features. Take it from me. Marketing makes a huge difference in what people will spend money on. How is anybody supposed to know how great this place is if you don't show them?"

"Maybe somebody should take her own good advice," Fred hinted.

Catherine was so mixed up about what people thought of her and what she thought of herself that she didn't know how to answer. "I'm going to go change out of these wet clothes."

"Give them to me, and I'll pop them in the dryer, or else you'll leave a drip trail through the house, which would be sacrilege to you-know-who."

Catherine had her bathing suit on underneath her tank top and shorts, so she unabashedly stripped off the drenched garments and passed them to Fred.

"Thanks," she said—for the offer and for his recommendation.

The question was whether she could take it.

"Yoo-hoo," a female voice called. In walked Ina, rattling a portable thermos. "May I have some ice from the freez—?"

Halting in her tracks, she stared at a half-naked Catherine standing in the middle of the kitchen with Fred holding her clothing. Her expression pinched with disapproval.

"This isn't what it looks like," he explained.

Ina spun on her heel and marched out of the kitchen.

Frustration washed over Fred's face.

"The upside is this wasn't the other way around," Catherine offered. "What if you walked in on *her* taking off her clothes?"

"I'm getting that ice. For a martini!" he pronounced. "Here. Take this for her and this for you."

He hastily put some cubes in a small bar cooler for Ina and got an ice pack for Catherine's swollen eye, having wrapped the pack in a seafoam-colored dishcloth that matched the cabinets.

"Go make peace," Fred ordered, prodding Catherine out of the kitchen.

"For the record, this debacle wasn't my fault!"

She grudgingly brought the ice bucket upstairs and rapped lightly on the door to the room the sisters were sharing.

"Who is it?" Ina asked.

"Ice delivery."

The door opened a crack, and Catherine held out the bucket to her.

"Funny story. I got sunscreen in my eyes and—"

Ina snatched the ice; then the door shut on Catherine midsentence.

"Good talk."

Catherine returned to her room, flung herself on the bed, and laid the ice pack across her brows. It reminded her of being sick as a kid, when her mother would send Robert in to check on her. If he saw that her eyes were open, he would close the door and leave, so Catherine would pretend to be asleep to get him to flip the compress over to the cool side for her.

Now Robert was the one fooling her.

She set the ice pack on the nightstand and got out her laptop before remembering what Fred had said about guests damaging the furniture and grabbed the ice pack again. The floors were wood, as was the dresser. She couldn't put the ice pack on either. Since she didn't want to sleep under a wet duvet that night, Catherine stuck it in her purse for lack of a safer place, then started her search of the Florida DMV sitting cross-legged on the bed.

According to the website, all motorized vessels used on public waterways had to be registered, excluding nonresident boats. Catherine grabbed the paperwork that Latham had faxed her. The documents stated that Robert was a resident, though they listed no former address. The fact that her brother had erased himself from the records felt like he was intentionally concealing the truth.

To obtain certification of ownership on a vessel, registration had to be made at the county tax collector's office, which was a few blocks away from the Abbott House, on Truman Avenue. Because registrations were only valid for a year, Catherine thought the city must keep a history of ownership on file.

She jotted down the address and was about to shut the laptop when she typed the words "Travis Bradley" into the search bar.

A series of articles appeared. However, they featured pictures of a much older man, Travis Bradley Sr., a decorated war veteran, who had become a district judge in Chicago. The physical similarities were striking despite the age difference. Both men shared the same square jaw and piercing eyes. Next, Catherine found a picture from a ribbon-cutting ceremony that listed the judge and his wife, as well as their adult daughter and her husband and their kids.

There was no mention of a son.

Page after page listed interviews and convictions by Judge Bradley. Except he wasn't the one Catherine was curious about. She clicked on a news piece with a line that caught her attention.

"Judge Bradley has cited his strong stance on violence as originating from a personal place," Catherine read aloud. "When asked if he was referring to his years of service in the army, the judge declined to comment further."

Travis had mentioned going through what he called a "tough spot" when they talked. Had a run-in with the law contributed to a falling out with his father? A legal charge would certainly frame the judge in an unflattering light.

You could be jumping to conclusions. Like Ina did.

Travis's past wasn't nearly as important as the history of the boat.

Catherine needed to find out if Robert had been hoodwinked into buying the trawler Ernest Hemingway had allegedly owned or if he had been involved in the scam. The thought that Robert would be involved in anything illegal had never crossed her mind. Once it did, it gave her an uneasy feeling.

She didn't know where her brother had lived. Or what his job had been. Or what he was like. He was a complete mystery.

Even though there were more pieces of the puzzle missing than Catherine could account for, she was determined to learn what she could about Robert, whether he wanted her to or not.

21

The afternoon sun hung in a bald blue sky, magnificent yet unforgiving. Catherine considered applying another coat of sunscreen as she wheeled Arnie's bicycle out onto the street. She was more afraid of her eyes burning again than her skin.

Since interrupting Fred's martini after she had caused another scene with Ina wasn't advisable and Arnie wasn't around, she hadn't asked permission to borrow the bike again. Catherine made a mental note to get him something sweet as a thank-you gift, as Arnie had suggested.

The address for the tax collector's office wasn't far. While digging her phone out of her purse for directions, Catherine discovered that the ice pack she had tossed in there to protect Fred's precious antiques had melted, causing the colors to bleed and the street names to blur. She peeled apart the wet pieces, then flattened the map across her thigh, which turned her fingertips blue and red. A faint grid of Old Town transferred to her leg.

"More bizarre tan lines. Just what I need."

Catherine chucked the map, her purse, and the ice pack into the bicycle's basket, then was off, passing house after house with white picket fences. Many were bed-and-breakfasts. Some were ostentatious, with intricate filigrees on the facades. Others were artsy, with flashy paint jobs in peach, pink, and teal.

She found herself comparing them to the Abbott House. They all paled. Some were bigger, others grander, but none had what Fred and Arnie could offer.

Up ahead was the address she was searching for. The Monroe County Tax Collector's Office was situated in a bulky square building, white and squat as a sheet cake with odd shutters that covered the windows like blinders, giving the place a blank, expressionless look. Gravel crunched under the wheels as Catherine rode into the driveway. There was a bike stand, but she didn't have a lock.

Catherine hadn't thought to ask Arnie or Fred for one. This was an ongoing problem. She wasn't thinking ahead the way she normally would, and the oversights were stacking up.

Concerned about leaving Arnie's property unguarded, Catherine leaned in the front door of the office building, which was glass with windows on either side. An older woman was seated at the front desk, her white hair sculpted into a lumpy bun. Catherine cleared her throat to get the woman's attention.

"Pardon me. I have a teensy favor to ask."

The word "favor" didn't seem to sit well with the woman.

"I'm vacationing here, and I borrowed a friend's bike, but I don't have a padlock, so I was wondering if I could prop it by the door and perhaps you could keep an eye on it."

"That's not our policy," the woman stated lifelessly, as if years of being in civil service had ground her voice down to a drone.

"I'm here to register my boat," Catherine added to mollify her. "Making sure everything's legal. According to code. Paid in full."

That softened the woman slightly. "Make it speedy."

"Will do."

Catherine rested Arnie's bicycle against a window frame, positioning it within the woman's view, then dashed inside.

"What office should I be going to?"

"Second floor. Tags and registration."

The lady at that desk could have been a clone of the one downstairs, except her hair was dyed candy-apple red and she had a Southern twang to her monotone. A high counter separated a small waiting area from a bank of computers. Framed watercolors of local sites decorated the walls. Most were hung lopsided. This was as close to the island's famed hotspots as Catherine had come thus far.

"Do you have your paperwork?" the redhead asked before Catherine could make any inquiries.

"I'm actually here to ask you that."

A grimace stood in for the lady's reply.

"I recently came into possession of this boat." Catherine produced the faxes, which were also damp from the ice pack. She picked them apart and smoothed them onto the counter. The lady looked on, blasé. "I wanted to find out who owned it before me."

"You don't know who sold it to you?"

"Yes. Sort of. I'd like to get a history of title holders."

"You'd have to tender your registration fee first."

Loath as Catherine was to part with any more of her dwindling cash, she'd figured it would come to this. In order to sell Robert's boat, she would have to pay. She resentfully ponied up nearly one hundred bucks. She could almost hear her wallet crying.

"About those titles?"

The lady heaved an irritated sigh and typed something into her computer keyboard. A perplexed scowl formed on her face.

"Ain't got any."

"Come again?"

"Wasn't a dealer sale. It was used. Most states don't require boats to be titled. Proof of ownership on a used boat from a nontitle state is the vessel registration and a notarized bill of sale to transfer ownership. Which you got here. Name of Mr. Smith. From South Carolina. Sounds fake. Happens a lot with used boats."

It took a second for Catherine to comprehend what the redhead was explaining. Then the brunt of the bad news hit her full bore.

"You're saying the previous seller went by a fictitious name and because they were from out of state, there are no records."

"Yes, ma'am. It's pretty much a dead end."

The lady wasn't aware how apt her choice of phrasing was.

"There's also the matter of the sales tax you owe. You wanna pay by cash or check?"

Out of options and nearly out of spending money, Catherine handed over the remainder of what she owed and left. The air-conditioned building should have felt like a reprieve from the heat, yet she was sweating profusely.

"Can't be too careful," the white-haired woman at the desk downstairs cautioned as Catherine reached the door. "Best to get a bike lock. Especially if that bike isn't yours."

"Thank you," she said. "For watching it."

The woman was correct. Hard as she tried, Catherine couldn't be careful enough, and she still came up short.

The heat greeted her the second she stepped outside. Crickets rattled, making it sound as if the hot midday air were sizzling. The weather wasn't helping Catherine's withering spirits.

Desperate and in need of somebody to complain to, she contemplated calling her mom. Only that was liable to backfire. Catherine was in too deep, and there was no resolution yet, nothing that could validate her actions.

She guided the bicycle down the steps, ice pack dripping from the basket as if it were crying, then called Kenny.

"What's happenin', Cap'n?" he said jovially.

"I have another boat question."

"Shoot. Or, rather, row."

"I'm at the county tax collector's office."

"Not one of our more popular tourist attractions."

"Turns out the person who sold my brother the fishing trawler was from out of state, and they put a false name on the forms."

"Ah," Kenny sighed. "Oldest trick in the book. Lots of folks do it, including dealers. Makes mechanical problems disappear, so to speak."

"Like money laundering for boats? To hide the original owners and the vessel's history?"

"If you want to be sure of hitting a target, shoot first, then call whatever you hit the target."

Was that what Robert had done? Catherine hated to think of him as a hustler or as a sap who'd been duped. At that point, she didn't want to think about him at all.

"Who's notorious for running this scam around the island?"

"Why? You gonna put them under citizen's arrest?"

"Nope. I'm going to do what we do in Jersey."

"Make them an offer they can't refuse?"

"Sort of."

"Kiddo, I can't let you go see these people by yourself. They aren't the type of guys you want to monkey around with."

"Then come with me."

"I'm on the clock."

"I'll pay you for your time."

What is a little more money down the drain? Catherine thought.

If the plan percolating in her mind worked, she could pay off her mom's rent at Shady Ridge this month as well as some of her bills. Although it wasn't the cash haul Catherine had been hoping for, it was better than nothing.

While she pushed Arnie's bike along the sidewalk, a lukewarm breeze kicked up by passing cars blew through her ponytail. A convertible limo crammed full of tourists taking selfies cruised down Truman Avenue, followed by a local schoolkid riding a skateboard and wearing headphones. Key West was a constant study in contrasts. The divide between the natives and the vacationers wasn't subtle.

Catherine decided that could work to her advantage.

"Come on, Kenny. Please," she begged.

"I'm an old man with a bum knee and a beer gut. I won't frighten these dudes, if that's what you're looking to do."

"You won't have to scare them. I will."

22

Catherine felt like she was walking the plank. The long boardwalk that led to the Sunset Marina stretched for what seemed like miles, giving her time to think over her plan.

And time to doubt it.

"You sure you know what you're doing?" Kenny asked, lumbering a pace behind.

"Not really."

"I had a feeling you were going to say that."

He'd picked her up at the Abbott House after she dropped off Arnie's bicycle; then they rode over to nearby Stock Island. Kenny tugged the brim of his hat low and tried to keep up with her. She'd never seen him standing up, and though he was taller than she had presumed, he appeared to shrink at the idea of locking horns with the men they were going to see.

"Are you certain this is the right place?" Catherine glanced around in disbelief.

The horseshoe-shaped marina had a parking lot on one side and pink-and-green condo complexes on the other. An elderly woman in a yellow sunbonnet was sitting outside reading the paper, with her walker and a white Maltese dog on a leash beside her. The hedges that grew along the boardwalk were being meticulously tended to by a groundskeeper.

"This looks like a retirement community."

"It is," Kenny replied.

"Then why are you so jumpy?"

"Sketchy people don't always live in sketchy places."

They reached a clubhouse, and Kenny was about to let her go in first out of courtesy, then changed his mind. "I'll point 'em out. After that, I'm not breathing a word."

The clubhouse had the worn air of a chain restaurant: shellacked tables and chairs, thick carpet, and pastel starfish wallpaper. This was hardly the den of iniquity Kenny made it out to be. The scent of piña colada swirled in the air as fans with rattan blades spun overhead.

"That's them." Kenny gestured toward the bar.

A pair of older men in khakis were seated on stools, nursing beers. One had combed his thin gray hair over his bald spot and wore a blue polo shirt. The other was sporting a turf-green visor and had the flat affect of somebody who would have to be bribed to smile.

"Those guys? You're spooked by two grandpas in golf pants?"

"Trust me. They're more dangerous than they seem."

Kenny's apprehension was starting to rub off on her.

"You can stay by the door."

"Really?" He seemed relieved.

"Unless a fight breaks out. Then feel free to step in."

"You fixin' on starting one?"

"Not intentionally. Anything I should be aware of before I go over there?"

"The guy in the visor is the tough one. The other one is his attorney. Loves to go on and on about how long he's been practicing law. Or, more likely, breaking it. Oh, and don't tell them your real name. Or where you're staying. Just in case."

Anxious, she mustered her nerve, straightened her posture, and sashayed to the bar, channeling the poise of Audrey Hepburn from the movie.

"Gentlemen," Catherine intoned. "I hate to interrupt."

Wary, the man in the visor looked her up and down. Meanwhile, his buddy in the polo seemed pleased to see her. "We always have time for a lady," he said, clearly trying to be smooth.

Catherine cozied up yet kept her voice low. "I hope this isn't too forward but—"

"Sorry, sweetie." The man in the visor curtly cut her off. "No working gals allowed in the clubhouse."

The shock on Catherine's face convinced both men that she wasn't what they had mistaken her for. "I am not a—!"

The guy in the polo made the apologies. "My friend, here, he needs to brush up on his manners."

Their accents gave them away as New Yorkers. Catherine latched on to that as she recovered from the insult.

"I was told I could see somebody here about a boat. I'm in town from the City, and my father, he's a big Ernest Hemingway fan. He would love to have a piece of history to call his own. Would either of you be able to help me with that?"

They traded glances.

"Boats?" the guy in the visor said. "Who says we know about boats? Your pal over there?"

Without looking, his back to the door, he had spotted Kenny. Catherine realized he must have spied him in the reflection from a window. Kenny was right. This was not somebody she should have been tangling with. Only she already was.

"He's my driver while I'm on the island. I asked him. He made a call. But if you don't know boats, you don't know boats. I'll have to take my business elsewhere."

She'd started to walk away when the man in the visor caught her arm. Out of the corner of her eye, Catherine saw Kenny take a step toward the bar protectively.

"Hey, hey, hey. We're not dealers, per se. Not in the business. We might have a connection, though. For a fellow New Yorker." The guy in the polo grinned at her.

The man with the visor was less enthusiastic. "Your dad, he's a fan, you said?"

"Huge. Even named me after one of the characters."

"Oh, yeah? Which one?"

It was a test. Catherine remembered Kenny had specifically warned her not to give them her real name. She raced to come up with a character from one of the books.

A memory of Robert flashed before her.

He was on the couch, glued to the novel where his namesake was the lead. Catherine had wanted him to play with her, so she grabbed the book from him, but he snagged it back.

"You've read that a million times," she had groaned.

"This is the best part. He's about to blow up the bridge. No more of that mushy junk with Maria."

Catherine could picture the worn paperback, dog-eared, the spine cracked, the cover split at the edges. Robert had worshiped it. It was his security blanket. Even though she had hated Hemingway, she had to admire the author for what he had done for her brother. In a way, he was the father Robert didn't have.

"Maria," she told them. "From *For Whom the Bell Tolls*."

The man in the visor nodded, as if she had passed. "Give us a minute, will ya?"

She headed over to where Kenny was standing by the door while the two men talked.

"Well?" Kenny asked under his breath.

"They thought I was a prostitute."

He wrinkled his forehead. "You?"

"I'm not sure what's more insulting—that they assumed I was a call girl or that you think I couldn't pass for one."

"Maybe both are compliments?" Kenny reasoned. "How's it going otherwise?"

Using the reflection from the clubhouse windows, the same way the man in the visor had, Catherine saw that he was dialing his cell.

"Either my plan is working or we're about to get whacked."

"Oh, brother."

"My thoughts exactly."

Robert had gotten her into this. She hoped he'd also gotten her out of it and that the men believed her story. Catherine felt guilty for dragging Kenny into everything. He hardly knew her, yet he was putting himself on the line for her. Soon, the man in the polo motioned her back to the bar.

"Can we make this happen?" she asked, smiling, despite how scared she felt.

"It's a possibility," the man in the polo stated.

The guy in the visor sipped his beer. "How much are you looking to spend?"

"It's my father." Catherine acted as if price were no object. "Is twenty doable?"

Her research had told her that forty thousand was a reasonable starting point, so she intentionally lowballed them.

"What? Are we giving away boats here now?" the man in the polo chided, as though his hands were tied.

"Fifty and we'll have them put a bow on it." The guy in the visor pushed aside his beer. "It's a steal. Seeing as it's a gift for your dear old dad."

She pretended to consider her options. "Okay," she said, acquiescing. "For him."

"Excellent." The guy in the polo took out his cell. "Give me your number, and I'll call you when we can move forward."

Catherine gave him the information, then shook the men's hands, reeling at the fact that she had made an illegal deal with money she absolutely didn't have. Her throat was bone dry. Her legs were jelly. Kenny held the clubhouse door open, escorting her outside. She waved at the men as she exited, then nearly puked over a side rail into the bay.

"Did you just offer those old crooks fifty thousand dollars for a boat you already own?" he demanded once they were clear of the building.

"Yup. And now I'm kind of dizzy. Can we stop walking?"

"No," Kenny insisted, grabbing her by the elbow and pulling her across the boardwalk as quickly as his injured knee would allow. "Do you want to get arrested?"

"I want to get the money Robert owes me."

"Your brother died in debt to you?"

"In a manner of speaking."

He gave her a look.

Catherine didn't waste time defending herself or her grudge. "You said dealers run this out-of-state sale scheme all the time. Vic must be one of them, or else those two wouldn't have said they could get the boat. If Vic wants them to pay him, he's got to pay me first."

Kenny stopped, and they caught their breath. Then he snickered. "That was pretty crafty."

"Thanks."

"Only the jig will be up if Vic figures out your angle and tells his pals at the clubhouse."

"By then he'll have paid me, and I'll be on an airplane. He'll have to answer to his buddies. Not me. Serves him right for doing this to unsuspecting Ernest Hemingway fans."

"Yeah, you're a real champion of the people. What about that dude living on the boat?"

"What about him? I told him he had to be out in a few days."

"For somebody who claimed to be a rotten liar, you're not too shabby."

"Maybe I lied about being a bad liar," she said with a wink.

Inside, however, Catherine was worried too.

23

Sunset draped the sky in pink and gold. Catherine couldn't believe how the day had gone by in a blink. Kenny pulled his cab up beside the Abbott House and shifted the car into park, causing the Jimmy Buffett bobblehead to quake, as though everything that had gone on gave it the shivers.

"Sorry for dragging you into my personal three-ring circus."

"This is the most excitement I've had since two college jocks got into a fistfight in the back seat of my cab."

"How did you break it up?"

"Jammed on the brakes. Both of 'em bonked their heads on the plastic partition."

"Inventive."

"You gonna be okay?"

Catherine gave him the money she owed him for the fare and as much of a tip as she could scrape together.

"It's like I'm jumping out of a plane and hoping my parachute opens."

"Remember, you don't need a parachute to skydive. You only need it if you want to skydive twice. Keep me posted, kiddo."

She got out, then was left standing in the street, alone, unsure what to do next.

"Some vacation this is turning out to be. I blame Hemingway."

Catherine held him responsible for a lot that had gone wrong. Because of Hemingway, she had a name she disliked, a brother who'd chosen books over her, and a boat that was becoming a bigger burden than she could ever have conceived. She had an axe to grind with a dead man she had never met.

Since she couldn't yell at him, Catherine decided to do the next best thing.

She headed to his historic house a few blocks away, taking Duval Street. Crowds overflowed from the sidewalks, lights twinkled, and neon bar signs beckoned in patrons. Resisting the temptation to linger and people watch, she cut over to Whitehead, where Hemingway's former home stood behind a redbrick wall and a closed iron gate.

A sign said the place had closed an hour ago.

Bordered by palm trees and manicured grounds, the two-story house was a funky mix of cream stucco, black wrought iron, and lime-green shutters glowing around arched windows. The upper floor had a balcony with spindly railings. She pictured what it looked like inside, bookshelves everywhere, mounted fish, stuffed deer heads, masculine and writerly. Catherine rested her arms on the wall. She was stuck on the outside, gazing in at something she couldn't be a part of. She felt that way more often than she cared to admit.

Could she hold some stranger who had died before she was born accountable for what became of her family and her life? She wanted to. It was easier to lump the reproach on a man she had never known rather than on her father, her mother, her brother, or herself.

"Fine," she relented, as if speaking directly to Hemingway. "I didn't say it was your fault. I said I was blaming you."

Catherine stared at the home, as if expecting an answer she wouldn't get.

Hungry, she went in search of a cheap bite to eat. Menus pasted in restaurant windows boasted mouthwatering meals, but she saw nothing in her budget. What she could afford was a piece of pizza from a little joint with New York in the name. The irony wasn't lost on her as she took a slice of pepperoni to go.

Eating as she meandered, Catherine was on the lookout for a place to pick up some sweets for Fred. Streetlamps cast a glow on the happy tourists bustling about while people on mopeds zigzagged around traffic. She wanted their kind of a tropical getaway, not hers.

A line outside a restaurant named Blue Heaven caught her eye. Catherine entered through a path covered by a canopy of trees, which led into a courtyard where weather-battered buoys hung from a rickety fence. A collection of mismatched tables and plastic deck chairs dotted a bed of sunbaked sand. A chicken trotted by, head bobbing.

Catherine found the front counter and asked the young guy at the register, "Can I have a key lime pie, please?"

He returned with an enormous pie topped with a mountain range of caramelized meringue, then announced her total.

Cringing at the cost, she handed over her credit card. Telling herself she would soon be flush with cash didn't assuage the angst. She was squandering the scads of money requisite for an extravagant trip. Except she wasn't having one.

She didn't have any scenic pictures. She hadn't found any keepsakes. She didn't even have a tan, just a splotchy sunburn that ached as badly as her conscience.

The walk back to the Abbott House gave Catherine plenty of time to mull over her situation while she judiciously shifted the heavy pie from arm to arm, careful not to drop the towering confection with its magma-like meringue. First her legs hurt, then her eyes, now her arms. Her head was starting to ache too. Common sense was nagging at her brain.

Catherine was giving serious consideration to taking Vic's lowball offer and having Travis hit the bricks. Travis hadn't told her much, and she could barely stand to be around him as it was. If she put the brakes on her plan, she could call off the entire ruse, claiming her dad had a change of heart, this fictitious father whom she loved enough to drop fifty grand on.

As she traversed the island's pebble-strewn roads, sand crunching underfoot, Catherine had to remind herself that this was still a vacation of sorts, time away from the grind at home. Robert might have attempted to hijack it from the grave, but she could reclaim the remaining hours for pure rest and relaxation. All the lying and conniving she had done had twisted her mindset into a corkscrew. Catherine needed to get back on the straight and narrow as soon as possible.

"Hello, hello," she chanted, inching in the front door of the Abbott House as she cautiously navigated the cramped foyer with the big bakery box. "I have a special pie for—"

Sitting in the parlor were Fred, Arnie, Ina, and Lita, eyes trained on her.

"Everybody," Catherine ad-libbed. She couldn't give it to Fred with the others staring. "It's key lime."

Nobody said a word. The tension was palpable.

"What's wrong?"

"It appears that Lita's new gold necklace has gone missing," Fred said in a clipped tone.

"A tiny seahorse on a chain." She was visibly upset. "From Neptune Designs on Duval. I saved up for months."

"Oh, well, I can help you guys look for it." Catherine set the pie on a side table, ready to pitch in. "Where did you last see it?"

Her offer was met with impenetrable silence.

That's when it occurred to Catherine that they were accusing her of stealing the necklace. "You think I—?"

"Of course not, but . . ." Arnie began, then trailed off.

"I didn't touch Lita's necklace," Catherine insisted. "I don't even wear jewelry. Maybe she lost it at the beach or when she was changing clothes."

Ina drummed her fingers on her legs, clearly simmering with anger while Arnie and Fred gazed at Catherine helplessly, their hands tied.

Appalled at being accused of something she hadn't done, Catherine started repeating herself to convince them. "I swear I didn't take the necklace. I swear!"

Neither sister seemed convinced.

"She goes or we do," Ina told Fred; then she stormed out of the room with a distraught Lita in tow.

Once they were gone, Catherine pleaded with them. "I wouldn't take Lita's necklace. I may be close to broke, but I don't steal."

"We believe you." Arnie was adamant, no doubt relieved he could speak openly at last. "What would you want with a little golden seahorse? I'm not sure why she bought it. The poor creature would be swallowed up in her cleavage like a tsunami of grass-fed flesh."

"We don't need the visuals right now, darling." Fred rubbed his face, the stress of being trapped between a rock and hard place carved into his expression.

Catherine knew that look. She saw it every time she caught a glimpse of her own reflection after a beleaguering call from her mom.

"It's okay," Arnie assured her. "Right, Fred? We'll get this sorted out. Lita probably misplaced the necklace. Maybe it's in Ina's fanny pack."

Catherine could tell it wasn't all right.

The sisters had a bigger room and had been there longer, so they must have been paying more. What if they posted something terrible about the inn online? That would hurt the Abbott House's reputation as well as Fred and Arnie's business.

The answer was obvious. "No, I'll go. I'll be out tomorrow."

"Catherine, don't be silly," Arnie protested. He turned to Fred, who wasn't putting up a fight. "Fred, tell her. Tell her it's fine."

He didn't respond. He simply nodded at Catherine.

She wasn't sure if he was accepting her decision or thanking her.

As she went upstairs, Catherine heard Arnie and Fred arguing quietly. She closed her bedroom door and wiped her eyes.

Catherine ruefully checked her phone. The day had been so hectic that she'd forgotten to check back in with her mom. Between that and being kicked out, she couldn't help but cry.

Now where will I go?

She didn't have the money to stay anyplace else. She certainly wasn't going to stay with Travis on the boat. Nevertheless, Catherine got her bag and started stuffing her clothes in it.

Before that week, she had never done anything even remotely wrong—never hopped the turnstile at a subway station, never fudged her work reports, and never pasted together a successful lie. Since arriving on Key West, Catherine had been accused of being a junkie, a hooker, and now a thief.

This last affront solidified her resolve.

If people presumed Catherine was dishonest and immoral, she wasn't going to try convincing them otherwise. She would let Vic buy the boat from her to play off her scheme. She would kick Travis off. Then she would use the money to enjoy what remained of her vacation.

And she wouldn't shed another tear over any of it.

24

The sun rose as though it didn't want to. Amber light slowly inched along the skyline, dawn sluggishly giving way to day as Catherine watched from the open bedroom window. She could hear the plastic tarp on the roof fluttering in the morning wind.

This was only the second sunrise she had ever witnessed. Despite seeing another, she felt cheated, like it was her own fault that she had missed out on so many. She was tired of taking the blame for things she couldn't have known how to do differently.

It was a few minutes after 6:00 a.m. She had set the alarm to wake her up early enough to sneak down and ask Arnie for breakfast before she left. After taking a quick shower, Catherine got dressed, left her bag by the dresser, slung her laptop case over one shoulder and her purse on the other, then snuck downstairs.

Catherine peered into the dining room. The table wasn't set. She stole a glimpse around the doorjamb into the kitchen. Arnie was at the stove, pouring batter into mini-muffin tins.

"*Psst*," she said to get his attention.

"Get in here this instant," he whispered, mindful of the slumbering guests. "You absolutely can't leave. I won't have it. Camp out in the media room. Fred will be none the wiser."

"That's generous of you, except we'll both wind up in hot water if Fred busts us."

Arnie shook his head. “He’s been so preoccupied with keeping up occupancy so we can fix the roof. I hate to see him this way.”

“Me too. That’s why I can’t stay.”

He rubbed her arm appreciatively. “You may not know much about movies, darling, but you’re a star in my eyes.”

“Can the star get some food to go? I’ll be back at noon to get my bag. Before then I have a couple of things to attend to.”

“Such as?”

“I shouldn’t go into detail. You’ll think I’m as much of a degenerate as the sisters do.”

“Never. You’re fabulous. Even if your outfits do put the *duh* in ‘dumpy.’ And you don’t brush your hair.”

“Hey! At least my clothes don’t put the *whore* in ‘horrible.’”

“Touché!”

Catherine leaned against the fridge while Arnie prepped her paper plate of food, then sealed it in plastic wrap.

“It’s a breakfast burrito with chorizo and papaya chutney with a side of potatoes and spicy peppers. The corn muffins won’t be ready for a few minutes. Do you want to wait?”

“I wouldn’t want to bump into Ina or Lita.”

“Understood.” He packed the plate into a bag with some utensils and their signature seafoam napkins.

“Those are cute,” Catherine said. “I noticed earlier that they coordinate with the kitchen.”

“We designed them specially. I wanted to order more. Fred says we can’t until we fix the roof. How about a cinnamon bun from yesterday?”

“Please.” Catherine was still peeved that she had given hers to Travis and was thankful to get one after all.

Arnie set two in a napkin and packed everything for her to take on the road.

“Can I borrow your bicycle one last time? I hate to ask.”

“It’s yours.” He held out the bag to her. “Fred loved the pie, by the way.”

"Glad I did something right."

"He already devoured half of it. He doesn't want you to go either."

"That makes three of us."

"I really am going to miss you, Catherine." He hugged her tight and gave her a kiss on the cheek.

Footsteps resounded from the other room, so she hurried for the back door, then turned to him. "You and Fred have been the best part of my vacation."

Tearing up, Arnie fanned his eyes. "You're going to make my mascara run," he joked. "Now scoot."

After he shut the door behind her, Catherine rolled his bike around the side of the house to the road. The sun had risen, yet the air remained cool. Dew darkened the street, and the foliage seemed a deeper shade of green because of it. She set her food in the basket, then climbed onto the bike and crossed the straps of her purse and laptop case on each shoulder so she wouldn't tip over.

This wasn't how she had pictured her trip. Then again, her life wasn't how she had pictured it either.

Catherine pedaled to Edward B. Knight Pier. The steel railings running its span created an optical illusion, making the pale cement pier seem to stretch infinitely toward the horizon line. Even though a handful of men were fishing off the side, there was a poetic solitude to the place, as if it were meant to be vacant to show off the vastness of the surrounding sea and sky.

She rode toward the end of the pier and found a bench to sit on. With hours to kill before she needed to be at the dock to meet Travis, Catherine had ample time to enjoy her breakfast and the scenery before doing her research. As she unpacked the plate Arnie had made her, Catherine wondered where she would sleep that night. Perhaps the Casa Marina. Assuming she had played her cards correctly, Catherine thought she might just be able to afford that suite. If only for a night.

Catherine will get it when she gets it.

Robert's words from his note were on a loop in her mind. What did he mean? Was it a riddle or merely gibberish from a dying man?

When she was little, Robert would bet her that she couldn't finish her dinner. To prove him wrong, she would stuff herself sick so she wouldn't have room for dessert; then he'd eat hers. Catherine had fallen for the trick a few times, but she'd never forgotten that Robert would do what he had to in order to get what he wanted.

Seagulls coasted on the gusts coming in from the ocean, their calls reverberating off the water. Having a delicious meal by the sea, orange-tinged clouds streaking the sky—now that was relaxing, even if it was eating on a paper plate alone on a park bench. Catherine wished her watch weren't right when she glanced at it. It was almost nine o'clock.

She had important matters to attend to.

Full from breakfast, Catherine put the monogrammed napkin full of cinnamon buns into her pocket for later, then headed to the Casa Marina, though not to check in. She hoped she could hang out in the lobby without attracting too much attention and get cracking on the work she needed to do on Willford's high-interest-rate project. She was deplorably far behind.

After dusting crumbs off the bench, she pushed the bike toward land. Leaving picturesque Edward B. Knight Pier was like saying good-bye to Arnie. Catherine was sad because she knew she was going to miss it when she was gone.

When she rode into the hotel's driveway, she realized the bike might pose a problem. The valet looked at her quizzically.

"I'm here to meet a friend for breakfast," she lied. "Can I leave this with you?"

To her surprise, he said, "Sure."

Head down, trying to maintain a low profile, she slunk over to a spot on a cream-colored sofa with her back to the concierge desk. Sunlight streamed in the tall windows filtered through gossamer drapes, creating an otherworldly glow that reflected on the marble floors. It was as though the hotel couldn't help being heavenly in every way.

Once her laptop booted up, Catherine was about to start work but felt the urge to check something first. She went back on the Monroe County Tax Collector's website. According to state law, all taxes and fees would be Vic's problem after the sale, and he would have to handle them the way she had. Technically, she was off the hook once he paid her.

Fretful, Catherine went over the plan again and again, ironing out every wrinkle. There was one major flaw in her scheme. If the two older men described their buyer to Vic, he might recognize that this was a scam. Then again, he thought she was from an insurance company and was off-loading a repo. It was unlikely Vic would connect the dots.

She looked at her cap, which had been scrunched into her purse, and imagined what her boss, Willford, must have been doing. It was Saturday, yet he was probably knee deep in data and the latest stats, wishing he had forbidden her from leaving. Catherine took out the hat and thumbed the stitching that spelled the company name.

The bleak realization that she had spent the lion's share of her life in service to a firm that treated her like a cog in a wheel was hurtful. The fact that she wouldn't be able to retire for years to come so she could afford her mother's care cut even deeper. She felt irrevocably trapped.

Catherine hoped Willford wasn't leading her on about the promotion as she had done to him with the vacation. Even if Vic came through with Robert's boat, Catherine couldn't keep paying for Shady Ridge without multiplying her debt. She desperately needed that raise.

Concern mounting because she hadn't even touched the mountain of work her boss was expecting her to tackle, Catherine dialed Gloria's cell.

"Your ears must've been burning."

"Why?"

"Willford stayed late last night, picking up the slack for you. Before I left, he asked what day you were returning. Said I wasn't sure. Then he went on about how you were supposed to report your vacation days to HR before taking them."

"I totally forgot. Everything was so sudden. I'll send an email now."

"I'll do it. Say it was my mistake. Can't miss an opportunity to get in tight with HR. Portrays me as a considerate coworker."

"Part of your master plan to bilk the company for millions?"

"Naturally. I wish I worked in the accounting department and could steal money from this company the old-fashioned way." She sighed. "When are you back?"

"Monday." Catherine's stomach heaved at the fact that she had so little time left in Key West.

"Oh, and I changed my mind about the mug. I want something pretty I can wear out with Tito. Seashell earrings, maybe."

"Another date? That's fantastic!"

"Tonight, as a matter of fact. I really like this guy. I'll strangle him if he's a con artist. Or an ex-con. Anything with a 'con' in it."

Catherine hadn't heard Gloria this excited since the elevators in the building had to be repaired and everybody was ordered to come in an hour late.

"Then you'll have to get in line behind me to strangle him."

"What? You go away for a few days and transform from kiss ass to badass? About time!"

Without Catherine realizing it, that was precisely what had happened.

"Yeah," she said with a hint of pride in herself. "Kinda."

25

Change was something Catherine usually weathered like a hailstorm, hiding and huddling and waiting for the pelting to pass. As she sat in the palatial lobby of the Waldorf, she opted to embrace the changes as best she could, the way she aspired to be a "badass." After she disconnected with Gloria, she heard someone say, "Ms. Moran? Is that you?"

The silver-haired man she had met the other day was standing behind the couch, impeccably dressed, hands laced behind his back like a general.

"Somebody takes their work seriously," he intoned. "Aren't you supposed to be on vacation?"

Catherine scrambled to come up with a suitable cover story. "You'd think the company had shut down because I was away."

"You must be hard to replace."

I wish they thought that!

"You really got me thinking after our conversation the other day. Your ideas were quite well framed and on point."

"Thank you." Catherine was flattered yet preoccupied.

He remembers your name. He'll probably check the guest registry and realize you're a faker five seconds after you leave. If he hasn't done that already.

"Could I ask what your thoughts are on brand loyalty? I mean, why stay here over another hotel?"

She gulped.

"That's what we constantly ask ourselves here to stay on top of trends," he added.

Catherine felt as if she had dodged a bullet.

Much as she enjoyed discussing anything involving research, Catherine needed to get out of there. She scrabbled to sum up her philosophy as concisely as she could. "Uh, well, what the studies show is that if you don't want your customer 'cheating on you,' so to speak, it's up to you to make them fall in love and stay in love."

Seriously? Catherine thought.

She could have kicked herself, hearing how she sounded. She was the last person to be making analogies about romance.

"Smart advice for business affairs. As well as matters of the heart. You must have men falling at your feet," the man retorted with a glimmer in his eye.

Is he flirting with me? He can't be.

"Oh, the stories I could tell." She laughed off the joke while collecting her purse. "I'd better be going. I have a . . . meeting at the marina."

"Buying one of those boats you were perusing the other day?"

Catherine was astounded that he recalled what she had been looking at online.

"Selling, actually."

"We have a fine marina here, should you be interested in a slip for any future purchases."

This man thinks you're loaded when you could barely afford pizza last night.

"Duly noted." Catherine excused herself. "A pleasure to see you again."

"You, too, Ms. Moran."

She hurried for the door and paid the valet extra to bring her bike around far away from the front of the hotel. Even if she did receive a big chunk of change from Vic for Robert's boat, Catherine was too humiliated to return and stay in a room.

"Bye-bye, beautiful hotel suite," she told herself, uncertain where she would be spending the night. "Hello, limbo."

There was no pelican perched at the end of the dock when she arrived. Catherine was disappointed not to see it again.

Her symbol of atonement had flown the coop. The concepts of making amends and reconciling hadn't been far from her thoughts since arriving in Key West. Was the bird's absence an unfavorable sign?

A white sheet of clouds hung over the marina, blocking the sun and turning the bay a deep turquoise color. While many of the other ships were gone, a few remained, each shabbier than the last, like a reverse evolutionary chart of fishing vessels.

Robert's boat was last in the row and at the bottom of the scale.

Catherine parked the bike beside the piling where the pelican had been and was about to climb aboard but hesitated, feeling like she was barging in somebody's front door, unannounced.

"Travis? You here?" she hollered.

No response. She noted the time. Her watch read ten o'clock on the dot.

While taking a tentative step onto the rear deck, the tide raised the stern, which sent the laptop case forward on her shoulder, the momentum hurling her onboard. Off balance, Catherine lurched sideways and accidentally knocked over a cardboard box full of heavy scrap wood and nails. The bin tumbled with a thud that resounded through the hull.

Once she had regained her footing, Catherine set down her bags, then started picking up the spilled scraps and loose nails, glad Travis hadn't witnessed her clumsiness.

Without warning, he flew out the wheelhouse door, no shirt on, ear pressed to a cell phone.

Catherine jumped up, thrown by his sudden arrival and by how attractive he looked.

"Yeah, yes, I have to go. I'll call you back." He shot her a furtive glance, hung up, and shoved the phone in the pocket of his board shorts. "You're early," he said, sounding on edge.

A terrible thought clamped down on Catherine.

Following her talk with the two guys at the clubhouse, she had assumed that their contact to procure the Hemingway boat was Vic.

What if it was Travis? He had been so vehement about protecting Robert's property. Had she inadvertently forced his hand?

Catherine knew virtually nothing about Travis except that he had a troubled past. And no place to go. That could turn him into a very desperate man.

"What?" Travis asked since she hadn't answered him.

"Nothing, nothing. How are you?" she asked awkwardly, buying time until she could figure out what to say.

"Peachy. Packing up all my belongings."

Her brain brimming with possibilities, Catherine dug the cinnamon rolls wrapped in the napkin from her purse and munched on them nervously while Travis gathered the rest of the scattered scrap wood back into the box. Now both of them were on edge.

Catherine knew what was making her uneasy. What had Travis so rattled?

"Bring any for me?"

"Not this time."

Catherine finished the mini cinnamon buns, crumpled the napkin, and tossed it in the cardboard box with the wood.

"That isn't trash. I said I was packing."

She was about to grab the napkin when she noticed a wooden statue in the box along with the items she had mistaken for refuse. It was an intricately carved figurine of a pelican.

"What's this?" she asked, picking it up. "It's beautiful."

Travis grabbed it from her protectively. "A gift. After I got out of the navy, I went to South America. Wanted another adventure. Someplace where I didn't have to follow so many rules. Or be who I was expected to be."

As if sensing he had divulged too much, he tried to wipe the last sentiment aside with a quick shake of his head. He rubbed the stubble on his chin contemplatively, and Catherine found herself transfixed by his face. Even though he was avoiding looking right at her, it was as if she was stealing glimpses of the real him.

"I was in Peru, going from village to village, teaching kids English. It was hard for some of them to learn, so I'd use stories to help them get the hang of it. 'Little Red Riding Hood.' 'Goldilocks and the Three Bears.' 'Snow White and the Seven Dwarfs.'"

Travis appeared to sink into the memory as if it were a comfortable chair, a place he could relax.

"One of my students gave the statue to me. The people were dirt poor, and they wanted to pay me but couldn't. I slept in the back of the schoolhouse. Ate whatever they had left over. When it was time to head to the next village, a boy asked his father to carve the pelican for me as a present. To them, it was a symbol of sacrifice. The pelican would wound itself to feed its young and keep them alive. It was an honor for them to give it to me."

The story framed Travis in a totally different light. Could a guy who taught English to impoverished children be a complete jerk?

"Question number one?" he sniffed, suddenly eager, it seemed, to get this over with because he had been a little too open and vulnerable with her.

"Number one. Number one is . . ."

Nothing came to her.

Think, think, think.

She combed through her memories of Robert. Catherine could picture him rushing into the kitchen to grab a soda from the fridge. Brushing past her on the stairs on his way to school in the mornings. Jockeying with her at the bathroom sink as they brushed their teeth at night. The ephemeral snippets didn't amount to a question.

Or maybe they did.

"What's your favorite memory of Robert?"

Travis was taken aback.

"That's a good one," he admitted, raking a hand through his wavy hair. He took a seat on the side of the boat. After a moment of mulling, he let out a soft laugh, remembering.

"It was in the chow hall. At basic training. First week. They gave us ten minutes to eat. Ten. Had to get your food, get a seat, and get your food down your gullet. I hadn't met Bobby yet, but he was in line behind a guy who'd dropped his tray. The jackass in front of him had purposely backed into the guy, knocking it out of his hands. Kid was skinny, green, and about to get reamed for the mess. Bobby helped him clean it up. Didn't get to eat his food. Just stayed and gave him a hand. I never forgot him after that."

Tears were poised in Catherine's eyes.

For so long, she had wanted to believe that her brother had a decent heart. Hearing that he'd forfeited his meal for a stranger confirmed she'd been right, if only in some small measure. Yet it hurt that she had rarely gotten to see that side of Robert.

The story gave her something almost solid to cling to. It surprised her that Travis had chosen that instance to relate, instead of talking about the time when her brother had bailed him out by giving him a place to live on the boat.

That said as much about Travis as it did about Robert.

She sat down near him, and he smiled, a fleeting grin that was gone before she could smile back. She blinked away the tears. Travis lowered his gaze, as if to give her some privacy.

Catherine had never wanted to hold a man's hand so much in her life. Even though they were less than a foot apart, their knees almost touching, she felt an ocean away from Travis. He held answers she couldn't get anywhere else, and if he was the link to sell the boat, she had to pretend to trust him.

The hard part wasn't pretending. It was hoping she genuinely could.

26

A flood of questions about her brother sprang to Catherine's mind, yet she was careful to select one that was general enough to keep Travis talking.

"Did Robert ever say why he was in Key West?" she tried to ask offhandedly.

"Come to think of it, he didn't. Couldn't believe my luck at bumping into him at the Green Parrot. We hadn't spoken for years, but it was like it'd been a week. Sailfish were running that time of year. We shot the breeze about that—then he told me about the boat. I moved on the next day."

Catherine could have burst. It was hard not to demand answers.

"You didn't ask him what he did for a living, where he was staying, what he was doing at the tail end of the country? What about a wife? Kids?"

Even though she had never married or had children, it hurt her to think that he hadn't. Robert had been such a dutiful brother to her until those last months. He would pack lunches for her if their mom was too harried. He reminded her to take her coat on cold days and would put on her mittens for her. Catherine could envision him making a great dad, far better than their father had been.

Travis's flat expression stood in as his answer.

"Those were . . . rhetorical," she said, composing herself. "Let me rephrase."

He plucked a few stray nails from the deck. "I think he mentioned he was retired. Had been in Naval Intelligence. Had a place on the south side of the island. That's just not what guys discuss. We don't do . . . personal. Bobby didn't seem to want to rehash his past, and I was more than happy not to bring up mine."

Travis had evidently let the last part slip and brushed it off by veering onto another topic. "What I can tell you was his nickname: Night-light."

"Night-light?" Catherine was wasting a precious question. After such an obscure reference, it had to be done.

"Bobby couldn't fall asleep unless he read before bed. Kept his bunkmates up because his light would be on until the wee hours of the morning."

That was her brother through and through.

When Catherine would wake up in the middle of the night to get a drink of water, his bedroom light was always on. Robert would read until he couldn't hold his eyes open, like he wanted to stay in the world of his books rather than be where he actually was, no matter how tired he had been. Reading was his escape.

Until he escaped for real.

"Night-light," Catherine repeated with a smile.

Robert seemed more alive than ever. She felt Travis staring. Only it wasn't with ridicule or indifference as usual. It was as if he saw in Catherine what she had seen in Robert's nickname—something real.

"There was this time Bobby fell off a dock in Naples when we were stationed there," he volunteered.

Catherine hadn't asked another question. However, she wasn't going to stop Travis, not if he was going to give her another story for free. She recalled his "Napoli" T-shirt and encouraged him to continue with a shrug.

"A bunch of us were on leave for the day. We'd go off base. See the sites. Drink way too much vino," Travis began, his expression growing animated with the telling of the tale. "Sun's setting, so we decide to go by the water. We walk out onto this rickety old dock that looks like it's been there since Mount Vesuvius blew. Your brother, he's three sheets to the wind and loses his balance. Into the water he went. Came up covered in seaweed. The stuff was dripping from his head and shoulders. He looked like a mermaid."

Hanging on every word, Catherine pictured it vividly while they shared a chuckle.

"Wait, you have to hear about when Bobby got stuck in the mud. We'd had these rainstorms, and he had to cross the base, but nobody'd warned him about how thick the mud would get, so he wound up ankle deep, stuck in the middle of the field between two barracks. A couple guys had to haul him out." Travis slapped his knee at the thought of it. "It was priceless."

Even though he and Catherine were barely acquaintances, sitting on a run-down boat under a cloudy sky, she felt as though they were old friends, reliving the past together. Their camaraderie wasn't strained. It was genuine, natural, despite the circumstances.

"Then there was the prank with the toilet paper. This is a classic," he assured her. "Bobby gets dozens of the rolls of toilet paper from all over the base. Had to be every single one except from the officer's toilets. Then he—"

"Stop," Catherine ordered, cutting him off harshly.

From a distance, she saw Vic coming straight toward them. She leaped to her feet and grabbed her purse.

"I need to go."

"Go?"

"Or hide."

"What for?"

She broke for the door to the wheelhouse. Travis got there before she did, barring her path with his muscular body, which was its own distraction, although not enough to outweigh Vic's impending arrival.

Catherine couldn't let him see her on the boat or palling around with Travis.

"What's going on?"

"I should ask you the same. Why won't you let me inside?"

He seemed to be holding in what he wanted to say while Vic was approaching fast.

"Travis, please."

The urgency of her plea evidently softened him.

Begrudgingly, he opened the door, and she found herself transported to a totally different world.

The entire interior of the fishing trawler was immaculately refurbished. The honey-colored wood walls and floors gleamed. The brass fixtures had been buffed to a sparkling shine. Inside was a small dinette, a smaller kitchen with a miniature sink and two-burner cooktop, as well as four bunks hollowed out under the prow. Every centimeter had been lovingly restored to its original glory.

"This is amazing. You did this?" she asked in awe.

"It's what Bobby wanted." His allegiance to her brother was broadcast in his voice. "Now tell me why you're hiding."

Tight as the quarters were, she and Travis were nearly face-to-face, his chest close to hers. Catherine was having trouble focusing. Despite the kinship she felt after the stories he had shared, she wasn't sure she could trust Travis, and she needed Vic out of the picture, or he would ruin the house of cards she had so artfully constructed.

"Get rid of Vic and I'll explain everything."

"Catherine."

"I promise."

The vow must have swayed him.

"Stay out of sight," he said, shutting the door behind him.

She ducked low, peeping through a side window.

"Morning, Trav," Vic declared, ambling toward the boat officiously.

"Morning."

Their dislike for each other was clearly mutual. Vic maintained the high ground by remaining up on the dock. His shirt had a smear of grease on it, a black slash across his chest.

"You seen a lady around? Short. Brown hair. Ball cap. The one from the insurance company who's got the title to Bobby's boat?"

"Insurance company?" Travis couldn't mask his surprise.

Catherine grimaced as she strained to listen in.

"Haven't seen her."

"Didn't she give you no date to be off the boat by?" Vic asked.

"Nope."

"Real cordial of her to let you stay," he said, sucking his teeth. "You sweet-talk her into giving you a few extra days?"

"Not my style."

Vic snorted, showing he was unconvinced. Catherine began to wonder if she should be either. Because he wasn't far off the mark. Travis hadn't asked her for any sort of extension, yet she had allowed him to hang around.

Had she unsuspectingly been duped?

"That's great news for botha us," Vic declared. "Means she hasn't sold it yet."

"What's it to you?"

"'Cause I'm buying it off her. Already got an interested party lined up."

Catherine was relieved that Travis wasn't the contact for the two guys from the clubhouse. Obviously, Vic was. As she crouched beside a built-in cupboard on the polished wood floor, the tireless hours of effort that had gone into renovating the boat were undeniable. She could tell it would wound Travis to have the boat fall into Vic's hands.

"We'll see about that," Travis growled, his arm muscles flexing as if he was about to lunge at Vic.

"Easy, tiger. You gonna put in a bid? You ain't got two nickels to rub together since your daddy sent you packing. Yeah, I heard all about you." Vic had a vicious glint in his eyes. "He might've gotten your charges dropped at Christmas, pulling strings or whatever you high-class people do to sidestep your responsibilities, but everybody on the island knows what really happened. You ain't fooling nobody."

Vic had noticeably gotten under Travis's skin. The rage was siphoning out of him, deflating into humiliation, as evidenced by his sagging shoulders. Catherine didn't need to see his face to guess how dispirited he must have looked.

"Beat it, Vic."

"I'm going, I'm going. Fancy wheels you got," he remarked, gesturing at Arnie's blue bicycle mockingly. "You're gonna need 'em when I kick you off my boat."

Catherine had to bite the inside of her cheek to keep from screaming in frustration. She was furious at Vic as well as herself. But Vic was doing exactly what she had expected, and her plan had played out perfectly.

He wasn't in the wrong. She was.

27

Apologizing was Catherine's first order of business. Travis wouldn't let her.

He barreled through the wheelhouse door and came at her full force, shouting, "Is it true? Are you selling this boat to that scumbag, Vic?"

Cowed by his fury, Catherine backed up a step. In a space as tiny as the interior of the trawler, she soon found herself cornered, in every sense of the word. Travis wasn't giving her room to breathe or to evade his question.

"Yes and no."

"Which is it?"

"More the former than the latter."

"So yes?" His pupils drilled into her.

Ashamed, Catherine hung her head. "You don't understand. I need the money for my—"

"No, *you* don't understand. It would have killed your brother to have this boat fall into Vic's hands. I'm grateful he's not alive to see what you're doing. Here. Take these and go." He pushed a bag full of books across the top of a built-in cabinet toward her. "They were Bobby's. I found them while I was packing."

Catherine's attention seized on the small stack of her brother's possessions, then quickly rewound to the commands Travis had barked at her. She was too emotional to let them slide.

"Go? This isn't your boat. It's mine. You should be thanking me for allowing you to stay as long as you have. Little did I know you were some criminal. Must be convenient to have a judge for a father who can make your problems disappear."

Even before the sentence left her mouth, Catherine regretted it.

Travis narrowed his gaze on her. "Done some digging, huh? Believe what you want. I don't give a damn."

He shoved the bag at her, causing a few books to fall out, then stormed off, doubtless unable to be near her a second longer.

Hurting Robert's things was meant to hurt her. It worked.

Catherine delicately picked up the books, lovingly dusted them off, then put them back in the bag, muttering the entire time: "Who does he think he is? Treating Robert's possessions this way. It's completely disrespectful."

It occurred to Catherine that she wasn't treating Robert's prized possession very well herself. The indignity of her actions made her want to give up and go home. Anger overpowered embarrassment.

She hadn't put herself in this position. Her brother had.

Seething, Catherine slammed open the wheelhouse door, carrying the bag of his books in her arms protectively. Travis was standing at the stern, waiting for her to leave.

"To be clear, I got the papers from Robert's lawyer an hour after I first met you. I could have kicked you out that night."

"Why didn't you?" he asked, challenging her.

She didn't dare answer. It was another reply that would make her seem like a scammer, a liar, a cheat. He responded for her.

"Because you wanted something. Information about Bobby, right? Self-serving," he chided. "Not the way I pictured you."

That made Catherine livid. She had been the antithesis of self-serving since she was a kid and had put her life on hold to care for her mother, while Robert had abandoned them.

"What's that supposed to mean?"

"Bobby told me about you back in training. Said you were ten years younger than him but twice as smart as he was. Maybe he was right. Maybe he wasn't."

To think that her brother only spoke of her a single time was a knife in Catherine's soul.

She was too irate to cry. She buckled down her wrath, collected her purse, calmly walked past Travis, and climbed off the boat onto the dock.

"I let you stay because I felt sorry for you. Obviously, so did my brother."

Travis seemed to take the insult in stride, a verbal jab that didn't bruise him. At least he was doing an impressive job pretending that it hadn't.

"Be out by tonight," Catherine stated coldly, placing the bag in the bicycle basket and slinging her purse over her shoulder. "This'll be Vic's boat by tomorrow."

The brave front Travis had been holding up fractured. Grief was etched on his face. It was the same sense of mourning that Catherine felt drenched in. She didn't look back as she pedaled the bicycle off the dock.

She didn't want to see Travis or that boat ever again.

A blustery wind blew in off the bay, tingling her skin with water droplets. The clouds had parted in places, revealing rippled bands of blue sky behind them, as if to say the day could get better, even when it seemed ruined. Catherine pedaled Arnie's bike toward the marina's convenience store, certain of what she had to do yet in no mood to do it.

Since Catherine couldn't let anybody spot the bike, she parked it between a storage shed and a rack of empty dry docks. To her surprise, a pelican was roosting atop the dry-dock structure, staring down at her. Though she couldn't be sure this was the same bird from yesterday, Catherine was happy to see it.

"Well, I'm glad you're here. I need to atone for a whole lot of stuff right now. For lying. A bunch of times. For deceiving people. For . . ." She was about to mention hurting Travis's feelings, but hers had been bruised as well.

The pelican blinked at her.

"Watch the bicycle, too, would you? That falls under charity. Doesn't it?"

Unwilling to leave Robert's books unattended, Catherine was about to try stuffing them into her purse as she searched for her cap as part of her disguise, but they wouldn't fit. The hat was nowhere to be found.

Crap! Where could it have gone?

Sunglasses would have to suffice. She pulled her hair into a severe ponytail to look no-nonsense and decided to employ her brother's books as props. Catherine was about to head for the bait shop when the front door swung open.

Out walked the two men from New York alongside Vic, the former pair unmistakable with their trademark combover and visor. She stifled a gasp and quickly ducked back behind the storage shed.

Catherine watched with bated breath as Vic pointed in the direction of Robert's boat, where he had just argued with Travis, then shook his head as if he was about to teach him a lesson.

Craning to listen, she overheard the man with the combover say, "You get the boat from her for twenty—then we get the cash from her, and you get a finder's fee of ten from her forty. Not a bad day's work."

Twenty? Forty? Vic offered me five, and they asked me for fifty! Vic wants to keep more profit for himself on top of the finder's fee, and they're shorting him on the back end.

"Maybe we find another boat and paint the same name on it, try this again?" the man in the visor added archly.

Vic thumbed the stubble on his chin. "Easy enough. I got plenty of boats here."

While the members of the trio took turns shaking hands, Catherine held her breath. Both sides were playing each other, and the stakes were high. Their casual, unvarnished greed rattled her. Blood was pumping in her ears. Sweat beaded on her forehead.

At least you know your plan is working. No pressure.

After Vic waved them off with a mock salute, he returned inside. Catherine remained hidden, peering around the shed as the two men ambled to a Cadillac in the parking lot and pulled onto the causeway.

Wired from the stress, she patiently watched five minutes tick by on her phone before heading for the bait shop. Catherine glanced up at the pelican, who looked down at her like it disapproved.

"Wish me luck," she told the bird.

It simply turned away from her to face the water.

Inside, Catherine spotted the clerk with the crew cut stocking the shelves with packaged fishing lures.

"Is Vic here?" Her tone was crisp and professional.

Busy, the clerk answered without looking. "Something I can help you with?" When he turned to Catherine, he recognized her. "Oh, it's you. One sec and I'll get him." He was rushing as if he had been directed to keep an eye out for her.

Moments later, Vic appeared from a rear door.

"Hey, there!" he sang, uncharacteristically cheery. "I wanted to get in contact with you, but I didn't have your number."

Reserved, Catherine replied, "Oh? Why was that?"

"Still interested in selling that old fishing trawler? Happy to take it off your hands for parts."

"Actually, I am."

"Fantastic!"

Vic clapped his hands, obviously unable to contain his enthusiasm; then he and the clerk shared a sidelong glance.

"The thing is . . ." Catherine heaved the bag of books onto the counter by the register with a dramatic thump. "I've been doing some research on the vessel. Company policy. Turns out there could be a connection to a certain author who is renowned in these parts. It's come to my attention that this boat might be worth quite a bit more than we at the firm initially estimated."

Vic's slick grin drooped. The clerk dropped a packet of lures on the floor, then scurried to pick it up, acting like he hadn't been listening. Despite how mad she was at Travis, Catherine wished he could have been there to soak in Vic's dismay.

Recovering, he took a deep breath. "I can't go more than ten thousand."

Cha-ching. You've got him on the ropes. Now up the ante.

"That's a shame. Since you made the first offer, I wanted to give you a chance to stay in the running."

"There are other bids?" he asked, incapable of disguising his distress.

"Much as we prefer to stay out of any . . . untoward entanglements, the company needs to make it worth our while."

Vic chewed his bottom lip, deliberating. "Ten."

"I've already got fifteen from a friend of a friend at the A & B Marina."

The spontaneous addition was meant to lend credibility to her story. Vic's long sigh confirmed that it did. She patted him on the shoulder, then gathered the bag of books. Catherine had Vic right where she wanted him.

"Wait." He pulled her aside, out of the earshot of the clerk. "I can do seventeen. But I can't come up with it until tomorrow."

Desperation oozed from his pores. Vic had bought her lie hook, line, and sinker. His original bid of five thousand would have left him a hefty profit after his deal with the two guys from the clubhouse. The more Vic had to pay Catherine, the less he netted. She tried not to revel in his discomfort.

"A cash deal would certainly make the firm look more favorably on your offer."

"Yeah, all cash," he conceded.

"Then you have a deal." Catherine put her hand out, and they shook on it, though it evidently pained Vic to spend that much. "I'll be here tomorrow at noon with the paperwork."

He nodded, spent by their exchange. "Noon."

Catherine made a hasty exit, resisting the impulse to do a touchdown celebration dance once she got out the door.

A few more feet and you're home free.

She walked toward the parking lot, the opposite way from where the bike was parked, in case Vic or the clerk were watching from the windows; then she circled back, cutting behind some outbuildings to return to the location where she had left Arnie's bicycle. It was still there, as was the pelican. Wind ruffled the bird's feathers gently while it dozed.

"Thanks," Catherine said to the pelican.

Seventeen thousand dollars was a lot of money. It would go a long way toward her bills and her mother's room at Shady Ridge. However, it wouldn't make her any less tense about what she had done. Nor would it bring back her brother.

Robert had gone so far as to admit that she was brighter than he was. It might have been the one thing he told anybody about her, yet it was, unwittingly, the best compliment he could have given Catherine. She had always assumed she was the dumb one for sticking it out and manning up when the men had run off.

Regardless of everything Catherine had endured, staying was what made her smart.

Standing under a bird she had asked for a favor with a bag full of books by an author she'd hated since childhood, Catherine had to wonder: If she was the smart one, why did she feel like such an idiot?

28

Catherine should have been happy. Even though she would be coming out on top, nothing about what she had done seemed fair.

As she pedaled back across the island, Robert's books sat heavy in the basket, making the bike unwieldy and hard to steer. The bicycle was as off-kilter as her conscience. At a stop sign, she paused to adjust the load; then the weight shifted, sending the bicycle toppling over sideways. She tried to brace herself with her leg but skidded on sand underfoot.

Catherine slid and fell, catching herself on the curb; then she heard an audible gasp.

Except it wasn't her own.

"Are you all right?" a voice crackled over a loudspeaker.

A large green-and-orange sightseeing trolley loomed over where she was crouched. It had pulled up right next to her, and the passengers were gawking, passersby too. The conductor waved.

"Looks like you took a spill," he said, his comment amplified, embarrassingly loud.

"I bet it does," Catherine mumbled. "To anybody around, care of your PA system."

"You hurt yourself?"

"I'm all right." Catherine dusted herself off. "Carry on with the tour."

"See, folks!" the conductor remarked, mellow. "It's all good here on Key West!"

Not sure I'd agree with that, she thought.

It was as if having Robert's books with her was the cause of her problems. Somehow, he was able to flummox her, even in spirit. She tried to force away the gloomy feelings. It was like batting at flies. A swarm of emotions whirled around her, making her ears buzz.

Catherine had been too young to comprehend the implications of their father's departure. To her, the future had the quality of a blank coloring book, black-and-white outlines full of possibilities waiting to be filled in. She simply assumed he would come back. Her mother hoped the same, quietly yearning for him to walk through the front door again. Robert, however, appeared to know it would never happen.

After their dad was gone, Robert would snap at Catherine over the slightest remark about what was for dinner or who had to take out the trash. She had to walk on eggshells, fretful of upsetting him when she was still confused about their father running out. Nothing Catherine did could get Robert to treat her the way he had when their dad was still there.

Nothing.

Even in death, her brother was impenetrable and unreachable, and yet again, he had abandoned Catherine to tend to what he couldn't.

What would she tell her mom about the boat and where the money had come from? What if her mom never forgave her for getting rid of the one thing Robert had left behind?

At least Catherine had the books. She could say that was what he had willed her. But it would be another lie.

The harder Catherine tried to do right, the further she got from it. She was, however, closer to the Abbott House than she had realized. She had finally gotten the lay of the land, just as her vacation was coming to an end.

It was almost noon—the time she had promised Fred she would be out by. Catherine walked the bicycle back to the garage, wishing she'd stayed to finish *Roman Holiday* with Fred and Arnie. That was one of many regrets she would be packing up with her. Catherine loaded Robert's hefty bag of books into her arms and gave the bike's bell a farewell ring.

The fountain was burbling as she went to open the rear door that led into the kitchen. It wouldn't budge. She fumbled with the handle, thinking she hadn't pulled hard enough.

The lock held tight.

"They must really want you out."

It was as though Fred and Arnie's friendly open-door policy was shut for good. She went to the front and tiptoed inside, hoping to save herself any further humiliation. They had her credit card information and could bill her once she was gone.

Two steps in the door, Fred called to her from the parlor. She froze.

"Catherine, could you come in here, please?"

Waiting inside were Fred, Arnie, Ina, and Lita. Truman was on Arnie's lap. None of them looked happy, including the dog.

"Have a seat," Fred commanded. It wasn't a request.

She took a tentative seat in an overstuffed chair. The plump pillows covered in brocade fabric engulfed her, elevating her so her feet barely touched the floor. Catherine felt like a kid who'd been called to the principal's office.

Arnie cleared his throat, signaling Ina.

"I found this in the shower drain this morning." She held up a gold necklace with a delicate seahorse charm dangling from it.

"And?" Fred firmly urged.

Lita got to her feet, wringing her hands. "We owe you an apology."

Ina jumped to her side. "Uh, sorry. I see now that you're probably not a meth head."

"Probably?" Catherine said.

"Just a scooch high strung," Ina replied.

Lita nodded, siding with her sister. Fred and Arnie looked around, obviously avoiding eye contact because they couldn't disagree.

"Hello? Anyone here?"

Recognizing the voice, Catherine attempted to bound out of the chair, but the cushions were so spongy that she had trouble getting traction. She scrambled to her feet as Travis strode in, her laptop case in his hand, a blue Key West T-shirt on over his shorts.

Their eyes locked.

"You left this on the boat," he announced, his resentment at having to bring it to her broadcasting clearly. "Didn't want you to think it had been stolen."

She hadn't even realized that she had misplaced her computer. "Yes, thank you, because stealing is a bit of a sore subject around here."

The others were all staring at Travis for a long minute, mesmerized. The normally chatty sisters seemed starstruck. Catherine had to wave at the group to snap them out of it.

"Everyone, this is Travis."

"Well, alo*ha*," Arnie said, instantly taken, no doubt, by his good looks. "Aren't you the catch of the day?"

"Greetings," Fred chimed. "And welcome to the Abbott House."

"Travis," Catherine remarked, regaining her poise. "How did you, um, find me?"

"From this."

He held out the crumpled seafoam napkin she had tossed aside on the boat, flattened to reveal the name of the inn.

"There you have it, Fred. Handsome gentlemen are appearing at the door out of nowhere. That's our marketing dollars at work." Arnie pushed the dog off his lap, eliciting a bark from Truman, then delicately offered his hand to Travis. "Enchanté."

"Okay," Travis said as he shook Arnie's hand too hard, taking in the scene with a befuddled expression. "I'm gonna go now."

"No, no, stay!" Lita flashed a flirtatious grin. Plainly smitten, she sidled up to Travis, shucked the laptop case from his shoulder, and hurled it at Catherine, who caught the case squarely in the stomach, nearly knocking the wind out of her. "You're not her boyfriend, are you?"

Rubbing her ribs, Catherine put her laptop aside. "Nope, no, he isn't."

"She's already got one," Travis said.

"I what?" Catherine nearly choked.

"Come again?" Arnie asked.

"Perfect." Lita batted her eyes at him.

"Anyhow, Travis must be going. He's got a lot of packing to do."

Catherine's attempt to usher him out was met by Lita's rigid insistence that he stay. She was gripping his arm, obstinate as an anchor. Trying to move Travis, let alone Lita, proved impossible.

"What about your bike?" Travis asked. "It says 'His.'"

"That's the *him* in 'His.'" She motioned toward Arnie, who took a graceful bow.

"There are bike rentals here?" Ina piped up. "That wasn't in the brochure."

"It was a loaner," Arnie demurred.

"That is not our usual policy," Fred guaranteed Ina.

Travis frowned. "You're dating a . . . gay guy?"

"Yup," Lita retorted. "She's taken. Not available. Off limits."

"He's with me," Fred vouched.

The couple gestured at their matching Hawaiian shirts.

"She's as single as the ones in a stripper's pocket." Arnie had his hand to his heart, as if pledging an oath.

Catherine couldn't take this any longer. "Thanks. Thank you. Everybody. For this truly memorable moment. Now Travis will be on his way."

"Come to dinner," Lita cooed, mooning over him.

"Yes, do," Arnie insisted.

Travis looked to Catherine, searching her face. She wasn't sure what he would see there because she couldn't pin down what she was feeling.

"For my sister's sake," Ina pleaded. "Or I'll never hear the end of it."

"We'd love to have you," Fred told him.

"Sure," Travis relented. "If it's all right with you, Catherine."

Everyone was waiting on her answer.

"Yeah, yes, of course," she stuttered.

Except Catherine wasn't comfortable with Travis coming to dinner. Not because she didn't want him there. But because, in spite of herself, she did.

29

Dinner was slated for six o'clock that evening, hours away. Catherine was already nervous.

"You don't have to do this," she whispered to Arnie, pulling him aside in the hallway off the parlor.

Fred sauntered up behind them and answered for him. "Yes, he does."

Ina and Lita came down the stairs, large cameras swinging from around their necks, ready for sightseeing.

"Have a wonderful afternoon, ladies." Fred was all smiles.

Ina waved. "We're off to the cemetery!"

"We'll be back by supper." Lita cut a competitive glance at Catherine as she followed her sister out.

"Enjoy." Fred courteously escorted them on their way.

"Should I be worried?" Catherine asked after the door had shut behind them.

"Not unless Lita digs a plot to push you into so she can get her mitts on Travis," Arnie remarked.

"It's a historical tourist spot here in Key West," Fred clarified; then he took her hands in his repentantly. "I owe you a big apology, Catherine."

"No need. I'm just grateful that I get to stay."

"Aw, Catherine," he said, hugging her. "The fact that you were willing to leave to help us maintain our business means more than I can express."

"The fact that Travis is coming to dinner means more to me than *I* can express." Arnie playfully pinched Fred. "He puts the *ex* in 'sexy.' You sure you want to give him the heave-ho? How about just the *ho*?"

Catherine wasn't sure at all. She slumped down on the last step of the stairway. The bag with Robert's books lay nearby, alongside her laptop case, reminding her that Lita's infatuation with Travis was the least of her troubles.

"You haven't even seen him without a shirt on."

"You have?" Fred inquired.

"Somebody got a dose of Audrey Hepburn, and now men are literally ripping their shirts off for her. Are we talking six-pack? Eight-pack? Describe the scene, darling," Arnie said.

"His abs were like one of those rock walls at the gym."

"Get out the climbing gear." Arnie clapped. "I'm at your service as a sherpa, should you need my humble assistance."

"She won't," Fred replied pointedly.

Arnie stuck his tongue out at him. "You're adorable when you're jealous."

"We're going to have a civilized dinner, and it will be our honor to have your friend Travis join us."

"Of course we are," Arnie answered, humoring him. "Who knew the kooky cat lady would go gaga for your hunky boy toy?"

"He's hardly that."

"Then what is he?" Fred asked.

Catherine thought it over for a minute. "He's the guy I'm evicting."

"Ouch." Fred cringed.

"Honey, do you need glasses? Contacts? A Seeing Eye dog? Can't you reconsider? At least for my sake?"

Fred crossed his arms in evident displeasure.

Travis was the last link to her brother besides the boat, and she was about to throw both him and the trawler overboard. After the lengths she had gone to orchestrating the sale, she didn't see what other choice she had. Travis wouldn't forgive her for selling it. She wasn't sure if she would forgive herself.

"This is business," Catherine revealed heavily.

Fred nodded his understanding. "Let's get our grocery list together for tonight's festivities, dear."

He tugged Arnie's shirt, guiding him away to give her some space.

"We shall discuss it no more. I should warn you, though. I'm going to be preparing something romantic using sensual, sultry spices. I'm thinking coriander, fennel, ginger. FYI, they're all aphrodisiacs."

"Splendid," Fred sighed. "Throw in some wine and we're going to need a crowbar to keep Lita off the poor man."

He dragged Arnie into the kitchen with him, leaving Catherine alone.

Truman trotted out of the parlor, gave the bag of books a cursory sniff, then followed his owners. She wished she were as disinterested in Robert's books as the dog was, but Catherine had been dying to investigate his possessions. She grabbed the books and her laptop case, then took them to her room.

Her bag was waiting by the dresser. Much as she wanted to unpack, Catherine wasn't sure she should bother. Another day and she would be gone.

She dumped Robert's things onto the bed.

In the bag were about a dozen books by Hemingway, ranging from his most famous works, such as *The Sun Also Rises* and *The Old Man and the Sea*, to his nonfiction, like *Death in the Afternoon* and *A Moveable Feast*. Some were in hardback, others in paperback, each well worn and apparently well loved. Catherine could almost see where her brother had held the books by the way they were bent on the edges.

On the top of the stack was *A Farewell to Arms*, the novel from which her name had come.

Seeing it gave her a pang. She didn't care to confront what the similarities—or dissimilarities—she had with her namesake might imply. Catherine wanted to be her own person, not a knockoff of some fictional woman she could never stack up to.

The novel was covered in cellophane, like an old library book that had been checked out and never returned.

"If I have to pay a fine on this for Robert, I'm going to be pissed."

Through the grayed plastic, the colors on the cover appeared dim. A slit in the cellophane showed the deep-indigo background and stylized orange image of a man and woman entwined under a tree, which remained brilliant. While looking for the book's card pocket, Catherine noticed something on the title page.

A handwritten signature.

The name Ernest Hemingway was signed in black fountain ink, the mark of the nib evident in the tail of the "y."

"This can't be real."

Since it seemed as though Robert had played trick after trick on her, Catherine couldn't believe what she was seeing. A signed copy of a Hemingway classic would be worth a small fortune.

Her brother's boat could have been a fake. What if this wasn't?

She gently put the novel down, resting it on the fluffy duvet, while she grabbed her laptop case. If there was ever an occasion for research, it was now. When Catherine opened her laptop, the pile of Robert's books slid to the side, exposing a small photo album at the bottom. It was brown leather with a snap-button closure holding it shut.

An electric surge of excitement coursed through Catherine's body. The hope of seeing pictures of her brother had faded when the estate attorney told her that his possessions had been donated to charity. Her hands shook as she gingerly popped the clasp.

The first photograph was a baby picture. Except it wasn't Robert's. Catherine's spirits floundered.

"Who the heck is that?"

The image of an infant boy swaddled in a blue blanket was yellowed by time. The next image was of a family picnic, mother, father, brother, and sister seated around a checkered blanket, the dad with his arm over his son's shoulder. The wave in the boy's blond hair and the icy blue of his eyes immediately told Catherine it was Travis. She even recognized his father, the judge, as a younger man, muscled, tan, with a can of soda in his hand.

Sorrow flooded Catherine's rib cage, yet she felt hollow. It was as though she couldn't get enough air. Angry as she was at Robert for what he had done, she harbored the wish that someday she would see him again, if only in pictures. Dejected, she continued flipping through the album, yearning for the disappointment to fade.

There were Christmases with the kids in snowsuits riding sleighs and an Easter egg hunt where Travis was helping his sister search a stretch of backyard grass. Next came a graduation shot of Travis and his father, each in navy suits. Both their jaws were set. Neither smiled. The rift between them could be seen by how far apart they stood from one another. For a second, Catherine pitied Travis. Then she pitied herself.

At least his dad had been around.

Curiosity kept Catherine turning the pages of the album, as if it could tell her something about Travis she didn't know. Eventually, she came upon a picture of a summer trip by a lake. It was a bunch of high school boys on a dock, roughhousing, and Travis was in the water, covered in long strands of lake weeds, mugging for the camera and twirling the green stems like they were long tendrils of hair. He looked like a sea monster.

"Or a mermaid," she murmured in realization.

Catherine's mind shuddered. She yanked the picture from its sleeve to cxaminc it more closely. Her eyes weren't fooling her.

Furious, she flipped through the other photographs and found one of Travis in front of a house at night, his buddies by his side, reams of white toilet paper draped across the front door and windows, rolls dripping from tree branches. A few pages later, there was a shot of Travis knee deep in mud out in the country.

He had done the same thing to her as he had done to teach English to the kids in Peru—made up stories. The one Travis had told her about Robert was really about him.

"That bastard."

Her heart was pounding. She hurled the album across the room.

Why would Travis have swapped his memories for Robert's? To buy himself more time on the boat? To mess with her? To mislead her?

Whatever he thought he might gain by deceiving her, Catherine was not about to stand for it.

30

Being sneaky wasn't as easy as Catherine assumed it would be. She crept down the stairs, treading lightly toward the front door and thinking she could make it out of the house unheard. She was wrong.

"Where are you off to?" Fred asked from the dining room, where he was busily polishing the silver tea service displayed on the credenza.

Arnie appeared in the doorway to the kitchen. "Someplace exciting?"

Reluctant to broadcast her plans, Catherine fumbled for a reply. "Uh, the beach."

"But you don't have a towel."

"And you're not wearing a bathing suit."

"Or sunscreen."

"I meant Mallory Square," she tried.

"Oh, well the guy on the six-foot unicycle is pretty wild," Fred marveled.

"The bagpipers aren't too shabby," Arnie said.

"What about the contortionist who can fold himself into a tiny Plexiglas box?"

"Gotta love a guy who's flexible."

Fred flared his nostrils with displeasure.

"Aw, you're flexible, too, honey. In the compliant and accommodating sense. You're polishing the silver for me, even though you abhor doing it."

"That's being obedient. Like a dog," Fred countered.

"Oh, please. That's a baseless argument. Our dog isn't the slightest bit obedient."

With the minutes ticking by, Catherine needed to get on the road. "Well, gotta go."

"Be back by six," Arnie reminded her. "I've planned multiple courses. The first will be served promptly."

"Wouldn't miss it."

Catherine had plans of her own.

She walked straight to the Ernest Hemingway Home. After paying the admission fee, Catherine was told she could tag along on a tour that was already in progress, so she jogged through the front garden to catch up with the group.

Dozens of cats were lazing on chairs and meandering around as a male guide in a white skipper's cap was leading a group of Russian tourists through the home's elegant living room with arched French doors.

"These are some of the furnishings that Papa Hemingway's wife Pauline acquired while living in Paris," he announced to the group with the flair of a game show host.

The name on Robert's boat. Pauline's Escape.

"It's said that Pauline had exquisite taste and that upon buying this property, her coveted chandelier collection quickly replaced Papa's stodgy old ceiling fans."

One of the members of the tour pointed at the delicate crystal fixture that hung overhead, then rattled off something in Russian, translating for the rest.

Poor Pauline is probably turning over in her grave, having her name on some derelict fishing trawler she would never have set foot on.

As the guide spoke of priceless paintings and precious antiques, Catherine's resentment festered, and she nearly tripped over a friendly cat making a figure eight around her ankles.

"This is a fascinating item." The guide motioned to a clunky iron contraption holding a bottle of wine like a vise. "It's a Spanish bottle safe called a 'tantalus.' It prevents anybody from spiriting away the spirits."

The Russians didn't get his lame pun, so he pressed onward through the home.

A series of photos hung above a sideboard, featuring various portraits of Hemingway, his gaze perpetually challenging, his expression dispassionate for effect. Here was the person who she had held responsible for how her life had turned out, the culprit of her misery. Staring eye to eye with him, Catherine wanted to loathe Hemingway. She couldn't.

Be it the age of the pictures or the man's deliberately stern countenance, Catherine didn't see a villain staring back at her. She simply saw a man who had nothing to do with her father. Or her brother. Or her.

Catherine had put her past on an emotional payment plan. The family strife she had repressed was a bill that was long overdue and accumulating interest at a high rate. Ready or not, she had to accept the charges, before the cost became too much to bear.

Trying to get the tour group excited, the guide peppered them with more information.

"Some fun facts: Ernest Hemingway survived back-to-back plane crashes in Uganda. The first brushed against a telegraph wire, and the second plane he was on to head home caught fire."

The Russians grimaced uneasily.

"He also shot himself through both calves while trying to kill a shark he had reeled in."

They grimaced again, muttering the word "shark" among themselves, befuddled.

"Papa Hemingway also dabbled a little in gender fluidity. He and his wife Mary would swap roles in the boudoir. Supposedly, she went by 'Pete,' and he went by 'Catherine.'"

"What?!" Catherine demanded, aghast.

The tour guide raised his brows at her. "Probably best they don't get that one," he told her, thumbing at the Russians. "Oh, and Hemingway was recruited to be a spy for the KGB."

Every head snapped to attention at the acronym.

"He was only a wannabe spook, never gave much valuable information. He was likely just panning for material for a new book."

The Russians gazed at him unflinchingly, so the guide changed the subject.

"Ah, I see you've spotted these rare pictures," he said, pretending as if Catherine had shown interest. "Hemingway was born in 1899 and died in 1961. During those years, he covered wars as a correspondent, skied the Swiss Alps, hunted big game in Africa, won the Nobel Prize and the Pulitzer. He did a lot of living in his sixty-one years. More than most."

Catherine hadn't done enough. She had held Hemingway liable for her woes; however, he was no more there to answer for them than Robert. Who did that leave to point the finger at?

"This one is of Ernest with his brother and sisters when they were kids."

"Sisters?" Catherine asked.

"Marcelline, Ursula, Madelaine, and Carol. He was very close with Marcelline in their younger years, though they eventually drifted apart."

That fact hit her squarely in the chest.

"And he and Carol had a terrible falling out. He didn't approve of the man she was with. They never spoke again," the tour guide relayed. "Hemingway may have been a master at writing about battles, loss, love, and the human condition, but siblings weren't his thing."

Catherine could relate.

Lost in thought, she lagged at the back of the group as they continued through the kitchen, a nursemaid's quarters, and the primary bedroom, each replete with ornate objects and original artwork. More pictures hung on the walls, some of Hemingway posing with a huge marlin in Cuba or in his Red Cross uniform or jabbing away at his portable typewriter.

"This room has some unique memorabilia," the tour guide touted, surely hoping to rouse the unanimated Russians. "In this display is a clipping about Stanley Dexter, a salvage captain who gave him his first six-toed cat, the great-great-granddaddy of the felines roaming the grounds to this very day."

"Cats with many toes," one of the Russian men stated in a husky accent.

"Yes, cats with many toes!" the tour guide parroted back enthusiastically. Having finally gotten everybody interested, he went on in an animated fashion. "This image of Papa in uniform is especially significant, seeing as he was wounded in Italy and that was where he fell in love with a nurse named Agnes, who broke his heart by declining his marriage proposal. That, my friends—or should I say comrades—was the basis of the character Catherine in his renowned novel *A Farewell to Arms*, the book Papa was working on when he first arrived on this island. He seemed obsessed with that name." He gave her a saucy wink because she was the only one who'd understood his earlier reference.

It took a moment for Catherine to process what the tour guide had said. When she did, the anger that had hardened in her soul softened, like pottery turning back to clay. The woman she had been named after had broken Hemingway's heart. Her father had broken her brother's. Robert had broken hers. With that revelation came a peculiar sense of long-awaited balance.

What had happened to her wasn't fair and never would be. The scales had been largely to one side, uneven with old wounds and injustices. Knowing what the real Catherine had done somehow tipped them in her favor. She couldn't resent a heartbroken Hemingway for his stories when she knew the feeling all too well. He wasn't the source of her problems. He had been the scapegoat. At last, Catherine thought she might be able to find stability in her brother's absence, steadiness in her mixed emotions toward him, and equilibrium in the finality of his passing.

"Here we have some real treasures," the tour guide announced. "In these chests are vintage boots and saddlebags from Papa's trips out West as well as some first editions of his books. Rare commodities, these are. Rubies among gold."

"How rare?" Catherine blurted.

The group of Russians angled toward her en masse. Her outburst threw off the guide, who adjusted his skipper's cap to scratch his head.

"We normally wait until the end of the tour for questions, but . . ." He glanced at the Russians. They seemed to neither understand nor care what he did. "I'll entertain a query. A first edition is considered more valuable than subsequent printings. Papa's publisher, Scribner's, employed a variety of methods of defining first editions. In the 1920s, the dates on the title and copyright pages had to be identical, with no indication of later printings on the copyright page. Eventually, the letter 'A' was placed on the copyright page to indicate a first printing."

Satisfied with himself, he summed up his speech and knitted his hands together. The Russians stared at him blankly, as if voicing the same concern Catherine had.

"So how much are they valued at?" she asked.

"A first edition of Papa's works could retail anywhere from a couple of hundred dollars to a couple of thousand."

Catherine hadn't checked the copyright page, because she had been floored by the signature. "What if it's a signed first edition?"

"Well, then"—the tour guide snorted—"one would first have to ensure it wasn't a forgery. There are tons of them floating around."

"How can you tell an imitation from the real deal?"

"There's a telltale curve at the top of the *E*, a long line across the *h*, and the last *a* is open at the top. And the *g* has a straight tail, not a looped one. It's quite distinct."

She committed his words to memory. "What would something like that be worth?"

"Some are only worth a few hundred. Others could easily command tens of thousands of dollars, depending on the material."

"Say it was *A Farewell to Arms*. For argument's sake."

"You could be talking about hundreds of thousands of dollars."

The Russians whispered among themselves. Money, they clearly understood.

"Any more questions?" the tour guide asked wearily, as though Catherine had gone too many rounds with him.

"I'm good."

If Robert's book was a first edition and the signature wasn't fake, Catherine was about to be way better than good.

31

Passing clouds tempered the afternoon sun, and though Catherine wanted to rush to her next stop, she couldn't help but stroll. She had asked the ticket seller at the Hemingway Home where the city library was located and learned it wasn't far. Nothing in Key West was.

The New Yorker in Catherine had to shrug off the need to race onward. It was a hard habit to break; however, she wanted to savor the gorgeous weather, especially since it would probably be snowing when she returned home.

Unlike the busier streets on the island, Whitehead was wider and less congested, with fewer stoplights. Homes huddled beside bed-and-breakfasts, most in a scenic state of decay. Tourists coasted by on scooters while Catherine contemplated what would happen if Robert's book was the genuine article.

From behind her came the familiar tinny sound of a loudspeaker. It was a miniature train with a black engine and a string of yellow open-air passenger cars trailing behind. Printed on the engine were the words CONCH TOUR TRAIN.

In a practiced tone, the driver was regaling the passengers with island folklore, "While countless rich and famous people came to Key West, few realized that the island's fortune was built on bad luck. Once settlers arrived, the trade ships carrying cargo to them fell victim to our notoriously dangerous reefs and the ravages of hurricanes. Because of the hundreds of ships that were shattered trying to get to port, a new cottage industry sprang up called 'wrecking.'"

The train inched along as tourists onboard listened, bobbing their heads from left to right to take in the view. Catherine was practically keeping pace on foot.

"The wreckers made money hand over fist by salvaging the crippled ships and selling the bounty. For a time, Key West was considered the wealthiest and most affluent city in America. Wreck auctions, the sea-sponge trade, and the popularity of hand-rolled Cuban cigars brought visitors by the thousands, building the island into the tropical haven it is today."

If it weren't for Robert's death, she wouldn't have been on the island either. Catherine questioned whether Key West had that effect on everybody who wound up there. One person's misfortune was another's windfall. Here, the tides turned quickly. She prayed they would continue to flow in her favor.

In the distance, she saw a sign with a name she recognized: **THE GREEN PARROT**.

That was where Travis said he had run into Robert. The low-slung building had a wraparound awning and glassless windows that faced the street. Unable to resist taking a peek, she stuck her head in the door.

It was like a junk shop with a liquor license or an old attic that served alcohol. Bicycle wheels hung from the ceiling amid billowy fabric, and strands of twinkling lights did little to brighten the dusky ambiance. Kitschy pictures and trinkets were affixed to every surface.

"What can I getcha?" a male bartender with a scruffy beard asked, a dishrag threaded through the belt loop of his cutoff shorts.

"Who, me?" she replied. "I'm just looking."

"Aw, come on," he cajoled. "A beer in the hand is worth two in the cooler."

It was a boozy take on an adage Catherine should have been considering with care.

Since she had the Hemingway book to sell, was getting rid of Robert's boat necessary?

Catherine pictured her brother sitting on one of the stools at the bar and tried to imagine what had brought him to the Green Parrot. Would he have ordered a beer? A gin and tonic? A shot?

She felt a spike of disgrace that she didn't know the answer and never would.

That made her even angrier at Travis for muddling her scant honest memories of Robert with fakes. Worse yet, she liked the bogus ones far better than her own because in his version, her brother seemed happy.

She ducked out of the bar, back into daylight. Her watch said it was after three. Catherine needed to get going, but she wanted to check something first by searching back issues of the Key West newspaper online.

Since Catherine hadn't found anything when she investigated Travis by his name alone, she plugged in the time frame Vic had brought up when he and Travis locked horns at the boat. Vic had mentioned Christmas, which meant that whatever happened could have occurred earlier than the holidays.

Combing through the online archives, she skipped articles with pictures of tinsel-covered palm trees and bikini-clad girls wearing Santa caps, then came across a piece from the previous November titled "Melee at the Green Parrot."

Catherine didn't doubt that the bar hosted its fair share of brawls. However, the snapshot in the paper showed a far grimmer scene.

Taken from the street, the photo captured a mob of people jostling to exit the building, some holding bloody napkins to their faces, while others were being tended to by EMTs. Police were hauling a handful of men through the crowd in cuffs. Travis wasn't anywhere among them.

That didn't mean he wasn't there.

The article stated a group of locals and tourists had gotten into a heated argument after a male tourist accused one of the natives of swiping his wallet. Beyond that, the details were vague. Phrases like "damage to the establishment was not major" and "arrests were made" didn't provide Catherine with what she was after.

Going back to October and September to study the crime reports didn't yield anything else noteworthy. There were burglaries and scuffles between vagrants and an incident where a pregnant woman punched her boyfriend—nothing that jibed with what Vic had referenced. Catherine was forced to resort to her backup plan.

She stepped out of the library to call Kenny.

"What's shakin'? You need a lift?"

"What I need is some more info. I've been doing some . . . investigating."

"Into?"

A lizard skittered across the sidewalk by her feet, trying to soak in some sunshine.

"The bar fight that happened at the Green Parrot back in November."

"What the hell for?"

"Just tell me what you heard."

"Far as I know, a couple of drunk tourist dudes picked a fight with a townie. Said he was a pickpocket. The guy tries to calm them down. They aren't having it. Guy tries to defend himself. They jump him. Some other locals see him getting clobbered, and they get in the mix. Fists fly. Glasses break. Average fare for the Parrot. That is until somebody grabbed a pool cue and broke it across the side of some tourist's face. Shattered the guy's jaw."

"That wasn't in the paper."

"'Round here, the whole story rarely is."

Catherine chewed on that. Did Travis steal some guy's wallet? Vic had said he didn't have much money. Except that was after his father supposedly cut him off. The details didn't line up.

"Do you know the locals who were involved?"

"Once the rumors started spreading, any lowlife seeking some street cred claimed to be part of the brigade. Couldn't say for sure who was telling the truth and who was glomming onto the glory."

"It's something to brag about when you beat up a tourist?"

Kenny sighed. "When you have to depend on them for every dime and they treat your hometown like a toilet, where they can vomit in the bushes and piss in the streets, animosity tends to build up."

In a way, Catherine could relate. After working for her company year in and year out without a raise or much thanks, she understood how easy it was to become resentful.

"I'm not saying what went down at the Parrot was anything to be proud of. Fighting never determines who's right. Only who's left."

It was an axiom Catherine should have taken to heart. Except the desire to get back at Travis for lying to her was almost impossible to resist.

"Care to enlighten me as to why you're concerned with this particular incident?"

"You already think I'm a troublemaker. I'd rather not sully my reputation any further."

Kenny chuckled. "Better I think less of you than more."

"Why is that?"

"Leaves plenty of room for improvement."

Catherine's expectations of herself had certainly gone awry since arriving on the island. She had lied—frequently and with vigor—and had arranged to trick Vic into paying a higher price for the boat. She was thinking less and less of herself by the second.

That seemed like the opposite of what should have happened on a vacation. Catherine thought she would come away from the trip feeling refreshed and rejuvenated. Instead, she was resentful and regretful.

Life on Key West had seemed simple, a place where everybody was in a constant Margaritaville state of mind. Yet she couldn't forget that this was an island founded on wreckage. While she was there, Catherine had to be careful she didn't wind up running herself aground, stranding her own self-respect in the process. She wanted her proverbial ship to come in *and* go back out safely.

32

Though the skies were a bright, never-ending blue, the hour was getting late. Catherine hustled home, anxious to put Robert's copy of *A Farewell to Arms* under a microscope. She rushed in the front door of the Abbott House, took the stairs two at a time, and threw open her bedroom door to find Arnie sitting on her bed, arms folded, a peeved expression on his face.

"We have some talking to do."

Catherine's eyes darted to the cellophane-covered book resting on the duvet. Arnie carelessly tossed it aside, along with a few others, then patted the spot next to him, inviting her to sit for a chat. It took every ounce of her will not to dive after the novel. She sat beside Arnie, itching to open the book and inspect the signature. With him there, she couldn't.

"It obviously wasn't your idea to invite Travis to dinner this evening. Nevertheless, he is our guest, and we will all treat him accordingly. Okay?"

"Am I being chastised in advance? I haven't done anything yet!"

"That's the problem." Arnie got to his feet. "You haven't done a thing. Not with your hair, your outfit, or your makeup. I will not stand for Lita giving you a run for your money because she had the common sense to run a comb through her hair. It's unconscionable."

He summarily grabbed Catherine's bag off the floor and hurled it on top of the books. She had momentary palpitations until she saw that *A Farewell to Arms* was safely out of reach.

"Your clothes have been bunched up in here and are probably wrinkled to high heaven. Where is your brush? Please tell me you have lipstick?"

"I—"

"Never mind. I'll find it myself. You get in the shower. Everybody will be here shortly, and my salmon canapés are about to come out of the oven. Time is of the essence. March!"

Arnie spun her on her heels and pushed her out of the bedroom toward the bathroom.

"Your ensemble will be waiting on your bed. Here." He handed her a bottle of perfume. "A guest left it behind last month."

"Are you saying I smell bad?"

"Not bad. Bland. Like l'eau de manila envelopes. You'll never snag that man with the scent of stationery."

"Who says I want anything to do with Travis?"

"You didn't have to announce it," he informed her. "It was written all over your face."

"Trust me. You're totally off base with this."

"Let's put the *wash* in 'hogwash,' shall we?"

Arnie pushed her into the bathroom and shut her inside before she could state her case.

"I don't hear the water running," he scolded from the hallway.

Catherine did as she was told and took the fastest shower possible. Dripping wet but clamoring to get back to *A Farewell to Arms*, Catherine nudged opened the bedroom door, expecting another ambush from Arnie. He was gone.

All Robert's books had been stacked neatly on the dresser, and she was about to lunge for them when she noticed the bed, which Arnie had remade. A white gathered blouse was laid out on the duvet, along with a denim skirt. Catherine had forgotten that she had packed either garment. Lined up on the bedside table were her mascara and the tube of lipstick. Arnie had arranged the entire ensemble with care. Although the clothes weren't haute couture and the perfume was from the lost and found, Catherine felt like the princess Audrey Hepburn played in *Roman Holiday*.

Catherine shut her bedroom door, pushed back her wet hair, retrieved *A Farewell to Arms* from the pile on the bureau, and took a deep breath.

The cellophane crackled as she opened the cover, then flipped to the copyright page. The date for the title and the date for the copyright were the same. This was a first edition.

Her heartbeat started drumming in her chest as she turned to the title page, where she had seen the signature. She shut her eyes tight, recalling the specifics the tour guide had listed.

"The *E* has a curve. The *h* has a long line across it. The last *a* is open. The bottom of the *g* is straight."

She went over every letter with the tip of her finger, confirming whether each matched the rules.

They did.

Ecstatic, Catherine could have wept. Robert had left her something of value, something that he valued. In that moment, the gaping chasm her brother's absence had created closed a little.

Money wouldn't replace what she'd lost or make up for what she had missed out on. It wouldn't bring Robert back to her. However, the gesture was bigger than the gift.

A knock came at the door.

"T-minus ten minutes," Arnie reported. "If you're not decent, get that way. And don't skimp on the lipstick!"

Catherine wiped her eyes and placed the book underneath her pillow tenderly.

A week before her father had walked out, she'd lost a tooth. Robert had reminded her to put it under her pillow, saying the tooth fairy would come in the middle of the night and replace the tooth with money. Though she knew there was no tooth fairy, they both played along. She had awoken to find a dollar as well as four shiny quarters.

The bill was creased and thin, clearly from her mother's wallet. The quarters had come from Robert's piggy bank. Despite everything he had done, Catherine's faith was renewed. Her brother had cared for her, even if it was from a distance.

As she threw on her clothes, her phone rang. In a rush, Catherine debated whether to pick up. But it was Gloria's office number, not her cell. On the weekend, that made no sense.

"Are you being held hostage?" Catherine asked. "Should I call the SWAT team?"

"No, girl. I'm here with Tito, showing him my desk. He asked to see where I work. Isn't that sweet?"

Catherine heaved a sigh of relief. "I'm shocked that you wanted to show him the office, given that you spend your lunch break plotting how to blow the place up and not have it traced back to you. Where's Tito now?"

"I let him use the executive men's washroom. Told him to swipe me some mouthwash or shoe-polishing cloths or whatever goodies they stash in there. Then we're going for sushi. This'll be our third date. Hot and heavy, ay? I'm hot. He's slightly heavy. I don't care. He treats me nice."

"That's all that matters, Gloria."

"How about you? You havin' a nice time?"

From the instant she'd gotten the plane ticket, Catherine's trip had been a roller coaster. Instead of lazing on the beach with a drink in her hand, she had spent almost every waking minute crisscrossing the island in service of Robert's run-down boat. Uncovering *A Farewell to Arms* changed her outlook on the vacation entirely.

"It's been . . . different."

"You need different," she declared.

In the background, Catherine heard a man saying, "Ay, Gloria, they had packs of toothpicks and mints. I took 'em for you. Think they'll notice?"

"You two enjoy your evening."

"You do the same with the rest of your days off," Gloria urged.

Catherine was certainly going to try.

She shoved her phone into the pocket of her skirt, twisted her wet hair into a loose bun, quickly applied her makeup, then hurried downstairs to the dining room.

A disturbing sight was waiting to greet her.

Sisters Lita and Ina were already seated at the table, and they had evidently gone to the beauty shop. Lita's blond hair was curled into crispy ringlets, and she had overdone it on the eyeliner. She had donned a new cat T-shirt, which featured a picture of a white Persian perched on a baby grand piano like the Sphinx.

"Nice shirt," Catherine commented.

"Thanks," Lita replied, stroking the image. "It's my fanciest one."

Ina had also taken a spin in the stylist's chair. Strands of her pin-straight hair had been plaited into cornrows with shells holding them together at the ends. Whenever she moved, they jangled, hitting her in the cheeks.

"That's the most clothes I've seen you wear," Ina told Catherine as she stood there debating where to take a seat.

The head chairs were for Arnie and Fred, and Ina was beside Lita. Catherine got the feeling Lita was saving the spot opposite her for Travis so she could be directly across from him.

"I'll take that as a compliment."

Even though it wasn't one.

"Who's hungry?" Arnie trilled as he entered, carrying hors d'oeuvres; then he nearly dropped the tray, agog to see the way the sisters were dolled up.

Fred followed with more appetizers, and his eyes went as wide as Arnie's. "My, my, doesn't somebody make a fine Bo Derek."

"Who?" Ina furrowed her brow.

"And you, Lita, you look . . ." Arnie evidently couldn't find the appropriate phrase.

"Stunning," Fred declared.

"Yup, I'm stunned," Arnie said awkwardly. Then his gaze fell on Catherine. He beamed with pride, then gave her an impressed wink. "Let me see how the Parmesan crisps are coming."

He flitted back into the kitchen while Fred busied himself by arranging the platters of appetizers. "Goat cheese puffs anybody? Mini crab cakes? Crudités?"

Right as Catherine took a spot on the other side of the table, Lita looked put off by the seating arrangement and went to forcibly shake her sister out of her spot.

"Switch seats?" Lita ordered.

"Switch seats?" Ina repeated, midbite with a cheese puff.

Arnie reappeared with more food, saying, "Here's the prosciutto-wrapped cantaloupe and phyllo dough stuffed with . . . What the hell?"

Lita was jerking Ina up and wrangling her into the chair across from Catherine, braids jangling wildly.

"Gentle, gentle!" Fred warned as the stemware on the table clanked and the dishes rattled.

Clearly satisfied with the revised seating, which ensured her position directly across from Travis's empty seat, Lita sat down and smoothed a napkin on her lap.

"We're one guest short," Arnie noted, checking the time. Travis was late.

"I'm sure he'll be here," Ina insisted, busily chewing.

"I'm sure he will," Lita reiterated excitedly.

Fred turned to Catherine, who shrugged and smirked.

For a change, she wasn't the one causing the problems.

"This is going to be a fantastic dinner," Lita declared, plucking a carrot stick from the vegetable tray. "I can't wait for the next course."

33

A sophisticated evening of conversation to go with the fine dining wasn't on the menu that night. Every minute that ticked by without Travis cast a pall over the table. Arnie had served a soup course of lobster bisque, and everybody was quietly slurping away while Lita was nervously jiggling her leg under the table, making the plates vibrate.

Catherine looked at Arnie apologetically. Even she wondered where Travis was.

Fred went around, topping off each person's water glass. "A toast to good food, good times, and good friends."

"We've got one out of three," Catherine whispered, and Arnie pursed his lips at her.

Then Truman started barking and the front door swung open.

In walked Travis, a cascading bouquet of flowers in one hand, a bottle of wine in the other. He had on pressed khaki pants and a royal blue button-down, a shade that showed off his tan and electrified his eyes. Lita blushed at the sight of him, which was a feat, given how red her cheeks were from her sunburn. Catherine had to pull her eyes away from Travis.

"I'm sorry I'm late. It's been a while since I ironed a shirt. Not as quick a process as I'd thought it would be." He gestured at his clothes, sheepishly.

"It was worth the wait," Arnie assured him, shooting a glance at Catherine. He grabbed the flowers from Travis before Lita could intercept them. "I'll put these in water. Fred, be a dear and show our guest to his seat."

Lita corralled Travis into a chair. "You're across from me."

"Hey," he said softly to Catherine.

"Hey."

The outrage she had felt toward him after she discovered he'd lied about Robert had dwindled. The book was a potent balm for her ire. How could she stay angry when she knew she had a first edition Hemingway novel under her pillow?

It was also tough to be mad at a man that handsome.

Arnie reentered with a bowl of soup for Travis.

"Do you like lobster?" Lita asked, vying for his attention. "The soup has lobster in it."

"Who doesn't?" he replied congenially.

"Never had it before," Lita said between bites.

Fred tried not to stare as she wolfed down the rich soup. "So, Travis, tell us about yourself."

"Not much to say. I've traveled around a lot. Not one for staying any one place very long, but I got to Key West, loved it, and couldn't leave."

The response struck Catherine as intentionally ambiguous.

"Tell them about Peru," she suggested, putting him on the spot. She wondered if his tale about the pelican statue was a fabrication, too, and Travis had just picked the statue up at some swap meet.

"Ooh, what was that like?" Lita asked, enthralled.

"Amazing. I backpacked throughout South America. Went to Carnival in Brazil. Climbed mountains in Patagonia. I'd teach English classes or do carpentry to repair churches or help build irrigation systems for villagers to water their crops. Anything to barter for meals and a place to stay. You can get by there without much money, which was great because I didn't have much. Material stuff never really did it for me. Reminds you that there's a difference between what you want and what you need. Your ego can't get too big when you realize how small you are compared to the world."

"Quite the adventure," Catherine said, dubious. "Why run so far away?"

Travis squinted at her warily.

"Sometimes you have to leave what you know to learn where you're meant to be."

Much as she wanted to argue with him, Catherine was now of the same opinion.

"With all that traveling, you must not have had time for a wife," Lita inquired coquettishly.

"Uh, no. No wife."

As she fluttered her lashes at him, Travis fixed his gaze on his bowl of soup.

"Finish up, everybody. The entrée will be ready in a few minutes," Arnie announced, a welcome distraction.

Dean Martin started to sing from Catherine's pocket.

"Sorry. I thought I turned the ringer off." Aware it was her mom, who she had been avoiding, Catherine decided to quickly take the call. "Only be a sec, everybody."

"Manners," Ina snapped, ever critical.

"Hey, Mom. Can I call you back?"

"You haven't called me back since Jesus Christ was on the cross, so no," her mother blared, loud enough that the whole table could hear.

She pressed the receiver to her ear to muffle the sound. "I know. And I'm really, really sorry about that. But I'm at a . . ." Catherine had to come up with something fast. "A business dinner. I can't talk."

Catherine caught Travis narrowing his eyes at her, listening.

"Why are you whispering?" her mother shouted, as if to compensate.

"Because my boss is here. I don't want to get in trouble. Please, let me call you back," she implored.

"Forget it. My shows are coming on, and I don't want you interrupting them. Call me tomorrow. If you remember."

With that, she hung up brusquely.

"Night, Mom," Catherine told the dial tone.

“First, you work in insurance. Then you’re at a business meeting with your boss,” Travis remarked, glib. “How do you keep everything straight?”

The undercurrent of sarcasm in his voice instantly set Catherine off, uncorking a blast of the emotions she had been holding in. “I should ask you the same thing. I found your photo album. It was in the stack of Robert’s books you gave me.”

Travis’s expression grew taut. He glanced away, then back at Catherine, as though preparing to accept his punishment.

“Admit it. Was the seaweed a lie? Was that my ‘Little Red Riding Hood’? A story like you told the kids in Peru?”

“Yes,” he answered, noticeably ashamed.

“What seaweed?” Lita asked.

“Was the mud a lie?” Catherine demanded in disgust. “Your spin on ‘Goldilocks’?”

“Yes.” He gritted his teeth.

“Why are we talking about fairy tales?” a bewildered Lita wondered aloud while sopping up the dregs of her lobster bisque with a dinner roll.

“The toilet paper too? Was that your rendition of ‘Snow White’?”

“Yes.” He shook his head as if to shrug off the humiliation.

“Uh . . . what’s going on?” Fred asked.

“And the mess hall?”

“No,” Travis insisted. “That was true. Every word of it.”

“Then tell me why you did it.” Tears welled, burning Catherine’s eyes.

“Catherine, please,” Arnie said, attempting to keep the party from going any further off the rails.

Fred stopped him, allowing her to speak her piece for a change.

“Why?” she yelled. “I may not have meant a lot to my brother, as you took so much pleasure in telling me, but he meant everything to me. *Everything.*”

Lita inched away from Travis after hearing that. Ina glared at him as the rest stared silently.

"You told me those stories about him, and they made me think that even if he didn't want me in his life, at least his life was normal when mine couldn't have been further from it."

Travis got to his feet to face her, except Catherine wouldn't let him talk. "Vic was right about you. I know what you did at the Green Parrot. You bashed some poor tourist across the face with a pool cue and broke his jaw—then you got your father to pull strings and expunge the records."

Lita let out a gasp, her perfect image of Travis plainly shattered.

"I may be a liar, a bad one," Catherine said, "but I don't hurt people the way you do."

"That isn't what happened," Travis bellowed. He paced, circling her and working up to the truth.

"I did *not* steal that guy's wallet. And I did *not* start the fight. He was tanked, completely wasted, and he must have lost it someplace. I happened to bump into him, and he assumed I lifted it, so he took a jab at me and missed. His friends thought I threw the first punch. Before I knew it, the bar was in chaos, and everybody was involved. I don't know who swung the pool cue, but it wasn't me. Yes, I was arrested along with a dozen other people from the bar that night. Once my dad found out, he realized it would hit the papers, so he called in a favor with the local PD to keep my name off the record. I didn't ask them to do it. He did. He doesn't care about me. He only cares about himself and his reputation. As always."

Although it obviously stung Travis to retell the tale, that didn't quell Catherine's temper. "I'm supposed to feel sorry for you because your dad bailed you out?"

"No," Travis admitted. "You feel sorry enough for yourself. There isn't anything left over for anybody else."

Fred was about to defend Catherine, but Arnie gave him a look to quiet him.

"Then you and I have more in common than we realized," she shot back.

But Travis's comment was painfully accurate. It cut her to her core.

"I told you those stories because I wanted you to like Bobby again. Your brother was a good guy. I didn't want you to hate him anymore, especially since he's gone. Because I know he never hated you."

Catherine deeply resented what Travis had done. However, she had been doing the same thing to her mother by not telling her about Robert's death. Protecting a person had a price.

"I apologize to everyone for ruining dinner." Travis pushed in his chair. "And Catherine, I apologize for lying to you. You don't have a single reason to believe that I'm being sincere, but I truly mean it."

He dug a folded envelope out of his back pocket and handed it to her.

"What's this?"

"It's from Bobby."

A small gasp escaped her lips.

"I have a PO box because I can't get mail at the boat. I was busy and finally picked it up today. Said to give it to you."

Catherine's heart lifted with hope as she took it from Travis. He stormed out, and the front door slammed behind him, reverberating through the house. A shudder went through her as if it were from the weight of holding something her brother had sent for her.

The letter bore her name in his handwriting. She recognized it instantly. All she could say was his name.

"Robert."

34

A heavy hush gripped the room, faces frozen in a tableau of anticipation. Catherine stood by the dining table, her brain slowly coming to grips with what she was holding. Fred and Arnie exchanged tense glances. Even Ina knew better than to chime in at that fraught moment.

"Read it," Lita said simply.

Arnie interjected, "You can go in the parlor for privacy."

Catherine could barely move, let alone think. Her fingers slid under the flap. She tugged out the letter and started reading aloud as if to ensure the words were real.

Fred glanced around, silently asking the others whether they should leave, yet nobody moved.

"Dear Catherine," she began, her voice cracking.

"I want to tell you why I left you and Mom. I owe you that and so much more. The night she and Dad had their big fight, he had come home early and caught me kissing a boy from school I was secretly dating. That was why he never came back. Because of me. He told me that I was a pervert, that I shouldn't be around a little girl your age, that I was a bad influence, that I was no son of his. He said he couldn't stand to see me ever again."

Tears streamed down Catherine's cheeks at the revelation. Arnie dabbed his eyes with a napkin as Fred hung his head in consternation.

"I was so ashamed. I thought I was doing the right thing by leaving and staying away. Now I know how wrong it was. Every time I wanted to reach out, the shame was still there."

Catherine wiped her eyes as Ina's and Lita's faces framed their solemn compassion.

"I hurt Mom. I hurt you. I hurt myself by missing out on everything in your lives. I apologize. I hope you'll find it in your heart to forgive me. Check my favorite book. It's on the boat. I left something for you. I hope it will make up for how wrong I've been. I always loved you and Mom more than you'll ever know. I'm sorry I'll never have the chance to say it in person."

The letter ended. Catherine stared at the page.

"He loved me," she said. It was as much an epiphany as a fact she could hold dear.

"Somebody say something," Ina declared, visibly uncomfortable in the gaping silence.

"This may be cold comfort," Fred began. "However, I know exactly how your brother felt."

"I do too," Arnie agreed. "He must have been very confused."

"And very alone," Fred added.

"That makes two of us," Catherine whispered.

"I'm not absolving him," Fred stated clearly.

"Or making excuses," Arnie went on.

"I hope you can put yourself in his shoes," Fred urged.

"You have no idea how difficult it was to be gay back then," Arnie admitted.

"The stigma, the fear, the ostracization, the danger, it was always present," Fred explained.

"It's better now, especially in places like Key West but . . ." Arnie began.

"But it's never easy." Fred had a hitch in his voice as he took Arnie's hand.

"He thought he was protecting you," Lita said simply yet firmly.

"He hoped your father would come home if he wasn't there," Ina added.

"He sacrificed himself trying to give you back your dad," Arnie told her gently.

Catherine thought of the story of the pelican that Travis had told and how it would sacrifice itself for its young. She felt like she was caving in. A rockslide of emotions threatened to bury her.

"I didn't want him back," Catherine admitted. "I wanted Robert. I wanted my brother."

"But now you know he loved you," Lita proclaimed, like that was more than enough.

Then she started to cough. Her rasping rapidly turned into hoarse choking. She grabbed her throat. Her face was getting redder by the second.

Ina hurried over as Lita croaked, "My throat."

Fred jumped from his chair. "What if she's having an allergic reaction to the lobster?"

"She said she hadn't eaten it before." Arnie wrung his hands. "Her tongue could swell and block her airway."

"Someone call 911," Ina yelled, yet she stood stock still, paralyzed with fright.

Catherine was about to grab her phone from her pocket when Lita's coughing got more guttural. Ina went pale as her sister's cheeks began turning purple.

Thinking fast, Catherine shoved Lita's chair, ramming her ribs against the dining table with all her might. Then she gave her an almighty slap on the back. Suddenly, Lita hacked up a sprig of chive from the soup onto the table. Once her breathing was restored to normal, Ina clutched her sister closely, and relief washed over everyone.

"Damn garnish," Lita grumbled, wiping her mouth. "What's the point of spices anyway?"

Arnie bristled but held his tongue.

"Amen to that." Fred mopped sweat from his brow, palpably grateful the crisis had been averted.

Ina tore herself away from Lita's side to go to Catherine. She stood before her for a long, awkward moment, bumbling over whether to shake Catherine's hand or pat her on the shoulder, then ultimately embraced her in a hard bear hug.

"You saved my sister. I can't thank you enough."

She wouldn't let go, and soon enough, Catherine couldn't either.

Eventually, Ina stiffened, embarrassed by her outpouring, then released Catherine and straightened her clothes. She straightened Catherine's clothes, too, as if doing her a favor.

Bashfully, she began, "When we were girls, we were swimming in a pool. I was supposed to be looking after Lita. Be a good older sister. Take care of her. Turned my head for a few minutes and she was gone. She had slipped under."

"I don't remember swimming." Lita looked around plainly, like the story was a pleasant memory from the past rather than a horrific trauma, one that humbled Ina.

"A lifeguard found her, dragged her out. She wasn't breathing for a minute. One long minute. That . . . changed her. Such a small thing can change everything."

Lita smiled. She had no clue what Ina was driving at. Everyone else did.

"My fault." Ina carried the responsibility like it was a wound that ached every day of her life, or so it now seemed to Catherine. "That's why I take care of her. Because I didn't when I should have."

"I like swimming," Lita announced. "We like swimming, don't we?"

"We do," Ina told her sister, patting her shoulder sweetly.

Lita's happiness had become Ina's reason for living after her sister almost died. Catherine saw the bond in their eyes. Instead of envying it, she aspired to it.

"You're nobody 'til somebody loves you," Dean Martin sang merrily.

Catherine checked her phone. She hadn't assigned that ringtone to anyone besides her mother, but because it read Private Number, the tone defaulted.

"Hello?"

"Is this Maria?" a male voice asked.

She was about to tell the caller they had the wrong number. Then the name clicked.

It was one of the men from Sunset Marina. Aware everybody at the table was listening, Catherine answered neutrally.

"This is she."

"Your dad's gonna be one happy camper."

Catherine knew it had to be the lawyer rather than his distrustful friend, who would never have used the phrase "happy camper."

"We'll have the Hemingway boat for you by tomorrow night."

"Okay, great," she answered with forced cheer.

"Let's meet at the dock, and we'll sort things out there."

All eyes on Catherine, she replied, "Excellent. Bye."

In a daze, she hung up. Ina stood at her sister's side while Fred and Arnie looked at Catherine expectantly.

Despite everything she had done to orchestrate the sale of Robert's boat, she simply couldn't bring herself to go through with it. Now that Catherine had his book, she didn't have to. But how was she going to get out of the underhanded agreement she had struck with the men from the marina?

Catherine could only think of one way to sabotage the deal.

"Listen," she announced. "As if this evening hasn't been strange enough, it's about to get a whole lot stranger."

"Lord in heaven and Liberace save us," Arnie muttered.

"You." She pointed to Ina. "You owe me for those baseless accusations of theft and drug addiction."

Ina shrugged as if to say *Fair enough.*

"And you." Her sister was next in Catherine's sights. "You owe me for trying to steal the one datable guy I've met in ages."

Lita tried to hide behind her curls. "I couldn't help it. He's just so handsome."

"*So* handsome," Arnie concurred emphatically.

"Fine," Fred moaned. "We all agree. He's hot."

"Meh," Ina muttered as the rest gazed at her in disbelief.

"As for you two." Catherine gestured at Fred and Arnie on either end of the table. "You don't owe me a thing. You've made a hellish trip into the most amazing vacation I could have dreamed of. However, I need your help too."

"Count us in," Fred told her as Arnie agreed, game to pitch in.

"I suppose it would be the proper thing to do," Ina huffed, then elbowed her sister to chime in.

"Sure." Lita was willing.

"Tomorrow we're . . . going somewhere," Catherine said obliquely.

"Sightseeing?" Ina asked, hopeful.

"Nope."

"Shopping?" Lita inquired.

"Not exactly."

"Then what is it that we'll be doing?" Fred folded his arms.

Catherine wouldn't have the benefit of a memorial. There would be no church service, no condolences, no sympathy, no laying Robert to rest. She had spent so many years believing he was in the wrong. This was Catherine's chance to pay her final respects and prove him right.

"Honoring my brother the only way I know how."

35

Sleep evaded Catherine that night. She tossed and turned, unable to shut off the many thoughts battling in her brain. As she nuzzled her head into the pillow, she felt the hard corners of Robert's book below yet wouldn't move it.

Moonlight streamed in through the lace drapes. On her nightstand, the bedside clock read close to 2:00 a.m. The pit in her stomach wasn't from hunger, but Catherine padded down to the kitchen anyway.

Fred was emptying the dishwasher in his robe, which was also a Hawaiian print, same as his shirts. This pattern was surprisingly sedate, the colors pale and muted, as if his normally sizzling hues were too much in the mornings, even for him.

"Did I wake you?" he asked as Catherine poked her head in.

"No, I couldn't conk out. Where's Arnie? Asleep?"

"In New York."

"What?"

"Via the DVD player," Fred explained. "He's watching *Arsenic and Old Lace* for the billionth time. Refers to it as 'his sojourn to the city.' Cary Grant always gets him out of a mood."

"That doesn't sound like a feel-good flick."

"It's a dark comedy about a man who discovers his dotty old aunts have been bumping off lonely old bachelors by poisoning their wine. Then his uncle buries them in the basement."

"Cheery."

"Watching the characters poison people will make him glad our guest only gagged on a hunk of chives."

"Is he really upset?"

"Lita's choking fit. Your brother's letter. Even a tiny disruption throws Arnie into a terrible tizzy."

Catherine wasn't so different. Each of her carefully laid plans had been unraveled or bungled or upended. She couldn't seem to get much right.

Lying hadn't leveled out her problems. It had made them worse.

"It wasn't my intent to spoil the dinner party. Or to start a fight with Travis. Okay, the second part was kind of deliberate."

Fred was somberly washing off a baking tray, scrubbing it with steel wool as if he wanted to scour away any memory of the evening's calamities.

"You're afraid the guests won't come back, aren't you?"

"Who says I want them to?"

Catherine was taken aback to hear him being candid.

"I can only be sociable for so long. It's exhausting," he confided.

"You mean doing the right thing is exhausting."

Fred grimaced. "Yup."

As someone who'd spent her life trying to do that, Catherine was tired too. Taking the easy way out wasn't any simpler. To her, that was a backhanded kind of comfort. It meant her efforts weren't in vain.

Being the bigger, better person might have been frustrating, but in the end, it was worth it.

"Need help with those dishes?" she offered.

Fred glanced at the teetering heaps stacked throughout the kitchen. "How can I say no?"

She joined him at the sink and pitched in, rinsing out the pots from dinner. Catherine was about to take a scrub brush to a frying pan when Fred grabbed her arm protectively.

"You can only use the foam sponge on nonstick pans. Arnie will have an embolism if there's a single scratch."

"I'll see your scratched pot and raise you a call to the governor's office."

"The what . . . ?"

"My mom phoned them to report that her room at the memory-care facility wasn't being properly cleaned. She wanted the staff investigated by Immigration. And Homeland Security. And the CIA. She said she suspected the place was bugged with recording devices. Suffice it to say neither the nursing home nor the governor's office were amused."

Fred tried not to laugh. "If it's any consolation, Arnie lines the food up by expiration date in the fridge. He also organizes our sock drawer by the size the socks make when they're balled up into pairs. And he won't buy a carton of eggs if each egg isn't the same shade of white."

It was Catherine's turn to stifle a snicker. "That's . . . endearing."

"Isn't it?" Fred made a face.

"One time, my mom insisted that there was an intruder in the room in the middle of the night. Woke everybody in the facility up. Had the staff and residents in a panic. Turns out she had locked herself out of her room and mistook the news anchor on TV for the intruder."

Soon, both Catherine and Fred were giggling, dish-soap bubbles wafting in the air between them. For as awful as those incidents had been, and as much as they scared her, if she didn't laugh, the other option was to cry. She didn't want to cry anymore.

Her mother was who she was. Instead of resenting her mom's eccentricities, Catherine decided she ought to embrace them, crazy voicemails, repetitive text messages, wild updates, and all. She would rather have her mother around and acting the way she did than the alternative.

As they stood together at the sink, Fred playfully bumped Catherine with his hip. "I was rougher on you than I should have been."

"That's okay. Usually, I'm roughest on myself. You gave me a day off."

He flicked water at her lightheartedly. "Travis would be lucky to have you."

"Yeah, well, I don't think he's in the market."

"He did say he wasn't married."

"He didn't say he wanted to be."

"Do you?"

"When every man in your life disappoints you, it's hard to trust any of them. Especially one who intentionally lied to you."

"Didn't you lie to him a little, too, about the boat?"

"That's not the same."

"Are you sure?"

The more she thought about it, the more she realized her lies to buy time may have been worse than Travis's. He had been trying to help her. She had been trying to help herself.

"See that? It's me not giving you side-eye." Fred glanced away, then looked sidelong at her, then away again.

"You are literally giving me the side-eye."

"Well, now you have two new men in your life—me and Arnie. And I'd let Ina make a quilt out of my beloved Hawaiian shirts before I'd break your heart."

Touched, she smiled. "Don't give her any ideas."

The dishes done, Catherine retreated to her bedroom and crawled under the covers. She wasn't the least bit tired. In the moonlight, the lace curtains were aglow, and she could make out everything in her room perfectly, including the stack of Robert's books sitting on the dresser.

Catherine got up and thumbed through them in search of *For Whom the Bell Tolls*, the novel that starred her brother's namesake. She carried the book over to the window and read the flap copy.

It said that Hemingway had journeyed to Spain to cover the civil insurrection for the North American Newspaper Alliance, and three years later, he had completed the greatest novel to emerge from that era—the story of Robert Jordan, a young American in the International Brigades attached to an antifascist guerilla unit in the mountains. Perhaps her brother had envisioned himself running off in search of his own heroic journey.

According to the book jacket, the novel told of loyalty and courage, love and defeat, the tragic death of an ideal. While Catherine had shunned her alter ego, she imagined Robert wanting to emulate his and live up to the moniker, striving for the impossible. He was real. Robert Jordan was imaginary.

Characters always had the author on their side. In life, people had to create their own happy endings.

Catherine got into bed, then settled under the covers with *For Whom the Bell Tolls*, eager to see what Robert had left her. Suddenly, two folded pieces of paper fell from behind the back cover.

She squinted at the pages, which were stapled together. At the top was the name of the boat, *Pauline's Escape*. Beneath it was a lengthy list of the previous owners dating back decades, almost to the year the boat was built.

A small hand-drawn star stood out in the margin. Beside it was the name Franklin R. Moran.

That was her father.

Astounded, Catherine flipped on the bedside lamp to get a closer look. After a second, her eyes adjusted, and she was able to read every letter clearly. It was him, all right. Not Francis or Frank. Her dad's full name was Franklin, and his middle name was Reginald.

"Catherine will get it when she gets it," Catherine said, recalling Robert's note to her.

Relief mixed with a swell of desolation. Her brother wasn't a chump who'd fallen for a long-standing Key West scheme. He had found something that had belonged to their father.

How he had tracked the boat down, Catherine couldn't know. The point was that he had and that he had bought the vessel to restore it. Not because it was Ernest Hemingway's but because it was a memento of their dad's. Despite the terrible falling out, Catherine imagined he yearned to be close to their father the way she had yearned to be close to Robert, the longing more powerful than the pain.

Catherine clutched the document to her chest.

Robert's departure had been a turning point in her life. Their father's departure was the turning point in Robert's. Each of them had coped with the loss differently. Maybe not correctly or responsibly, yet they had dealt with it the best they could.

Sorrow spun logic inside out. Mourning addled the mind. The anguish of missing a loved one made people irrational. Catherine had come to the island to dispose of the only thing her brother had willed her. That was nothing if not foolish and absurd. In the lamplight, with the list in her hands, a star beside her father's name, she saw that clearly at last.

For Robert Jordan, his story ended with the tragic death of his ideals. That was fiction. Catherine would make sure at least one of the real Robert's ideals didn't die with him.

36

Catherine was convinced her plan would work. However, persuading everybody else was a tall order. She had gathered them in front of the Abbott House the next morning, birds atwitter in the trees, promising to spell out the entire plan in detail.

"We're going where?" Ina groaned. Her braids were frizzy from sleeping on them.

"And we're doing what?" Lita's skin had broken out from the heavy makeup. A pair of blue-eyed Siamese cats stared out from her shirt, as though they fervently wanted to know too.

Fred folded his arms. "Who are we supposed to be?"

"Tourists?" Arnie asked.

Before she could explain, Kenny pulled up in his cab.

"You rang?" he hollered through the open windows.

"Okay, everybody in." Catherine herded them toward the taxi.

"All of us?" Fred asked. "In one car?"

"It'll be . . . cozy, but we'll fit," she assured him.

"Welcome, welcome. In you go!" Kenny coaxed them. "Hospitality is making your guests feel at home. Even when you wish they were."

"You need that printed on an apron," Fred grumbled as he squeezed next to Ina while Arnie wedged himself beside Lita.

Catherine closed the doors, sandwiching them inside, then hopped into the front with Kenny. From behind the plastic partition, the four of them were squashed together sardine-style, limbs entwined. The Jimmy Buffett bobblehead appeared to be quivering at the sight.

"The marina, please," she told Kenny.

He snuck a glimpse in the mirror. "I'd say buckle your seat belts, but that could get kinky."

"This puts the *ug* in 'snug,'" Arnie wheezed as Lita's meaty leg pinned him against the armrest.

"Step on it," Fred commanded, his face compressed against the window because Ina wouldn't share an inch of space.

"Are you going to tell us what's going on?" Arnie asked.

"The four of you are going to bid against each other to buy a boat."

Lita clucked her tongue. "That sounds expensive."

"You're not really buying it," Catherine informed her.

Ina dug into her fanny pack for a stick of lip balm, which she applied liberally, elbowing Fred in the ribs with every move. "Then why are we bidding?"

"So I don't have to sell it."

"I don't understand," Lita stated.

"I think I do," Fred lisped, his cheek mashed against the glass.

"Then you can explain it to your wife, played by Ina. Arnie, you're going to be 'married' to Lita."

Objections erupted from the back seat. Kenny closed the sliding partition, putting a lid on the noise. "Want me to hit the brakes to shut 'em up?"

Catherine waved him off and reopened the partition. "I need two couples to make this believable."

"We already are a couple," Arnie reminded her.

"Can you two pretend to be in love?" she asked the sisters.

They gave one another uncomfortable sidelong glances. Then Ina grabbed Fred's hand to hold. Lita followed suit, clasping Arnie's.

"I now pronounce you temporary husbands and wives."

"We are *not* kissing our brides," Fred declared.

When the cab finally pulled into the parking lot, Catherine turned to Kenny somberly. "Would you mind staying? To keep an eye out in case this goes south?"

He nodded gravely. "Key West may be called 'south of normal,' but this scheme isn't even on the map."

Arnie tapped Catherine on the shoulder from outside the car, reaching through his open window into hers. "Um, hello, Mademoiselle Mastermind? Why is it that we need a bodyguard for this recital of our ad hoc repertory troupe?"

Kenny shot her a fidgety glance as Catherine attempted to dream up a reply.

"Uh, it's because . . ."

He answered for her. "The men she made the deal with aren't exactly what you would call upstanding citizens."

"They're criminals?" Lita asked fretfully.

"Let's just say they have questionable pasts," Catherine replied.

Ina tsk-tsked, saying, "I once saw an episode on *Dateline* about a dismembered—"

"Not now, *pumpkin*," Fred urged.

A serious mood gripped the passengers, including Catherine.

Kenny came to a stop; then everyone in the back seat piled out, thankful to extricate their arms and legs from the cramped quarters and breathe normally again. Catherine got out her wallet to pay. Kenny declined the money.

"I hope you know what you're doing."

"That makes two of us."

As he pulled over to park, Catherine directed Fred, Arnie, Ina, and Lita to Robert's boat, saying, "I'll meet you there in a minute."

They each hesitantly assumed their roles, linking hands with their new partners.

"Come, darling," Arnie told Lita, who sauntered along the dock with him.

"Yes, let's get this over with." Fred gestured for Ina to lead, and she took off, ferrying him behind her at a brisk clip.

Once they were gone, Catherine composed herself and entered the bait shop, heart racing.

The show must go on.

At the register, the clerk with the buzz cut had his nose buried in the latest issue of *Salt Water Sportsman*. He sat up attentively when he saw Catherine approach.

"Please tell Vic to meet me at Mr. Moran's boat," she announced pertly.

Catherine was out the door again as quickly as her legs could carry her. She had to beat Vic to the boat if this was going to work.

The gang was waiting for her at the end of the dock, gaping at the boat in astonishment.

"We're supposed to be bidding on . . . this floating disaster?" Arnie asked dubiously.

The dilapidated fishing trawler no longer looked that beat up to Catherine. The chipped paint added to the character. The barnacles speckling the sides gave the boat an honest sense of history. The creaky, splintered masts with threadbare nets were a nautical version of wind chimes. To her, the disrepair now read as charm. Like most things, it came down to a person's point of view.

Thanks to her brother, Catherine's had changed.

"Follow my lead and say as little as possible."

"Is that one of the bad guys?" Lita asked timidly, motioning at the man who was walking toward them.

"No," Catherine asserted. "That's the guy you need to outbid. We have to get to forty. Fast."

"Forty thousand?" Lita audibly gulped.

"That's far too much for this floating kitty-litter box," Ina declared.

"Okay, act natural," Catherine announced.

She panned the row of them. Ina had an iron grip on Fred's arm. Meanwhile, Lita was glued to Arnie's side, while he was blatantly ignoring her, nose wrinkled at the seagull droppings stippling the stern.

"On second thought, don't. Just be yourselves."

Vic lumbered up in his heavy work boots, taking in the scene. "Who do we have here?"

Who, indeed?

Catherine hadn't come up with names for her pretend couples and groped for an answer.

"This is Mr. and Mrs. Higgins," she said, motioning at Fred and Ina. Then she presented Arnie and Lita. "These are the Navarros."

The group gazed at her in bewilderment. Those were the names of her mother's neighbors at the facility. They were all Catherine could come up with on the fly.

"They're also interested in buying this boat."

Agitated, Vic pulled her aside. "I thought we had an arrangement?"

"These bids came in late last night. I don't know how word got out that the vessel was for sale. I certainly didn't mention our agreement to anyone," she lied, planting a seed of doubt in Vic's head. She could see his wheels spinning. "The Higginses here have offered twenty-two."

Vic stunned her by saying, "I can meet that."

"The Navarros are at twenty-five."

That stalled him.

"Thirty," Ina stated staunchly.

Fred's eyes bulged. "Honey, we agreed—"

The door to the wheelhouse opened, and Travis came out, shirtless, carrying a stack of boxes. Lita and Arnie were instantly distracted by his physique. Fred cleared his throat to get them to stop staring. Arnie pretended to avert his eyes, while Lita twirled a lock of her hair shyly.

Travis's gaze fell squarely on Catherine. "What's going on?"

"Sir," she said, affecting authority. "I'm going to have to ask you to stay out of this. It's . . . business. Insurance company business," she hinted to tip him off.

Catching on, Travis put down the boxes, as if preparing to watch the fireworks. "Far be it from me to intrude on company affairs."

"We'll pay thirty-five if he comes with the boat," Lita piped up.

"Snookums," Arnie trilled, only to realize how effeminate he sounded. "Sweetness," he tried in a deeper voice. "That's a steep price tag."

"Thirty-eight," Ina retorted, a sisterly competition setting in.

Not one to be outshone, Arnie snapped, "Thirty-nine."

"Forty!" Ina shouted, determined to win.

"This is way too rich for my blood." Defeated, Vic hung his head, bowing out of the race and dialing his cell phone. Catherine could guess who he was calling.

"Going once? Going twice?"

"It's obvious who wears the pants in that family," Arnie muttered to his fake wife about Fred and Ina.

"Sold!"

"Yes!" Ina threw her arms in the air, then grabbed Fred, picked him up, and spun him around jubilantly.

"Whoa, honey. Whoa," he stammered. "Or I'm going to need a Dramamine."

"What are you smiling about?" Vic spat at Travis, who was grinning at him self-righteously. "It's not your boat."

"I'm smiling because it's not yours either."

37

A strong wind kicked up off the bay, rocking moored boats and buffeting flags. It was as though it were whisking away the lies, machinations, and confusion to wipe the slate clean. After Vic stormed off, Catherine gave Ina a hug, startling her.

"If I didn't know better, I'd think you were hitting on my wife," Fred quipped.

"Thank you," Catherine said. She glanced at Travis. "All of you."

"Maybe somebody needs help unpacking," Arnie hinted.

Still besotted, Lita took a fervent step forward.

He held her back. "Not you, snookums."

"I can stay?" Travis asked, leery.

"Well, I can't leave my boat here unattended. And it does need *a lot* more refurbishing. You cover the dock fees and the insurance—then we've got a deal."

This was the last time Catherine hoped to be uttering that phrase.

"Can you two please just go on a date already," Ina moaned, her braids flapping with the breeze. "Sheesh."

"Such a romantic, this bride of mine." Fred sighed.

"I suppose it couldn't hurt to treat my new landlord to dinner," Travis conceded.

Arnie beamed at Fred excitedly.

"How about lunch? My flight back to New York leaves in a few hours."

"That'll work."

Arnie, Lita, and Ina were staring excitedly, as if watching a movie unfold.

"We'll see you back at the inn." Fred ushered them away as they waved their goodbyes. Arnie gave her an enthusiastic thumbs-up over his shoulder, while Fred had to tug him toward Kenny's waiting cab.

Travis held out his hand to Catherine to help her onboard from the dock. When she took it, she felt the warmth again like before. It cut through the wind, stoking her heart.

He opened the door to the wheelhouse, inviting her in.

Waves lapped at the boat's hull as Travis emptied a cardboard box and retrieved a frying pan. The lulling sound of the water was soothing, the rocking motion reassuring, yet Catherine was slightly twitchy. She had a seat at the built-in booth, unsure what to say now that she and Travis were alone.

"I hope grilled cheese will do." He took a loaf of bread and a stick of butter from the small galley fridge.

"It's one of my favorites."

"Great. Because there's not much else to choose from. I was about to pack the last of the food when the gang showed up." He pulled a knife from the same box, sliced some butter, and spread it on the bread.

"About that. I can explain."

"No worries. Everything worked out in the end. It is what it is."

There was another cliché that got under Catherine's skin, a phrase so simple it was almost offensive, implying the facts were too plain to ignore, too obvious to be misunderstood.

"But this *isn't* what it is. It hasn't been from the start."

Confused, Travis turned from the two-burner cooktop, where the bread was already sizzling in the pan, as he added the cheese. "What do you mean?"

After the litany of lies she had told and her various schemes—from pretending she didn't have the legal documents to pulling her version of *Roman Holiday* on him—Catherine had to consolidate her thoughts.

"Look, we've both said and done things that we didn't mean."

"Agreed."

"Maybe we should start fresh. Put the last couple of days behind us."

"Works for me." He finished the sandwiches and placed each on a folded paper towel. "Sorry. Already packed the plates."

"Not a problem. I ate almost every meal of my childhood on a napkin. Robert hated doing dishes, so we'd use paper plates, empty pizza boxes, or our hands."

The ordinary memory took on a tender significance to Catherine in light of what had transpired. For years, she had fixated on what she and her brother hadn't shared. Focusing on what they had done together and what they did have in common reframed the pictures of the past. The memories didn't all miraculously turn rosy. However, many of them weren't as dismal as Catherine had perceived them to be.

"Before we call a do-over," Travis said, "I wanted to tell you that I may not have known your brother as well as either you or I would have wanted, but from what I saw firsthand, he was an upstanding guy."

That wasn't how she had seen Robert. Catherine owed it to him to try. Though her brother had passed, it wasn't too late.

"I was drinking too much when we ran into each other. He could tell. That's why he asked me to work on the boat. So I'd have something to keep me from drinking. The last drop of alcohol I had was with him at the bar that night."

Travis got two bottles of water for them and set them on the table resoundingly to underscore the point.

"Most people go into the military to serve their country and because they have a sense of duty. But also because it levels the playing field. It didn't matter how much money you had or how smart you were. That wasn't what you were judged on. You could remake yourself from the ground up. That's one of the reasons I joined. I would never be as rich or successful as my father. I didn't want his life. Or his judgment. I wanted a fresh start," Travis confided. "Your brother didn't bring up his past, but you could sense he always had something on his mind, like a weight on his back. Only he never let on what it was."

"Our dad left when he was seventeen. Robert never got over it. Then he left too. And I never got over him."

Travis absorbed the admission, seeming wounded on her behalf. "Makes sense now."

Catherine debated whether to tell him what Robert's letter had said, then thought better of it. It was her brother's story, his alone to share.

"I don't think he thought I knew," Travis said.

"Knew what?"

"That he was gay. Not that I would have cared. But given where we met, that wasn't something you discussed. Not in our generation, at least. I'm pretty sure that's why he kept things so close to the vest with me. Still a master poker player. Never showed his hand."

"I didn't know."

Travis studied her, trying to temper his response. "Would you have cared?"

"No. All I ever wanted was for him to come back." She took a bite of her sandwich, and it tasted like home. "Good grilled cheese."

Travis was quietly gazing at her, as if memorizing her face. "Thanks."

"We don't ever get what we want, do we?"

"Rarely," he sighed. "But sometimes. And those times are worth waiting for."

A calmness bloomed between them. The brittle spats and back-handed insults seemed so childish to Catherine now. Both of them had been too guarded for their own good. At last, she could be upfront. She could be herself.

"I realize I was prying into your business with the stuff about your father," she added. "Was what Vic said about him cutting you off true?"

"He's done it again and again, vowed to write me out of his will and his world. But I was never interested in his fortune. First time was my senior year of high school. He wanted me to be a lawyer, follow in his footsteps, become a politician. I told him I didn't want to go to college, that I wanted to be a carpenter. That did *not* go over well. He gave me a choice: get a university education, go into the service, or pack my bags. I went with door number two. We've been on and off ever since. He's almost ninety, and he still treats me like I live under his roof, like I owe him for every breath I've ever taken. That's who you heard me arguing with on the phone the other day. We have a ten-minute max before we're at each other's throats."

Where Travis's father had intimidated him and threatened to kick him out, Robert had encouraged his talents and given him a place to stay. It was no wonder Travis remained loyal to him. No stranger to familial friction herself, Catherine could empathize.

"Is that why you went to South America? To get away from your dad?"

"From him. From everything. You can't figure yourself out when somebody keeps forcing you to be something else."

Robert hadn't forced her to do anything. However, he had made Catherine into the person she was by default.

"I'm the last one who should be giving advice on this subject," Catherine said, "but no matter what he does, he's your dad. And he's still around. There's time to make things better between you two."

Travis nodded and continued to eat. Sitting across from him at the table, Catherine was no longer nervous. What she was saying to him was the truth. That she was comfortable with.

"I can't speak for Bobby, only for me," Travis told her. "But when you don't like who you've become, you don't think anybody else will either. You think you'll disappoint them. You keep people away to protect them, not you."

"I get that."

Catherine finally did. Though she wished things had been different, at last she understood her brother.

"I didn't lie about Bobby's nickname or about what went down in the mess hall. He really did help that guy who dropped his tray."

"I believe you."

That was the sort of thing her brother would have done. He wasn't as much of an enigma as Catherine had built him up to be. Robert had been gone for decades, yet he hadn't changed. Neither had she. She had always loved him and always would.

"What time's your flight?"

She checked her watch. "Soon. I've got to be going."

After Catherine finished the last of her sandwich, Travis walked her out to the rear deck. The sun was hidden behind a lone cloud. Within moments it was free again, shining down unfettered.

"There is a minor tidbit I didn't fess up about," he admitted.

Catherine's face fell. "You're joking?"

"Bobby did tell me one other thing about you. He said, 'If you ever meet my sister, you'll hit it off. You two couldn't be more alike.' I think that's why he mailed me the letter. So we would have to meet."

Catherine grinned. "By that he meant stubborn. We should probably both be insulted."

Travis smiled as well. "I've been called worse."

As he helped her onto the dock, she glanced back. "Say, did you come up with that name for the boat, *Same Ship, Different Day*?"

"Yeah," he confessed, ruefully. "It's awful. Bobby told me to pick something, anything to cover the old one."

"It's a new day. How about a new name?"

"Got any ideas?" Travis asked.

"Not yet. I'll let you know when I do."

He grabbed a scrap of paper from his packing boxes as well as a pen and wrote down his phone number. Then he dug the pelican statue out and gave it to her along with the paper. "I look forward to it."

"I can't take this, Travis. It was a gift."

"Still is, Catherine."

She clutched the pelican to her chest and walked along the dock, aware that she was leaving behind the one man she had ever genuinely been attracted to, a man who'd cared for her brother almost as much as she did. Nevertheless, a solid, hefty peace was welling inside her.

Catherine had learned that just because you weren't with someone, that didn't mean you wouldn't reconnect somehow. If Robert had taught her anything, it was that there was no distance in the heart.

38

Key West might have been famous for its tropical vistas, but a marina parking lot probably wasn't one of them. Yet to Catherine, it was worth memorializing.

She took in the view of Robert's boat, snapping photos on her phone. Unlike the sunrise at the Southernmost Point on her first day on the island, when she had missed taking pictures, this was a moment she could capture and hold on to.

Catherine texted Kenny to pick her up, then realized that he had been right. There was a secret to the sunrises in Key West. The difference between the truth and a lie had nothing to do with the facts. It was how the truth felt versus a lie. The truth only helped if it made her feel better.

Finally, it did.

Kenny arrived quickly, melodic jazz wafting from the windows. Catherine got in and pinched his shoulder appreciatively through the opening in the plastic partition, saying, "Thank you. You were great today."

"Me? I heard you put on a tour de force act."

She bowed from the back seat. "It's a one-time performance. Lying is a lot harder than I thought it would be."

"A clear conscience is a sign of a fuzzy memory. Smarter to stick to the facts."

"I second that," Catherine agreed. "Can we swing by a souvenir shop?"

"Given what you've been through, I'm surprised you want to remember this trip."

"The souvenirs aren't for me," she explained. "I couldn't forget this vacation if I tried."

"That's Key West for you. Excess in moderation."

Kenny swung over to Duval Street, where a flock of souvenir shops competed for tourists' attention, every window cluttered with a cavalcade of bric-a-brac and raunchy T-shirts. He double-parked in front of the biggest one.

"Eyes on the prize," Kenny warned. "We've only got an hour to get you to the airport, and boutiques like these can be a quagmire of irresistibly useless crap. When my wife goes in, I need a lasso and the promise of a foot massage to get her out. Don't get stuck."

"Got it."

Catherine jogged inside one of the shops and instantly discovered that Kenny wasn't exaggerating.

The store was a sprawling oasis of plastic ferns, rattan furniture, fishing-inspired ornaments, and objects of every variety encrusted in seashells. From the piranha-shaped pizza cutters to the watering cans made to resemble cows with holes in the udders, each strangely mesmerizing item was the shopping equivalent of quicksand.

She found novelty mugs for Ina and Lita that featured cats in bikinis, which read **KEY WEST IS CLAW-SOME!** Next, she grabbed a pair of dangly earrings for Gloria, along with a coffee tumbler that featured an image of a clock with palm trees as the arms that read **WHEN YOU'RE ON KEY WEST TIME, IT'S ALWAYS FIVE O'CLOCK SOMEWHERE.** Then she picked out a set of pink flamingo salt and pepper shakers. The birds were wearing identical Key West shirts, their necks lovingly entwined. Catherine hurried to the register to pay, then dashed out to the idling taxi.

"That place was wild."

"Close to perfect, far from normal," Kenny intoned, hitting the gas. "There's a reason that's our official motto."

"That's also going to be the official motto of this trip."

"Glad to hear it," Kenny told her with grin.

Seeing the city whiz by through the cab's windows gave her a twinge of longing, like she already missed the place. To Catherine, the gift store had been a microcosm of the island itself, full of wondrous natural creations as well as weird delights, something amazing to see wherever one looked. She had only experienced a fraction of what Key West had to offer, yet she felt full from the trip, as if she had gotten what she had come for and more. Although Catherine wasn't looking forward to returning home, she had the reassuring sense that Key West wasn't going anywhere, so it was okay if she was.

"Do you have a notepad?" she asked Kenny.

"Sure." He handed it to her. "Leaving thank-you notes for the cast of your production?"

"Sort of."

In the cups for Ina and Lita, she left notes urging them to go online and praise the Abbott House to offset the nasty remarks other guests had previously posted.

The one to Lita read "Your cat is going to ignore you if you can't say something kind."

The note for Ina said "I saw on *Dateline* that it's the polite thing to do."

By the time she had finished writing, Kenny was pulling up in front of the bed-and-breakfast. He glided to a stop. "I know you want to say your goodbyes, but you gotta hustle or you'll miss your plane. Unless that's what you're bucking for?"

Appealing as that idea sounded, she replied, "I'll be quick."

Catherine bolted in the front door, ran up the stairs, deposited the gifts outside the sisters' room, grabbed her bags with Robert's books tucked securely inside, and was pounding down the stairs when she found Fred and Arnie at the bottom, waiting for her. Their dog, Truman, was at their feet.

"Well?" Fred inquired.

"How did it go with Travis?" Arnie demanded. "I've been on pins and needles. Spill!"

"Nice. It was nice. Except he lives here and I'm in Manhattan. It's not as though it could have been like *Roman Holiday*, where we wind up together."

Arnie cocked his head quizzically. "That's not how the movie ends, doll. You didn't stay to see it. Audrey Hepburn and Gregory Peck don't become a couple. They're from two different worlds. A match made in heaven doesn't always work on earth."

Catherine hadn't expected that.

If Audrey and Gregory couldn't make it, what were her chances?

"Then this is pretty much like *Roman Holiday*," she replied, shielding her dismay. "I'm going my way, and he's staying here. Anyhow, I have to catch my flight, so I need to settle my bill."

"It's on the house," Fred stated. "Or rather, it's on the inn."

The touching gesture was almost too much for Catherine.

"What about your roof? You need the money."

"Consider it a gift." Arnie squeezed her shoulder. "We needed you more than we need that stuff. You reminded us why we opened this B and B. To have amazing people in our lives, if only for a few days."

She blotted a tear. "I'm glad I already posted an amazing review for you online. And don't be surprised when I email you guys a comprehensive—okay, exceedingly lengthy—business plan about how to generate more revenue by optimizing your location, your amenities, your food, and your customer service. If you follow it, you should be able to afford the repairs in a few months—then you'll be generating pure profit."

"That's an answer to our prayers!" Arnie exclaimed.

"It's my job. I figured I could help you the way you helped me."

Fred gave her a tight hug; then Arnie wrapped his arms around them both as Truman wagged his tail.

"Even the dog is going to miss you." Fred sniffled. "And he hates everybody."

A horn honked. Kenny was signaling from outside. Catherine was halfway out the door when she called back, "Oh, wait. These are for you."

She pulled the pink flamingo salt and pepper shakers from her purse.

"They're adorable." Arnie admired them, then read the inscription on the backs of their matching shirts: "Birds of a feather. Meant to be together forever."

"They're very thoughtful," Fred added.

"They're you guys," Catherine told them. "Same outfits, different spices."

She blew them both a kiss, then ran outside and jumped in the cab.

Kenny hit the accelerator before she had even shut the door. Watching the Abbott House recede as they drove onward was tough. Catherine felt Kenny monitoring her in the rearview mirror.

"Don't cry, sugar."

"After a few days in paradise, the thought of going back to the cold and back to work would reduce anybody to tears."

"'Cold' and 'work': two of my least favorite terms."

"Think you could get me a job driving a taxi here instead?"

"Yeah, though I doubt it'd be your cup of tea. Sitting on your rump ten hours a day, dealing with crappy tippers and crazy people. I mean, colorful characters," he teased in reference to her.

"Sounds almost identical to my current job. Minus the tips."

They cut across the island, passing as many sites that were familiar to Catherine as those that weren't. They soon arrived at the airport. The mural of the Conch Republic flag greeted her, telling tourists where they had been and what they were leaving.

"Everybody has the same aspiration." Kenny sighed. "Visit Key West, then return someday to make a life here. A perpetual vacation. The island has that effect on people. They ditch what they know and come in droves. Heck, I'm one of them."

"If you did it and other people do it, maybe I could too."

The concept of upending her existence in the city to carve a new path here felt like a total fantasy. Pie in the sky. A pipe dream.

"Why not?" Kenny told her as he parked at the curb. "To steal ideas from one person is plagiarism. To steal from many, that's research."

Catherine cracked up.

"What's so funny?" he asked.

Instead of examining everything that wasn't working, keeping a tally of what might go wrong, and cataloguing what she had missed out on, Catherine decided she ought to count her blessings. She had to stop researching life and start living it.

"Nothing," Catherine said. "And everything."

After paying him twice the fare as a tip, she leaned through the plastic partition and gave Kenny a peck on the cheek.

"Look me up next time you're in town, kiddo. That is, if you're coming back."

It was part statement, part question, as though he didn't want to get sentimental and ask her directly.

Catherine wanted to come back, only she wasn't sure how or when. "Where there's a will, there's a way."

"There was a will, and you were in it. Next time, just come to Key West for the reasons everybody else does."

"Which are?"

"To get drunk, to get tan, and to have fun. You've earned it."

"Yeah," Catherine agreed. "I have."

39

The flight home was packed. The general mood onboard was gloomy, like nobody wanted to go. Catherine had an aisle seat, and the middle-aged man who wound up beside her had a Margaritaville tank top on and tan lines around his eyes from his sunglasses, the contrast in skin color making him appear wide awake, although he had dozed off within minutes of buckling in.

Other passengers filed in, wearing commemorative shirts and hats, their faces beet red from last-ditch efforts to soak up the sun, most of them sluggish, in no hurry to return to New York. Nobody was looking forward to trading this island for the next, including Catherine.

Her cell phone rang in her purse, and she rushed to get it, trying not to wake the guy next to her.

It was the same number from last night, the man in the polo from the clubhouse. She braced herself.

"Bad news, Maria," he said. "Somebody else bought the boat before we could get our hands on it for you."

"Aw, bummer," she groaned, feigning disappointment.

"We can find you some more options if you're still in the market. Plenty o' boats for sale in Key West."

"No, that boat was special."

"What are you gonna do? Everybody loves Hemingway. I'm sure your dad will understand."

"I think he will," she answered knowingly.

Catherine switched to airplane mode for takeoff and tried wrapping her brain around the fact that she had pretended to want to buy a boat that she already owned for her father, who had already owned it.

"Only in Key West." She sighed.

Soon the plane was in the air. Through the windows, Catherine saw palm trees blurring into a green smear against a backdrop of blue sky. Then the island faded from sight, though not from memory.

She had three hours to do three days' worth of work for Willford.

Even without finishing her quantitative analysis, Catherine was more certain than ever that his high-interest plan would bomb. She had been living that way for years, paying a steep emotional premium, the outstanding balance unsettled, deeply in arrears in her soul. Her tab wouldn't be squared until she told her mom the entire story, so she wasn't out of debt quite yet.

Catherine begrudgingly got out her laptop and prepared to dive into grueling reams of data. Before she could, curiosity got the better of her. She did a search for her namesake in *A Farewell to Arms*.

One article featured a scene with the fictional Catherine steering, rowing, and bailing out a boat as she crossed a lake in Italy.

"Seems fitting." She chuckled under her breath.

Online she read that when the character's lover said, "Nothing ever happens to the brave," she replied, "They die, of course."

Then that's exactly what her namesake did. She perished, retaining the courage of her convictions, the strongest of the cast despite her sedate modesty. Catherine didn't have to be the protagonist of the novel to matter.

Suddenly, the passenger next to Catherine snored loudly, as if to remind her to get back on track with work. After this trip, she no longer minded sharing certain qualities with Hemingway's Catherine. However, she was determined not to let the rest of her life unfurl quietly.

When her flight touched down, it was around 7:00 p.m., and it was fully dark. Snow buried the areas surrounding the runway, creating stark grids of black and white. Catherine caught a taxi at the cabstand, and the driver curtly asked her, "Where to?"

She gave him the address; then he promptly recommenced a conversation on his cell from his earpiece, content to completely ignore her.

Catherine wasn't in Key West anymore.

Outside, the streets were a sea of murky slush, which made a shushing sound under the tires. Icicles hung from streetlights. The grip of winter remained firm. The cabbie had the heat cranked high, yet Catherine shivered.

When she arrived at Shady Ridge, the woman at the front desk gave Catherine a limp nod and pushed the sign-in log toward her while scrolling on her phone. Then she glanced up, noting Catherine's bag.

"You been on vacation?"

"Yes," Catherine said confidently. "I have."

The woman checked the name she wrote in. "Oh, you're Mrs. Moran's daughter. She's a real handful." Embarrassed, the woman backtracked. "Um, I don't mean no offense. With what you go through, you deserve some time off."

Catherine wasn't offended. She actually agreed.

The linoleum halls of Shady Ridge were lined with identical rooms. From some, TVs blared. Others sat silent, doors halfway closed. Inside, the elderly sat in chairs or lay in their beds alone, some asleep, others with vacant stares. She was the only guest around.

When she got to her mother's door, she paused, hand hovering over the doorknob, much as she has stood before Willford's door days earlier.

She had a flash of him implying there might be a raise and a new title in it for her if she kept her vacation short and did her end of the work, which she had wrapped up in record time on the plane. Robert's book might only cover a portion of her debts and her mother's expenses, depending on its value. It wasn't as if Catherine could quit.

The thought of returning to the daily grind wasn't as annoying as returning to her old self. Same job, same responsibilities, same her.

Because Catherine didn't feel the same. It was as though she could feel the weight of *A Farewell to Arms* in her bag.

Catherine knocked, then pushed open the door.

Her mother lay asleep in her bed, the hospital rails up on one side, a half-finished cup of pudding on the bedside table, the TV clicker grasped in her hand. Catherine turned down the sound, then rubbed her mother's hand to rouse her.

"Cath?" she asked, bleary eyed. "What are you doing here? Aren't you supposed to be at work?"

The wrath over Catherine avoiding her calls was nowhere to be found.

"It's Sunday, Mom."

"Oh, right. You're right," she replied sleepily.

Catherine sat down in a chair and got out the book, the file, and Robert's letter.

"What's that bag for? Am I leaving Shady Ridge?" her mom asked hopefully. "Am I moving in with you?"

The request pained Catherine deeply, almost as much as what she was there to tell her mother, who spotted the bathing suit bulging from the zipper.

"Were you on a trip? Yes, you went to Ohio! To give that speech and you got sick! Did your hotel have a pool?"

A year earlier, Catherine had flown to Dayton for work, where she had caught a nasty case of the flu. To her amazement, her mother remembered as if it were yesterday. Her recall was as intermittent as it was accurate.

Catherine would have preferred to wipe the entire journey from her own memory if she could have. She had been flown out to the Ohio branch of the firm, where she was giving a presentation on brand-equity data gathering. A dry subject to most, but she was excited to lecture to such a large group about new methods for extracting consumer feedback. It made Catherine feel like her arcane, meticulous research mattered, that her expertise was valuable, even in some minor way.

Public speaking wasn't her strength, and she had come down with a sore throat the night before the big meeting. Catherine wound up coughing and sneezing during the entire seminar. People could hardly hear her, even with the microphone, and she had mangled her presentation by sniffling from beginning to end. On the flight home, she was curled up in a ball with a high temperature and the chills.

She had blocked the entire debacle from her mind, yet her mom could practically recite it chapter and verse. Maybe the memory loss was the best thing that could have happened. Even if it was a burden to Catherine, it spared her mom vast stretches of a painful past.

Catherine clutched Robert's book to her chest. "Listen, I have something—a lot of things—to tell you."

"About the trip?"

"About *a* trip."

"What do you mean?" she asked, an alert edge creeping into her voice.

Catherine held out the book to her, and her mother narrowed her eyes to squint at the author.

"Hemingway," she huffed, unenthused. "If we're going to talk about that macho geezer, can we order pizza? The pizza here is soggy. I miss crispy pizza. With pepperoni. Can we have pepperoni?"

Her mother's disposition switched on a dime, going from disinterested to gleeful in a second flat.

Catherine put her bag by the bed and shut the door to tuck in for the evening. It would be long. But it would be worth it.

"We can have whatever you want, Mom."

She had done her best to give her mother what she could. That was why Catherine had held a grudge against Robert. He hadn't. He'd given up, shirked his duties, split. That meant she couldn't.

The tenacity it took to hang on was a trait her brother had inadvertently instilled in her. She hugged his novel against her ribs. Catherine never imagined she could be thankful to Robert for anything. As she sat there holding *A Farewell to Arms*, she was grateful for far more than the book.

40

Catherine got to work early the next morning, hoping to put Gloria's present on her desk as a surprise. Except Gloria was already there, sitting primly at her desk.

"Good morning," she singsonged brightly.

Stunned, Catherine almost dropped her purse and laptop case to the floor.

Gloria hadn't been on time since they first met. Over the years, she had slowly been coming in a minute later and a minute later, keeping a spreadsheet to chart her arrival rate and how that shaved down her total day's work. She devoted more hours to keeping that tally than to her actual job.

"Why are you here *before* work starts? This must be one of the signs of the apocalypse. Are the four horsemen in the break room?"

"I'm early? I didn't notice." Gloria admired her nails, feigning innocence.

"Did you get a concussion?"

"My head's fine. It's my heart that's changed."

Gloria swiveled her computer monitor around, affording Catherine full view of her screen saver. It was a giant picture of Gloria and her new beau, Tito, cuddled together at a restaurant table and toasting sushi rolls with chopsticks.

"I'm picking out stuff for our wedding registry in my mind," she sighed dreamily.

"But you only met him a few days ago."

"Listen, I've dated every different flavor of jackass, and if it's taught me anything, it's that you don't give any man your ATM PIN, and if you do find a decent guy, you hold on to him for dear life because good guys are rarer than a seat on the subway that has never been peed on."

Catherine was about to protest her rushing in. But Gloria was spot on. Finding a good man, one she felt safe with, one she could trust, was indeed exceptional. With a wistful smile, she pictured Travis.

"Tito said being late isn't just disrespectful to one's employer, it's disrespectful to yourself. Makes you look tacky," Gloria clarified, as though Catherine wouldn't get the gist.

"Given this renewed commitment to professionalism, I'm not sure you'll appreciate your gift."

Catherine handed her the earrings as well as the printed tumbler; then Gloria burst out laughing.

"You leave, and I fall head over heels for a guy who makes me want to do my job right. How crazy is that? It's like you gotta have a change to see why you need one."

Catherine couldn't have said it better herself.

"Anyhow, Willford wants you at the morning meeting in ten minutes," Gloria informed her. "Hard copies of the files you need to get caught up on are in your office."

Opening her door, Catherine discovered the top leaves of her plant peering meekly from between the piles.

"Welcome back," Gloria deadpanned.

"Thanks." Catherine chucked her laptop case onto her chair.

"*Soooo?*" she asked deliberately. "Did you tell your mom?"

"I did."

"And?"

Her mother had taken the news about Robert and the truth about why he had abandoned them as well as expected, which was not well.

When Catherine had explained the letter, the book, and the history of the boat, that seemed to soften the blows.

"I'll probably have to tell her again."

"And again?"

"Maybe that could help both of us."

Although Catherine was aware she would have to relive the sad tale over the coming weeks, she was prepared for that. She hoped the retelling would forge a way toward forgiveness for her mother.

"We'll get through it. We always do."

"I know you will. Just remember that 'we' doesn't have to mean you shouldering all the weight." Gloria gave her a wink as her phone rang; then she went to grab it.

Reaching out to book dealers would have to wait. While mustering the energy to embark on the workday ahead, Catherine overheard Gloria talking.

"Yes, Ms. Moran is here. May I ask who's calling?"

A spark of fear that the men from the clubhouse had figured out her scam and tracked her to Manhattan flared in Catherine's mind.

Gloria rolled her desk chair into the doorway. "You heard of a Mr. Jacoby?"

She shook her head.

"He's heard o' you. Line three. Make it snappy. You've got to be in the conference room stat."

"Right," Catherine replied, frantically excavating her phone from the mountains of paper.

"Ms. Moran?" a familiar voice said when she answered. "You may not remember me. We met at the Casa Marina."

It took a second; then she placed him as the gentleman with the silver hair from the resort.

Uh-oh. What could he be calling about?

"Of course. How can I help you?"

"I have your hat."

"My . . . oh, my baseball cap! I was wondering where that had gotten to."

There was a pause as Catherine contemplated why the man had gone to the trouble to track her down for some measly hat. With the meeting minutes away, she was scrabbling through piles of paper while turning on her computer.

"I'm happy to send it to you."

"That'd be terrific. I need to run, but I can have my assistant give you the corporate address—"

"I promise not to take much more of your time, but I do have another reason for phoning."

He realized you weren't a guest, and you owe him for the cabana!

"I was impressed with your enthusiasm for your work, your passion for research. So much so that I mentioned you to the head of marketing at our parent company, the Waldorf Astoria, who's very interested in discussing an employment opportunity with you. As you said, any business driven by consumer needs would be remiss not to invest in market analysis."

On came Catherine's computer, the palm tree and daybreak beach scene appearing in brilliant hues amid the mounds of files.

Her mind reeling, she numbly repeated what he had said. "An employment opportunity?"

"Yes. We have properties all over the globe, from London to Hawaii to Shanghai to our home base in New York, where you are."

"Key West?" she asked, more to herself than to him.

"As well as this property, yes. There would be travel involved in the position, but your base could be here, if you like. I hope that wouldn't be a problem."

"No, nope, not a bit," she stuttered.

"Excellent. I'll put the necessary contact information in with your hat and overnight it. I do hope you'll consider the offer. We'd love to have you."

"Yeah, I mean, yes. Of course. Thank you."

Gloria was peeking around the doorframe from the perch of her rolling desk chair, eyes wide from eavesdropping on the call. "Did you just get a new job?"

Catherine hung up in a state of utter shock. "I think I did."

Gloria did a triumphant, arm-pumping spin in her chair.

"Take it. Leave. Vamoose. Scram. Don't let the door hit you in the caboose on the way out. This company is run by a bunch of free-range morons who don't give a damn about anybody who works for them. Get out while you can!"

"Didn't you say being disrespectful to one's employer is being disrespectful to yourself?"

"Ah, screw 'em. This is the chance you've been waiting for!"

It was. Only Catherine hadn't been aware of that until it happened.

Gloria hopped up, manhandled her out of her winter coat, and forcibly adjusted her clothes to make her presentable. "Don't be late for the meeting."

"A second ago, you were—"

"Because Willford needs to be reminded of what he's about to lose—a smart, confident, sometimes decently dressed researcher who he'll miss when she's gone."

"You think I should be honest and tell him?"

"Don't you dare!" Gloria stealthily glanced around the office to see if anybody had been listening.

"But he might finally give me that promotion. Made it seem like it was mine if I came back by today."

"Then use it against him in the salary negotiations. Jeez, do I have to teach you everything? Now put on some lipstick and pull yourself together." Gloria pinched her cheeks hard to bring color to them, and Catherine flinched. "How did you come back without a tan?"

"I am tan!"

"Then you better move back to Key West because this is pathetic. You're the same color as the copier paper."

"What about my mom and Shady Ridge?"

"You think you're going to have trouble finding a retirement home in *Florida*? Take her with you! She might get her memory back just by getting the hell outta Jersey. Or at least forget about what she's forgotten about and have a blast by the beach. The botha you could."

Travis sprang to mind, along with the memory of the first time he had held her hand. That was as close to happy as she had felt in as long as she could remember. The idea of seeing him again made Catherine flush, as if the sun were dawning inside her. She dug into the zipper pocket of her purse for her lipstick and came across the map of Key West, the street names hazy, the pages crimped together.

Catherine did deserve more out of life. Her mother did too. She was sure Robert would have agreed. He was the one who had set things in motion. Now the mark he had left on her life seemed less like a wound and more like an arrow on that map, urging her to go a different way. Despite all the lying she had done, in her soul she was certain it was true.

On her desk, green palm fronds were poking out on the computer screen from behind the heaps of paper. Golden rays of dawn and a stretch of white sandy beach were visible in slivers between the folders, as if presenting her with a choice.

She could be like the palm tree on her screen saver, alone and stuck where she started. Or she could head out into uncharted waters in search of a brighter future waiting off in the distance with the sunrise.

Fortunately for Catherine, she had a boat.

~

Acknowledgments

I am deeply grateful to my friends for their unwavering support. Heather Stober, Sally J. Smith, Ann Biddlecom, Tracy Milenkovic, and Sara Barthol deserve my heartfelt thanks for their encouragement on this project. I also want to thank my literary agent, Joanna MacKenzie, for her insightful feedback and my editor, Selena James, for her expertise in transforming my manuscript into the book you now hold.

About the Author

Ellie Block began her writing career under her given name Brett Ellen Block—she, too, was named for a Hemingway character. She is the author of the critically acclaimed novel *The Grave of God's Daughter* and the Macavity Award–nominated thriller *The Lightning Rule*. Her debut short-story collection, *Destination Known*, won the Drue Heinz Literature Prize and garnered her the distinguished Michener-Copernicus Fellowship. As Ellen Block, she also writes women's fiction, including the internationally lauded novels *The Language of Sand* and *The Definition of Wind*.

Ellie received her undergraduate degree from the University of Michigan, where she studied fine arts and won the Hopwood and Haugh awards for fiction. She went on to earn graduate degrees from the Iowa Writers' Workshop and the University of East Anglia's esteemed fiction-writing program. Her work has been translated into numerous languages around the world. For more about the author, please visit www.brettellenblock.com.